POISON FOREST

LAURI STARLING

Poison Forest

Lauri Starling

Sword and Silk Books
105 Viewpoint Circle Pell City, AL 35128
Visit our website at SwordandSilkBooks.com
To request permissions contact the publisher at admin@swordandsilk-books.com.
First Edition: October 2022

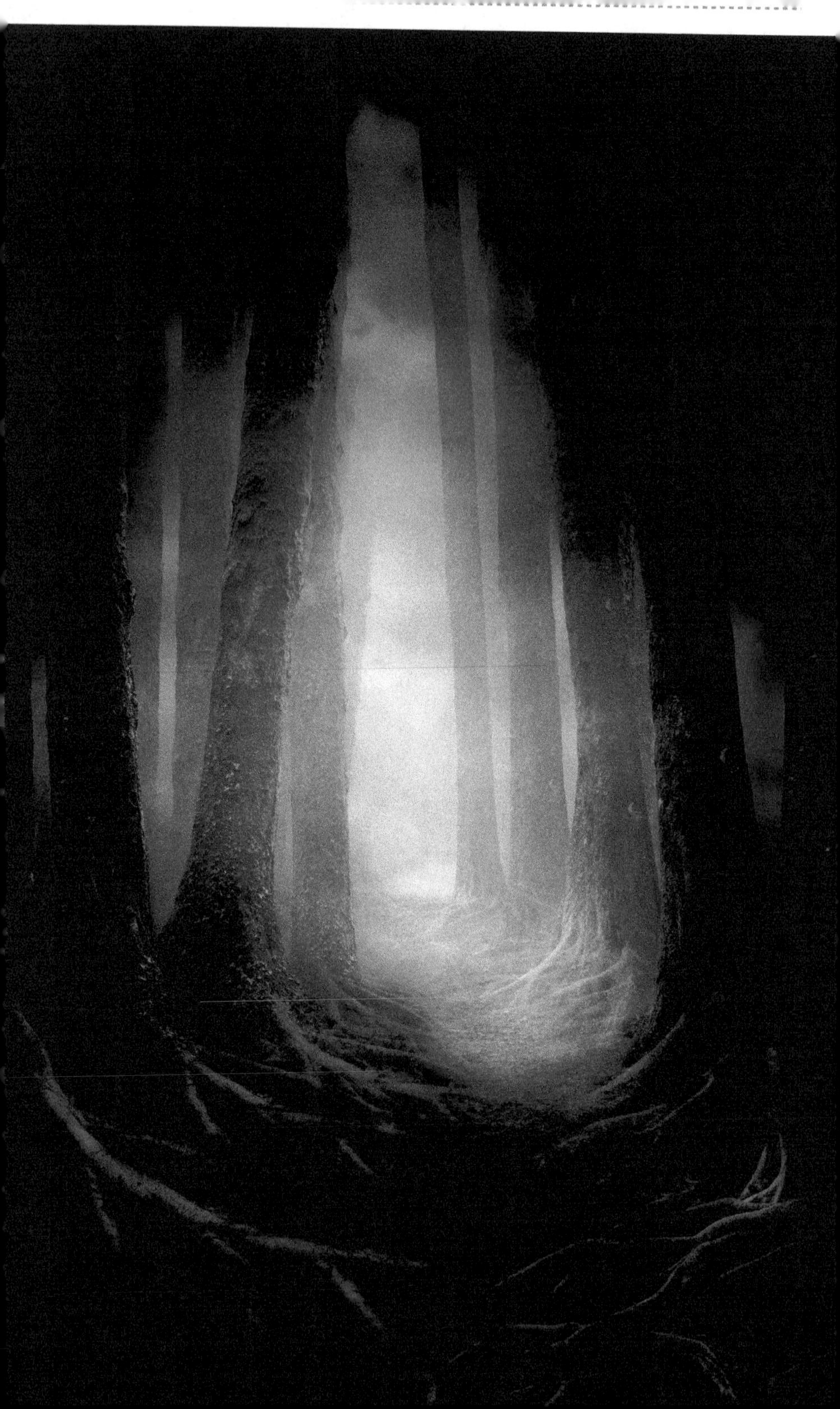

Part One: Walking the Dead

Who can tell where the dead walk?

Whether they meet on dark paths or distant shores?

Only one who has met Death themselves.

–Lazulian Book of the Dead

Chapter XV, Verses 12-14.

CHAPTER ONE

PRAYERS in the Temple of the Dead are twice as long today. The chanting usually lulls me into tranquility. Boredom, even, if I'm honest. But today is different.

I made my sacrifices and underwent the sacraments before the sun rose in preparation for my death ceremony tonight. The priestesses bathed me the way corpses are bathed in the mortuary, anointed me with blood, ash, and scented oil.

Here in my country, Lazul, death ceremonies are held in the ancient burial ground a few miles from the capitol. Tonight, I'll walk there to wake the shade of Zori, our goddess of death.

A young acolyte crosses the nave and touches a set of hanging spirit chimes with fingertips light as moth antennae. A crystalline note hangs in the air for a moment, clear and sharp as an icicle. This is the signal to end morning prayers, and I scramble to my feet as my knees crack in protest from kneeling so long on the stone floor.

The temple keeper, Garneta, pads over as I begin

extinguishing the numerous tapers arranged on the marble altar.

She pulls a dagger from the folds of her white robes, used for scraping dried wax from the altar. “Never mind the rest of these. Won’t the Empress be arriving soon?”

The candle snuffer trembles in my hand, and I take a shuddering breath. “Yes, any time now.”

Queen Akina, High Empress of the Triumvir, is bringing her daughter Dette for my death ceremony. We’ve known one another since we were eleven, and when we fell in love one summer, our parents stole the opportunity to betroth us to one another. But it all fell apart after my mother died.

Once I thought not being with Dette would destroy me. I cried like I was dying the night our betrothal was dissolved, and eighteen months later I still can’t stop thinking about her. Her home is in Thistle, the capitol of Zelen, and it’s nearly a week’s ride from here on horseback. I haven’t seen her since the night her mother broke our engagement. *They’re only coming for political reasons, Thedra.*

Garneta gives my arm a comforting squeeze and takes the snuffer. “Don’t be anxious,” she says. “You know the rituals.”

I nod. She thinks I’m only nervous about my death ceremony, and I’ve no reason to inform her of my inner turmoil. I may be a princess, but inside the temple, she has always treated me like any other acolyte, and I prefer it that way.

As I leave, I hear the clamor of a crowd gathering in the understreets, and the breeze in the open courtyard brings the scent of roasting mutton. The city is up and about early—peddlers will be selling meat pies and cups of mead for flin'pennies. My father's guard has assembled in the courtyard below the palace. Sunlight glints off the gold details on their uniforms, dazzling my eyes as I stride across the balustrade.

Father is sprawled beneath a covered awning with his lover, Onyx. They're sharing a chaise and breakfasting on summer fruit and bread with broiled goat cheese. "Good morning, Thedra."

"Morning."

"You look surly." He licks a drip of melted cheese off his thumb. "Aren't you pleased you'll soon see, Dette?"

"I'm pleased."

I turn and grip the balustrade's marble banister until my knuckles turn white. Father looks thoroughly relaxed, like he's on holiday in the Glittering Caves, but a flush is building beneath his translucent skin. Sun and wind burn him, and his complexion betrays emotion like a bog, giving up hidden detritus in the heat. He's nervous, too.

I brush my palm across the diamond vial hanging from my belt. My touch awakens the lightning inside, and it skitters across the surface like an anxious spider as the courtiers and servants gathered behind me chatter. Even the guards' steeds on either side of the gate seem edgy.

High Empress Akina has this effect on everyone.

She is a stone elemental, which means she has the power to move earth and rock, and to petrify flesh. Although she hasn't turned anyone to stone in decades, one doesn't tend to forget her history. At age fourteen, she inadvertently petrified a young nobleman for being too handsy with her in the palace gardens. Dette says his condition proved irreversible despite the efforts of Zelen's court physicians and mages, but the statue was bronzed and served as both a fine garden ornament and a reminder of Akina's power.

We wait and wait, as the sun rises and glitters off armor and horse livery. Just when I think I can't wait another minute, the roar of the crowd greeting the Empress reaches us.

When the royal litter alights on the cobblestones in the courtyard below, I push away from the marble banister eagerly.

"Wait, Thedramora." Father's voice is indolent as always, but he uses my full name, so I know he's serious. "Don't run to them like an eager pawn."

I glare at him over my shoulder, annoyed that he would call me a pawn in front of his lover. "It's rude to stay up here when they journeyed all this way to meet us."

He twines a finger in one of Onyx's chestnut ringlets. "This is our stronghold. Make them come to us. If you're so concerned about etiquette, you should've made yourself presentable for their arrival." He glances at the worn breeches and loose, belted linen tunic I always wear to the temple. "You look like a stable hand."

He's been like this since my engagement to Dette was rescinded. It was my fault, after all.

I turn away, refusing to rise to his bait. I watch Empress Akina make her way toward the steps leading up to the balustrade. Dette runs ahead of the gaggle of courtiers and attendants and skips past her mother to climb the stairs. Zelen is a warmer country than Lazul, and she has on a light summer dress embroidered with pink buds and green vines. Her white, feathery wings are folded, trailing on the ground behind her.

Dette is half-sylph, the long-lived, winged race of people who share our world. They're something of a mystery to us humans. Some of them can fly, and their mythology and anatomy are different from ours, but occasionally we join our races for the benefit of each. Dette's father is King Cygnus, the leader of the sylphan realm.

Dette mounts the stairway to the upper tier in a flash, taking the steps two and three at a time. Court etiquette requires that she let her mother come first, but she has either forgotten or doesn't care. Two of her ladies-in-waiting are on the cobblestones halfway between the stairway and the litter. They look confused, but they lift their skirts and follow her.

When she sees me frozen on the balustrade, she calls, "Don't just stand there, silly."

She sounds unbothered and slightly teasing, like she's daring me to jump into the freezing lake back at Alder Tower, the summer home where we first met. I don't understand how she does it, how she acts completely normal when every time I see her, I feel like I'm slowly dying of longing for her like an unprepared traveler dies of thirst in the desert.

I meet her halfway with open arms and she hits me square in the chest. We're the same height, and anyone else her size would've knocked the breath out of me, but Dette's sylphan heritage makes her bones lighter than a full human's.

Dette's gaze doesn't leave my face. "I missed you." She pecks me on the lips with a quick dart of her head and her feathers tickle my cheek. It feels like a careless, impulsive kiss, but my mouth tingles. I thought we'd never kiss again.

"Dette," barks Empress Akina, "control yourself." I was so focused on Dette that I didn't notice her enter the upper tier. From the corner of my eye, I see Onyx flinch and I have to bite back a snort of laughter. Empress Akina is a short, broad woman with a gravitas that would brook no nonsense even if she didn't have the power to bring the stones of the castle down on our heads.

Dette shrugs and flips her curls, completely uncowed. "You look wonderful, Thedra."

"And you. I've been informed that I'm dressed like a stable hand." I cast my eyes at Father, and Dette laughs.

"I meant your face," she says.

She's the one who looks wonderful. The sunlight brings out the pale green undertones from the verdant blood in her

veins, and her rosy cheeks and light brown skin glow like a ripe summer apple. As another gust of wind billows the flags and banners, she opens her wings to their full width, letting the breeze ruffle her downy feathers. Dette's wings have never been strong enough for flight, but they're beautiful, like the rest of her.

"How was your journey?"

"Pleasant enough, but Momma grumbled over the state of the roads for half the journey."

"Some of us are not so young that bouncing in a litter for days upon end is a treat."

Father deigns to leave his lounge so he can kiss Dette's cheek and go down on one knee before Akina, who extends her right hand where she wears a massive ruby signet ring. He places his lips on the gem with indifference. The whole procedure reeks of boredom and habit. And he accuses me of behaving like a pawn.

I can tell Akina is waiting for me to genuflect too, and the fact that everyone is watching me, wondering if I will, only makes me more averse to the idea. She might be High Empress in title, but constitutionally, she and my father are equals, and I'm first in line for the throne of Lazul.

She fixes me with her stony gaze, and I hold back a tremble at making prolonged eye contact with her, still refusing to bow. I wonder if it hurts, being turned to stone, or if it happens so fast you don't even have time to flinch.

"It's a great honor that you've come," I say finally, lowering my chin a bit.

Father's mouth and eyes look tight. "Our children seem to forget their court manners as soon as they're together."

"Agreed," says Akina smoothly. "Although it's a mystery which of them is worse, and who has influenced the other more."

Dette links her arm through mine. "It's been an equal exchange. Will you show me inside, Thedra? I'm starving and need a good soak."

As she steers us toward the palace, I see the two ladies-in-waiting who followed her scamper behind us like obedient puppies.

Fruit, wine, bread, and water are set out in the spacious dining hall, where the windows have been opened to admit the breeze. The gusts blow the heavy draperies away from the casings in billowing arches, like the sails in a fleet of ships. Autumn will come early this year. Late summer gales never lie.

We sit at the long table and the ladies-in-waiting hang back until I beckon for them to join us. Dette reaches for a ripe plum. "Oh, I almost forgot. Thedra, meet Henbane and Neev."

Henbane looks like a Zelener, her complexion the same shade as the dark velvet center of the flower she's named for, her long locks dyed brilliant green and decorated with beads. Neev is more than likely from Dendronia, the snowy country to our north. She's pale-skinned with large gray eyes and short, chin-length hair dyed deep purple. She is wearing a pair of silk gloves, which I find odd. Lazul is a colder country than Zelen because we're farther from the warm sea breezes and closer to snowy Dendronia. But it's not that cold here in summer.

Both women bow deeply to me before taking a seat.

As usual, all this bowing and scraping makes me uncomfortable, but Dette is too busy eating to notice. She finishes the plum in several bites, then spreads a slice of dark, thick bread with yak butter. My stomach rumbles, but I shake my head when she offers me the platter of fruit.

"I'm fasting until tonight."

The corner of her mouth turns down. "Ascetic Lazul."

"Self-indulgent Zelen," I return. "It's tradition. And for my benefit, I've been told."

Servants scurry in and out in a flurry of preparation for tonight's festivities. There is a ball planned for after my death ceremony tonight. Father takes any excuse to throw a ball, but I do find it odd, given that some acolytes don't return from Zori's tomb alive. My mother was the only other royal to become a Priestess of Death, and she suggested the food from her ball be given to the poor in the event of her untimely demise. My mother had a strange sense of humor.

Dette opens her hands. "I can ease your hunger if you want."

I stare at her hands—the long, capable fingers, the soft

palms, the neat nails. I bite my lip involuntarily as I imagine the warmth of them on my belly, soothing the gnawing discomfort of my hunger the way she used to soothe my menstrual cramps or the headaches I got when my mother wrote to me of Lazul's suffering and political unrest. But the weight of being Priestess of Death is mine to bear, not hers, so I shake my head.

When she's finished eating and her ladies have been sent to prepare her rooms, I lead Dette down the corridor to the palace baths. I remove my boots at the entrance and turn them over, spilling sand onto the tile.

"Do you keep half of Lazul's sand in your boots, Thedra?" asks Dette teasingly.

"I rode across the Fallow Dunes before I went to the temple this morning," I say, referring to the strip of desert between here and the Dendronian mountains.

Dette selects a bottle of scented oil from the menagerie of skin treatments arranged on a marble table and pours some into her palm, infusing the heavy air in the room with the scents of vanilla and chamomile. "You'll have to take me with you tomorrow."

Two servants, a man and woman clad in loose, sleeveless robes, come forward to attend to us.

"Welcome, Your Highnesses. What pleases you today, Princess Thedramora? A bath? Steam?"

"No, thank you. They… they bathed me in the mortuary this morning."

"Oh good goddess," exclaims Dette, annoyed once more by Lazul's morbid rituals.

I shrug. "It's tradition. A bath," I say to the attendant, "for Dette."

Dette unpins the tower of hair atop her head and it springs loose in a cloud of black curls. "I'd like my hair washed, please, for the ball."

As Dette soaks in a vat of soapy hot water, the woman washes her hair and takes time untangling and oiling it. The other attendant pares my cuticles and rubs rose-scented balm into my hands and arms while I wait.

"A massage, perhaps?" he asks. "Your shoulders are up by your ears."

He has dimples and blond hair, and Dette arches a querying brow at me. I shake my head at her, not wanting to be teased in front of the servants. She only likes women, but you could say I like everyone. Potentially, anyway. "I'm fine."

As we leave the baths, I pause to look at the statue of Zori tucked into an alcove. Her flowing hair is painted dark brown, and she is covering her eyes with one hand. She is always depicted in one of two forms in reliefs and statues: the Slayer, who carries an executioner's axe, or the Blind, like this one. Her covered eyes represent her indifference to human mortality as a death goddess.

But what if she looks nothing like these portrayals? In my worst nightmares, she's a monster with teeth that craves human souls. The Devourer was what they called my mother when she was Lazul's High Priestess and executioner. It was said she could take off a man's head in one terrible bite, and although I loved her, I also feared her. In my early childhood nightmares, she and Zori were one and the same.

Dette takes my hand and squeezes it, sensing my mood. "You've been learning the rituals for your death ceremony since we were children, Thedra. You'll be fine."

I go to the ancient burial ground in the Fallow Dunes at sunset and wait among the gravestones for the priestesses from the Temple of the Dead to join me. I like to think it takes a lot to scare me, but my heart is beating erratically against my ribs, a wild bird fighting the bars of its cage.

The sun sinks quickly, taking the heat of the day with it. The cool of night falls, leaching the warmth from the sand beneath my feet. I lean against the stone of an ancient grave, its inscription long worn away by centuries of wind, sand, and snow. The limestone digs into my back, and I wish the priestesses would hurry, but I know they're chanting rites and walking slowly. It's bad luck to trip on the way to a meeting with Death.

Finally, I hear their footsteps on the path, and the crystalline ringing from the spirit chimes they wear around their necks.

I stand and meet them at the entrance to the burial ground. Garneta is at the front, and she pads over and pulls a dagger

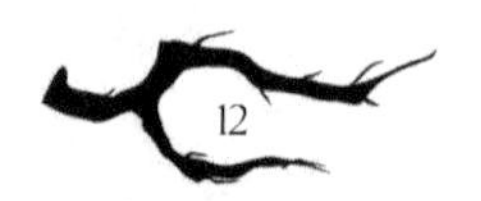

from the folds of her white robes. I extend my hand to her from habit.

She pricks my palm with the point of the dagger and I tilt my hand, letting the blood run in a thin rivulet to the sand—an offering to Zori. My palm is mottled with thin, interwoven scars from my years as a temple acolyte. A scarlet droplet runs along one of the raised lines, reminding me of the tiny red sand beetles that hide in the rocks of the palace gardens.

Two priestesses catch some of the blood from my hand and mix it with temple ash to draw runes on my face. Then they drape a sheer black veil over my head that reaches my elbows—a death shroud—and take each of my hands to lead me to a large sarcophagus in the center of the graveyard: Zori's tomb.

Zori was mortal, once. But legend says she grappled with Death until he fell in love with her, and when they were married, she stole his power for herself by learning his secrets—the power to move between worlds, to raise the dead and steal the living, to come back to life. It's her power that we take for ourselves.

Garneta presents me with the necessary items for the ceremony: an unlit lamp, a stick carved with ancient death rites, and a dagger. I take them silently, willing my arms not to tremble and betray my fear. The ritual to awaken Zori is a secret kept from acolytes, and I don't know what will happen. I only know what I'm supposed to do.

The caged bird in my chest has frozen nearly to death. I take a deep breath, bursting the icy bubble of fear.

"You'll be all right," says Garneta. "I know you will. You're Mora's daughter."

As I cross the threshold of the crypt, my palm brushes the diamond vial hanging from my belt and the lightning inside glitters, awakened by my touch. It skitters inside the confines of the vial like an anxious spider, illuminating the walls of Zori's tomb so it looks like a subterranean cavern. I clasp one hand around my vial, letting its buzzing energy fill me.

I hold the stick before my eyes and run my fingertips over the runes carved into its surface before using it to draw a circle in the thick dust around the tomb.

I light the lamp with a spark from my vial and speak the ancient rites. "I summon the one who lies buried here—Zori, Bride of Death, Goddess of the Dead, protector and executioner of the living. Awaken and speak."

There's a rushing in my ears, maddeningly loud in the dark, silent crypt, and I'm grateful the rituals for the ceremony include fasting. If I had anything in my stomach, I'm certain it would come up from terror.

I stand still, blinking at the shadows cast by the lamp as my pulse pounds in my ears. I hear a rustling like old, dry fabric brushing against stone, and I picture a shroud being dragged along the floor. I give a start as the flickering flame in the lamp snuffs out. One second, I'm alone, and the next I can sense something beside me in the darkness. My heart lodges in my throat. I thought a shade was unable to leave the circle. And no one said anything about the lamp going out.

A voice cuts through the silence, stirring the air next to my ear. "What do you want?"

I close my eyes, recalling the proper words for this part of the ritual. "Zori, G-Goddess of Death, bless me, make me your consort. Imbue me with justice and mercy. Help me raise the dead and put the living to rest."

Her voice is a death rattle, a droplet of water on a searing hot stone. "What's your name?"

"Thedramora. Daughter of Queen Mora, who was Shapeshifter, High Priestess of the Dead, and of King Thede, son of —"

"Enough," she interrupts.

"But...I'm asking to be high priestess. Don't you want to hear my—"

"Entire genealogy? I've been dead a millennium and heard enough bloodlines yammered by trembling proselytes to last me two."

I can't see anything in this suffocating tomb, but I sense that she's standing in front of me now—I can feel her breath through my thin veil, cold and stale.

"Why do you want to be my consort?" she asks.

"I..."

No one has ever asked if I want to be Zori's consort, let

alone why. I was just expected to do it, as I was expected to eat a wholesome breakfast every morning, or learn combat, diplomacy, and foreign languages.

"It's in my lineage," I say finally. "My mother was High Priestess."

"Lineage means nothing. Why should I make you the arbiter of who lives and dies in Lazul?"

"Because it scares me," I blurt. "I saw what it did to my mother. She used to lock herself away after an execution. There was plague and then famine when I was a child and people started murdering one another, eating one another… It was up to her to decide who deserved justice and mercy."

"I didn't ask for your kingdom's entire tragic tale," she interrupts. "Lazulians stink of grief. We'll be here all night."

I bite my lip savagely beneath my veil. I've worshipped Zori my entire life, but only because I had to. It's wise to honor the Goddess of Death in a country like Lazul, and when I was a young child, my mother made me.

The commoners bring Zori monthly offerings of first fruits and small game in hopes of appeasing her through hard winters and drought. But despite being the daughter of the king and the Priestess of Death, I never trusted Zori. A goddess who craves so much blood always seemed suspect to me. And now that I've summoned her, I hate her.

"I won't take the responsibility lightly," I say, and I can hear the bitterness in my voice, cutting through the air like a

sharp blade.

"You despise me." She sounds amused. "I hear it in your voice. Do you fear me, too?"

My eyes have finally started adjusting to the dark and I can see her outline, but it shifts and changes, unbound by the laws of the living. She smells of decay and grave mold, and I close my eyes so I can't see her wavering shadow. "Both."

"Well, at least you're honest. I never bless liars."

"Then you'll bless me?"

"If you're brave enough."

I stretch out my hand. "Let it be done."

Her hand clasps mine. It's so cold and dry that I suppress a shudder. "Kneel and give me the knife."

A deal-making. I sigh with relief, but it quickly turns into a gasp as she throws back my veil, revealing my face like a groom about to kiss his bride.

"Oh. They painted you for me."

I kneel on the hard floor of the tomb, flipping the dagger around and shoving the handle at her. "Fuck off."

As she takes the dagger, I extend my palm for the blood pact. But instead of cutting my offered palm, she plunges the long blade into my chest.

Chapter Two

I slump sideways. Even if I scream myself raw, the priestesses won't help me. They would never go against Zori's will, even if it involves killing me. I'm too stunned to let out more than a croaking wheeze, anyway. Slowly, I sink to my knees as blood seeps between my fingers.

Zori reaches for the blade still buried in my chest. As her hand wraps around the hilt, I shake my head, begging her not to pull it out. She ignores me. The blade is sharp as a carving knife; the priestesses made sure of it, and she slides it free like it's nothing.

The knife is replaced by a razor-sharp lance of agony. The blood doesn't seep now; it gushes and spurts with every beat of my heart. That's when I know it's over. I won't get out of this alive. They prepared me like a corpse because soon I'll be one.

Zori watches me fruitlessly clutch my chest as my lifeblood flows between my fingers. I don't remember lying down, but at some point I must have, because now I'm reclining on my side as bone-deep cold sinks through me. Drowsiness replaces the throbbing pain until I lose consciousness all together.

When I become aware of myself as a vessel once more—a thing with extremities and senses—there is warmth on my face and wet sand beneath my back. I open my eyes and I'm lying on a pebbled beach, frothy waves lapping the shore. A turquoise sea stretches to the horizon and a tall woman in flowing robes approaches me from the shoreline. She has black hair festooned with shells and pearls, and she's pale. She doesn't look much like the statues we have of her all over Lazul, so I don't recognize her until she speaks.

"Welcome."

I scramble up from the wet sand. "You stabbed me!"

She smiles. "Do they no longer teach acolytes the ancient rites? How can you be a corpse-waker if you have not conquered Death yourself?"

That's when I notice the knife wound in my chest no longer hurts. I look down, expecting to find a gaping hole, but my skin is unmarked. My toes are sinking into the soft, sucking sand. I lift my head and look at Zori in horror, realizing where I am. I'm on the shore beyond our world, beyond the Endless Sea. The place we call the nextworld, the entrance to our afterlife.

This place reminds me of the few journeys I took to the eastern shore with my parents as a young girl—the cries of gulls and the frigid, deep blue of the wind-tossed Sapphire

Sea. But this is a very different ocean, this tranquil blue-green mirror. It looks warm and calm.

"You spoke of your mother," says Zori, as if getting down to business. "If you want, you may stay here and find her."

"I know." I've been memorizing the regulations since I learned to read. I stare at the calm, teal water, the cloudless sky. I imagine my mother walking toward me across the pebbled shore, the feel of her hand on my cheek, just like all the times I dreamed it. "If I stay, can I go back?"

Zori shakes her head. "You will remain dead. And if you return, you may not resurrect her. Corpse-wakers are forbidden from raising the dead for their own benefit."

She studies me, her gaze stern. "Fine, I'll send you back. But you will see the dead, Thedramora of Lazul, and walk among them. Death's mark was on you before I ever touched you."

"Anyone with a dead parent would."

Zori smirks, takes a step forward, and places both hands over my heart, pressing firmly. I awaken with a gasp, my lungs burning as they inflate with air. I'm back inside the dark tomb and I fumble on the packed dirt floor, rolling onto my side. The fresh warmth of the shore is gone, replaced by stale air. I put my hand inside the neck of my tunic and my fingers graze a thick scar that wasn't there before.

When I step out of the tomb on trembling legs, Garneta

and the other priestesses kneel before me, but I toss the bloody dagger onto the ground without ceremony.

"Oh, get up," I say irritably, tired of formalities. "One of you might've said she was going to murder me."

"But Your Highness, no one would go into the tomb if they knew!" Garneta sounds amused, which annoys me further. "Zori kills us all. She only brings us back if we choose for her to do so."

So that explains why some don't return. They don't *want* to. Disgusted by this artifice, I shake my head and replace my lace veil to hide the bloodstain on my tunic.

Chapter Three

When I reach my room back at the palace, I'm met by my seamstress Godwin and Dette's two ladies.

"Dette sent us," says the one called Neev. "To help you dress."

"Why? Where's my maid, Beryl?"

Her gaze flicks to my face and then back to the polished marble floor. "She's ill, Your Highness."

"The gown is breathtaking," says Henbane.

Godwin designed it to symbolize the union of the Triumvir and she stands back, admiring her handiwork as they help me into it. The fabric is a pale blue silk embroidered with red roses and green vines for Zelen and snowflakes for Dendronia, with gemstones sewn into the hem and neckline for Lazul.

It's impressive as dresses go, but it pinches my ribs and it weighs at least fifteen pounds with the heavy embroidery, jewels, and yards of silk. After the night I've had, I don't feel like being laced into another dress, much less one that requires hefting its weight all over a ballroom, but I try to bite back my grumbles. It's not like I've worn many in my life. As a young child, I put up a fuss over wearing ruffles and lace, so I was brought to court in a brocade tunic and breeches like a little prince.

When I've stepped into it, Neev laces the back. Unsatisfied, Godwin takes her place and pulls the laces tighter. Godwin has big hands with thick fingers and strong forearms, and I give a sharp intake of breath as the bodice cinches my waist.

"We're almost done, Your Highness," says Neev. Her voice is soft, soothing. She'd make a good midwife, I think. Or a healer. Both professions suit people who possess the gift of making torture seem like a normal, everyday occurrence.

"Sorry to complain," I say. "Hell of a long day."

Neev's gaze lands on the bright red, diagonal scar across my breast and she starts to reach for it with slow fingers, but I catch her wrist gently in midair. It is so slim that my fingers nearly touch.

She meets my gaze and I release her. "I'm sorry, Your Highness. But that scar looks so recent. What happened to you at the tombs?"

"I can't tell you that."

Her eyes grow round. "Your goddess is real, then?"

"You thought she wasn't?" asks Godwin, sounding insulted.

Neev blinks at her, quiet but uncowed. "Zelen's favored

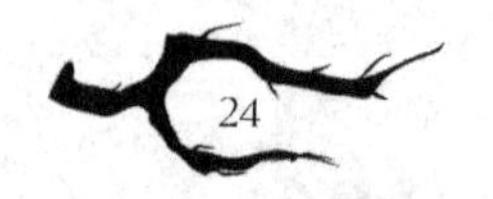

goddess is Thorne, and that's where I grew up. I know nothing of Zori."

"Thorne is patron of peasants, lovers, and well-fed nurslings," explains Henbane. "She makes trees grow tall, streams run clear, and men and women fall in love. At least for a night, so babes fill wombs. She is alive in everything living, she has no tomb."

Godwin snorts. Zeleners adore poetic prophesies and rhyming charms, but here in Lazul we are more practical. We take such things with a grain of salt. I find Henbane's description of Thorne unexpectedly beautiful, though. She sounds earthy, so different from cold, merciless Zori.

"Not everyone's as obsessed with their goddess of death as we are," I explain, "but in a country beset by unforgiving winters, plague, and famine, not to mention the snow beasts that wander down from Dendronia... Well, it's wise to honor her."

Godwin chuckles with approval at my explanation and makes the sign for Zori's favor by covering and uncovering her eyes with a flutter of her hand.

I've seen the sign made a thousand times by noble and commoner alike, but it looks strange now. Perhaps death has shown me how meaningless it is. Everything has a surreal tinge after the clarity of the far shore. The spicy scent of cinnamon tapers burning on my dresser and the glimmering stars in the window are distant and dreamlike.

When I'm dressed, Henbane does my makeup and Neev my hair. It's naturally wavy and messier than usual, frizzy with static from the veil I wore to the tombs. She combs it smooth and plaits it into multiple braids, arranging them atop my head in an intricate labyrinth of coils.

I turn my head to inspect the elaborate hairstyle in my vanity's mirror. She has placed the lapis hair ornaments that belonged to my mother among the loops of hair. I usually keep them in a jar on my desk and the sight of them shining brilliant blue against my dark hair makes my throat ache.

I swallow the painful lump in my throat. "This is impressive. How long have you been one of Dette's ladies?"

"Almost a year."

It makes sense that I don't recognize her then. Dette and I ended our engagement eighteen months ago. I can hear a hint of an accent beneath Neev's practiced court speech, and it makes me curious. "You said you grew up in Zelen?"

"That's right. My mother was born in Dendronia, but I grew up in the Eastern Zelen countryside."

"You parents were farmers, then?"

"Sheepherders, for a landowner."

When she was doing my hair, her palms radiated heat like coals, even through her gloves. I wonder if she has a fever. An outbreak of pestilence among the servants is the last thing my father needs. I meet her gaze in the mirror but see no hints of illness—her eyes are clear, and her cheeks aren't flushed.

Her touch is steady too, even though it makes my temples bead with sweat.

When Henbane has refreshed my makeup—dark green lipstick, shimmer on my cheeks, and black eyeliner—I hardly recognize myself. Flamboyant fashion is popular among the upper classes in Lazul, but it doesn't suit me, and I feel ridiculous.

As if she can sense my hesitance, Henbane says, "You look striking."

"Dette says the nobles here are superficial and obsessed with appearances," agrees Neev. "If you flout their trends, they won't respect you."

Dette's not wrong. I frown, glancing once more at my reflection in the oval mirror. I have my mother's dark hair and severe features: high cheekbones, a sharp jaw. The swirling wings of eyeliner and dark lipstick only intensify them.

"It's beautiful," I say, not wanting to offend them and their hard work. "My father says an occasional smile would go a ways toward softening my edges, but I believe you two have made me look fiercer than ever."

Neev gives me a small smile. "Then we did our job well. You look the part—powerful and determined."

I smile back. Perhaps she's right.

Neev leads me into the dining hall. It's lit by alchemical lamps from Zelen and bobbing lights of emerald green and amethyst created by the palace elementals. A long table is

laden with roasted fowl and swine, brined apples, savory hand pies, and goat cheese. Servants weave between the revelers with platters of sugared fruit and spitted dune lizards dipped in honey and grilled to a crisp.

My empty stomach rumbles at the smell of so much food, but I can't seem to make my taste buds comply after the day I've had. My legs are still weak, and I know I should eat something even though I have no appetite. I settle on a few bites of bread and drink some wine.

I stand on tiptoe to look for Dette. I glimpse her on the other side of the ballroom, talking with a girl named Topaz. Topaz's father is a marquess, the heir of the Glittering Caves near the Eastern Sea. They're some of the primary suppliers of the world's jewels and stones, making Topaz's family the richest in Lazul.

Topaz is wearing a fitted, one-shoulder, cropped top in persimmon fabric and a pair of matching billowy trousers. Her eyelids and hair are dusted with gold, and yellow diamonds gleam in her ears and navel.

Dette's full-skirted ballgown is the same shade of green as the dune lizards that sun themselves on the courtyard stones. "Hi, gorgeous," I blurt.

I immediately regret using the nickname I gave her when we were a couple. My cheeks flood with heat.

Dette looks unbothered. "Thedra. You look incredible!"

I manage a smile for her. Her white feathers reflect the

multicolored lights of the hall. Some sylphs have wings of thin membrane like dragonflies, and those who dwell underground have webs of skin like bats, but Dette's are soft with downy feathers like a cygnet, light as the sea foam that skitters along the beaches of her port home.

"Thedra," purrs Topaz. "You look *shockingly* splendid. I don't think I've ever seen you in a gown before."

Topaz and I have been going to the same parties since we learned to walk. She has definitely seen me in a gown numerous times. At a ball when we were twelve, she offered five queens to anyone who would kiss me to see if my lips shocked theirs. It didn't take long for this to lead to jokes about other body parts I might shock.

She's shorter than I am by at least four inches, and I make a point of looking down at her. "Thank you, Topaz. How is Olivine? I haven't seen them in some time."

I know from palace gossip that she and her lover broke up only two weeks ago. It's petty of me to put her on the spot, but she started it.

"Olivine and I aren't together anymore," says Topaz, as if this is old news. "Didn't you know?"

"I'm sorry to hear it."

"Yes, I suppose you know all about the pain of a fractured betrothal."

Before Dette or I can respond, the crowd of revelers parts as Empress Akina approaches us.

Tonight she's resplendent in a necklace of onyx and opals, and a velvet gown of rich burgundy and dark green, the royal colors of Zelen. The ensemble complements her deep brown skin and coarse black hair. She's a short, broad woman, with a gravitas that would brook no nonsense even if she didn't have the power to bring the stones of the castle down on our heads.

"I don't pretend to understand Lazul's ancient rituals," she says, "but I offer you congratulations on your success."

"Thank you."

"Would you like to dance, Dette?" Topaz asks. Dette smiles and gives Topaz her hand and Topaz pulls her easily toward the dance floor, grinning like a malicious little cat that has caught a colorful bird. I watch them and tip the last few drops of my wine into my mouth.

Dette walks in a circle around Topaz as she begins one of Lazul's sinuous traditional dances. This is one aspect of royal life that has never made sense to me. I don't see the purpose of prancing around in snug slippers and silk gowns while my makeup melts from the heat of a roaring fire and the press of too many bodies. I hate small talk, and the sour flavor of wine, and trying to dance in heavy skirts. It's not that I have anything against balls or ball gowns, or girls who like them. I've just always felt more myself in plain, serviceable items like tunics and boots.

But Topaz and Dette are both in their element at events like this. They are both wealthy, both noble, both beautiful. It occurs to me they would make a stunning match. I've known since we broke off our engagement that I'll someday have to watch Dette marry someone else, but even the smallest possibility of it being Topaz makes me sick with envy and regret.

I turn away, giving my empty wine goblet to a passing servant. I don't care that they're dancing together. It's not like I was going to ask Dette to dance. But the thought of watching Topaz home in on her like a nectar-thirsty bee after a flower is far from appealing.

I make my way to the terrace that leads out into the gardens, dodging a duke who looks like he wants to congratulate me, and the Master of Ceremonies, who will probably try to find me a dance partner if I linger. I've nearly escaped when I feel a hand on my arm.

I look up into the smiling face of Rothbart, my mother's former lover. During my childhood, he was Peakstone's chief sorcerer, but he has avoided the palace since Mother died, and I haven't seen him in some time. I recall the servants saying he was handsome back then, with his dark beard and slender build. He has grown too thin, his cheekbones jutting sharply above his beard, which is streaked with gray.

The silver robe he wears reflects the greens and purples of the orbs floating around the ballroom, and he makes me a courtly bow despite his haggard appearance. "Congratulations, Princess."

"Thank you."

"I have something for you."

He takes a small wooden box from inside his robe and presses it into my hand.

"You didn't need to bring me a gift," I begin, but he cuts me off with a wave of his hand, still smiling.

"She'd have wanted you to have it." Bowing to me again, he turns with a sweep of his iridescent cloak and disappears among the crowd.

I descend the terrace steps and follow the path of paving stones around scrubby trees and cold-hardy shrubs until I hear the trickle of a fountain. In winter it will be frozen, but now in late summer it's alive, gurgling and foamy with bubbles. Our gardens are nothing compared to those in the palace of Zelen, but my mother loved them. She often walked the paths regardless of the weather, and she kept her solarium full of succulents, bromeliads, and potted citrus trees from Zelen, donating the fruit she coaxed from the trees to Lazul's poor.

The fountain is tucked into a round alcove ringed with topiaries and lit torches. Sitting on the edge of the fountain, I slide open the wooden box's lid, revealing a filigree locket on a golden chain. I pull it free and spring the catch. The small hinge pops open with a *snap*, revealing an aquamarine embedded inside. The jewel glows with an eerie green light in the darkness.

Once an ordinary aquamarine, Mother had the jewel

enchanted as a gift for Rothbart. She called it the Speaking Jewel. It was meant to tell him her location whenever he wished to find her. When Mother died, Rothbart was the first person I suspected of being responsible. They were always cooking up spells together. Some were simple—an elixir to make bland food taste better, or charms to help her plants flourish in the cold. But she died by a spell so complex none of our mages could trace its origin. All that remained of her was a smoldering pile of bones and ash and a few feathers. It was assumed she died trying to transform into her bird form, but I didn't believe it. Transfiguration is challenging, and many have died trying it, but my mother was a natural shapeshifter.

I insisted to my father that something was amiss, and that I suspected Rothbart had played a part in my mother's death. He was questioned, but he had an alibi. He was at a meeting that night for court mages. My continued suspicion was considered further evidence of me being overcome with grief in the days after her death.

Now, I trace the mouth carved into the gemstone with my fingertip and it pulses with strong magic. I sense the agitated churning of the lightning in my vial, like it knows the magic isn't mine. The necklace's power feels impartial and synthetic, not organic like Dette's restorative greenhealing, or my static lightning. It does as it's asked, and no more.

"Where is she?" I say, my voice a high quaver. When the jewel doesn't answer, I say, "Where is Mora?"

When it speaks, the jewel has a voice like falling rock or the crack of diamonds. "She is no longer."

I snap the locket closed with a gasp, my throat suddenly choked with tears. What a horrid gift. I want to throw it into the fountain, but there's a part of me that can't bear to part with it.

I shake my head, angry with myself. Mother was a hard woman. She wouldn't want me to wallow. She wanted me to be strong and brave, worthy of my station and power.

I'm drawing my hand back to toss the locket into the fountain after all, when I hear Dette's voice. "Thedra? What are you doing out here?"

She's standing at the entrance to the alcove with one hip cocked, her hand resting on the dip of her waist. Quickly, I put the necklace's chain over my head and tuck the locket into my gown's bodice.

"I was just looking at the fountain. My mother loved it here."

She joins me on the fountain's ledge and trails her fingers in the water, which is tinted green and purple by the flickering torches. We watch the frothing, jewel-colored water.

"Are you going to tell me to cheer up?" I ask.

"No, of course not. Tonight must've been difficult for you." Dette flicks a few drops of water at me, and I giggle despite myself.

"How long will you stay?" I ask. "I've missed you."

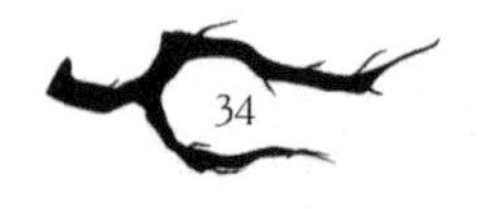

She winds a curl around her finger, not looking at me. "A few days. Then I'll follow the trade road to Thornewood Forest. I want to visit my father before they close the gates for autumn."

Dette's father is King Cygnus, the leader of Shoreana, the sylph realm. Shoreana is an independent country, not technically part of the Triumvir of Zelen, Lazul, and Dendronia. The sylphs have their own laws and customs, and we exist in peace with them.

"Give him our regards."

"I will. I plan to winter on Lebed. We've had no word from our steward for six months, nor the messenger we sent to him. Momma wants to make sure all is well there."

Lebed is the isle where Dette and I were fostered together in Alder Tower, her family's summer home. The castle once lit the isle for the ships crossing the Lake of Tears at night.

Lazul is a land of contrasts—frozen tundra and barren desert, black frost and blinding sun on white dunes. Icy Dendronia lies to the north, and lush, green Zelen to the south. Because we are mostly landlocked, we have few ships. When I was eleven years old, I crossed the Lake of Tears to Lebed for the first time in a simple dory. I remember asking the boatman why they called it the Lake of Tears and he told me to taste its waters.

I dipped my fingers over the side of the dory and licked at the water that dripped from them. It was saltwater. When we reached the isle, Dette was the first person I saw. She was lying onshore after swimming, drying her dark hair and silky white wings in the sun.

"Six months is a long time for no word," I say. "Wouldn't you be safer to send someone else ahead of you?"

"Don't worry. I'll be traveling with a large company."

"Promise me you'll be careful, anyway. You know my friend Vere of Albiton went missing three weeks ago."

"I know."

Several daughters of vassals and nobles in the Triumvir have disappeared since my mother's death, and they're almost always women and girls with powers. Some turn up dead, but most simply vanish. Father once demanded that I have an armed guard with me at all times, but so far, I've avoided that particular encumbrance.

"Of course I'll be careful," Dette replies, her tone brisk. "But it's not your place to protect me, Thedra. I don't mean to scold," she says more gently. "I only mean...make yourself your priority. You've had plenty to trouble you the past few years without adding me to the list."

Silence that's thick with past disappointment falls between us, and I stare at my hands, suddenly feeling vulnerable.

"I know you hate pointless ceremonies," says Dette, changing the subject. "But the ball is for you. You should be in there"—she nods toward the palace—"dancing like mad and drinking your weight in wine."

I shake my head. "The ball is really for Father. At my own ball, I wouldn't have to wear a dress or watch you flirt and dance with a girl who has never been kind to me."

Dette laughs softly, but she looks away.

"I'm serious. Topaz is a snake. If you must pair off, at least choose someone halfway civil."

"We were *just dancing*. I don't remember you being this possessive when we were engaged."

"I'm not being possessive," I choke out. "You can dance with whoever you want, but that doesn't mean I want to see it."

I trail off because she's looking at me solemnly, and even though she says nothing, I can read her expression. Her eyes glitter in the torchlight, the usual pleasantness banished from her face by my envy.

I want to tell her it hurts to think of her with someone else. Especially someone I know will act like a bitch every time I run into them. But I don't want to expose the soft underbelly of my insecurity. Dette was one of the only people I could be vulnerable with, but now I've lost that, too. I should tell her that, but I don't.

She stands up, her pale green ball gown shimmering like silver fish scales in the moonlight. "It isn't fair of you to be angry with me for this. You know I still care for you, Thedra, but..."

Dark goddess, she really just said, *I care for you, but*. My voice comes out in a hoarse whisper. "But what?"

She folds her hands. "It's time we let go of one another. We both have duties to uphold, countries to someday rule."

My tongue sticks to the roof of my mouth. "I'd never have given you up if Akina hadn't parted us."

"Don't blame Momma. She always puts the crown first. It's her sworn duty."

"Forget about duty for five seconds, Dette," I plead. "What is the crown? A piece of jewelry. An empty circle."

There is hurt in her eyes. "The crown of the High Empress is a symbol of three nations," she says, her tone cool. "And of their people. To wear it is to be reminded of one's responsibility. You'd do well to look to your own."

Perhaps this is wise of her, but it angers me she always takes her mother's side. Just once, I want her to see things as I do. To want me more than she wants to rule the Triumvir or please Akina.

"You've never loved me as much as I love you," I say. "You only agreed to marry me because your mother told you to."

"And you love some fantastical idea of me," retorts Dette. "An ideal I'd never have managed to live up to."

"I'd have relinquished my own crown to rule by your side. Even let my father's capricious nephew take Lazul's throne if it meant staying with you."

My dead aunt's son, Amonite, who she schemed and

maneuvered to place on the throne, has no real interest in ruling, but the luxury of court life would appeal to him.

"That would've been selfish. Handing your country to a fool just for youthful love."

She sounds a million years older than me when she says things like this, and I scoff, pushed past my breaking point by her condescension. The wine I drank gurgles in my stomach, and I silently beg Zori for it to not come back up. "Maybe I *am* glad we didn't get married," I say, "if it saved me from being lectured like this for the rest of my life."

Dette shakes her head at me and walks away with a swish of feathers and the tap of jeweled slippers on the stone path.

I rub my face, no doubt smearing my ridiculous makeup, and slip my hot, sore feet out of my shoes and into the fountain, hiking up my gown's heavy skirt. The water cools my skin and my anger, and I regret what I said, but Dette's words gnaw at me. Why wouldn't I idolize her? She has always been everything I'm not: sage, gorgeous, blooming with joy. But I don't mind. I've never minded, so long as I can bask in her glow.

CHAPTER FOUR

THE path from the fountain leads to a side passage into the palace and when I'm done soaking my feet, I carry my slippers and head that way rather than back through the crowded ballroom. The main corridor to the royal chambers is lit with flaming torches and more of the bobbing purple and green lamps. I flinch as someone steps out of the shadows into the shifting, multicolored light.

I relax when I see it's only a page, unclenching my fist from around my diamond vial and flexing my fingers. The page folds into a bow as soon as he sees the look of annoyance on my face.

"Why are you skulking there?" I snap. "You scared me. I might've roasted you alive where you stand. Don't you know people have been going missing?"

Zori have mercy, I sound as crotchety as my great-grandmother Dowager Em. Before she died, the servants used to hide in alcoves or behind the drapes when they saw her coming.

The page bows again, so low his nose almost touches his knees. “My apologies, Princess! But his highness King Thede has sent for you.”

I sigh. I was so close to making it back to my room to wrestle my way out of this getup.

Father is in the royal master bedroom with Onyx, eating candied figs in front of a cozy fire. The room is larger and fancier than mine, hung with velvet draperies and tapestries depicting hunts and ceremonies from centuries ago. Thick rugs cover the tiled floor and the bed is large enough for six or seven people. The flickering firelight glimmers off a suit of ancient Lazulian armor and the shiny pate of Father’s head.

I stalk over to stand between him and the fireplace, my gown rustling with every step. “Yes?”

He puts a hand up as I attempt to lower myself into a curtsy and am nearly thrown off balance by my pendulous skirt.

“Don’t be silly, Thedra. It’s just us. Have you left the party so soon?”

“I was tired. And besides, you left.”

“Only just.” His gaze runs over my decadent ballgown. “What a masterpiece.”

“I suppose Godwin was making up for all the gowns she never got to sew for me. She practically groans every time I ask for another new cloak or tunic.”

His mouth twitches. “Well, she certainly outdid herself.

Congratulations, by the way. Your mother would have been more than pleased."

I know he means well, but I'm so tired of being congratulated I nearly sigh. I opt for silence, as this barely resembles a compliment. He can tell me Mother would be pleased, but can't admit that he's proud of me?

Father nods to Onyx. "I'll speak with Thedra alone now."

Onyx rises from the floor and glides toward the door, the emerald gems in his ears glinting in the firelight. He's from one of the distant isles in the Sapphire Sea and he's beautiful—my father doesn't keep lovers who aren't—with sun-burnished golden skin and different colored eyes of hazel and blue. In the doorway, he turns to give Father a look and Father beckons to him. Grinning, Onyx returns for a kiss on the lips.

He brushes past me, blushing. He can't be older than twenty-three. Father's eyes glow with affection. I bite my lip to keep from gagging.

When he's gone, I ask, "Will you keep this one long?"

"Thedra," he demurs. Then he shrugs. "Perhaps. He's docile, affectionate. Unambitious."

"You're downplaying what he means to you. You've had lovers all my life, but never one with his own wing in the palace, or who wore Mother's emeralds."

He frowns gravely, as if he wonders why I have so little respect for his private affairs, but he waves an indifferent hand. "Go take them out of his earlobes, then. You're welcome to all Mora's jewels, if you want them."

I say nothing, letting my silence serve as an answer.

He takes a leisurely sip of wine. "That's right. You care nothing for gemstones, aside from the one that holds your lightning. I was surprised to see you wearing Mora's lapis tonight."

"I wanted to honor her."

"And you did. She'd be proud, truly. But you're seventeen, Thedra. You must marry and take the throne when you come of age next year. We've just come out of a five-year famine, with the moneybags repressing trade and Akina little more than a figurehead. Marry a royal or a noble, I beg you."

I cross my arms, frowning. Although Lazul's jewels could feed a country twice its size, they're owned and regulated by a handful of noble families who brood over their wealth like a horde of dragons. They'd rather watch the populace starve than share what's theirs.

"Akina could send us her greensmiths and make anyone who disagrees with her into a lawn ornament, but you want me to do things the old way. Save the country with an alliance through marriage."

A hundred times my mother proposed making the rich of Lazul share their wealth by heavy taxation so we could afford to trade with Zelen and the Sapphire Isles for grain and citrus fruit, and with Dendronia for more of their cold-hardy cattle and blocks of frozen yak milk. But Dowager Em, last of the old line who ruled through blood rather than power, refused. She'd not have a robber queen in Lazul, she said. Keep the nobles happy and there is peace. Displease them and there is war.

Father scowls. "Akina is a diplomat, not a tyrant. She never turns important people to stone. Lord Woodbine excepted, of course. You could learn from her."

I roll my eyes, and he sighs and slumps in his armchair, as if remaining upright throughout the revelry tonight and this conversation has drained all the life from him. He's so dramatic. At least he didn't have to survive being stabbed in the heart.

I walk to the table beside the massive fireplace and grab one of the candied figs he and Onyx were sharing.

Father frowns as the chain of the locket around my neck catches the firelight. "What's that?"

I bite my lip. "The Speaking Jewel. Rothbart gave it to me."

"Now, you see? Would a man give such a gift to the daughter of a woman he murdered?"

I shrug. *A strange gift, if you ask me.* "That doesn't mean I was wrong to suspect him," I say.

"When you're queen, you'll be free to look for treasonous plots behind every corner, although take my word that it will drive you mad."

I take a bite of the candied fig in my hand so I don't have

to reply.

"I know you think I care only for myself," Father says.

I glance at him, startled. The wine must have loosened his tongue.

"But I understand your lingering feelings for Dette," he continues. "When I was your age, I wanted to marry the crown prince of Dendronia. But sometimes you must hold your own feet to the fire. It's part of being a sovereign."

My eyes widen. I've never heard this story.

"Grandmother wouldn't hear of it," he explains.

"Oh." This makes sense. Dowager Em wasn't exactly known for being merciful. Or flexible.

He turns the crystal goblet in his hand, studying the jewel red wine. "Same-gender unions had just begun to be more common, and it didn't help that he'd lost his powers in an accident. *A powered heir must share the throne in Lazul's halls of jeweled stone*, and all that. Ah well." He shrugs, dismissing the love of his life with another wave of his hand. "He's been dead since the Giant Wars."

He sighs, pinching the bridge of his nose. For possibly the first time in my life, I feel a hint of empathy for him.

"I'll take the throne if it's what you really want," I say. It's noncommittal, but it's all I can manage just now. Too much has taken place in the past twelve hours.

He sits up a bit straighter, giving me a doubtful look, as if he's waiting for my conditions. "It is. I'm getting too old to make another heir."

"You should know that when I'm queen, I won't stand to see children starve in our streets. I know the royal family is in debt, but I'll confiscate the estates of the corrupt, sell the crown jewels and every tapestry in the palace if I must."

He frowns. "You think it will be so easy? That we wanted people to starve? That we had a choice?"

"I don't think you tried hard enough if you didn't."

Father exhales through his nostrils and takes another sip of wine. "Well. That problem will be yours if you take the throne, and I wish you joy in solving it."

"Is that all?"

"Yes." He gives me a wry glance. "It was a pleasure visiting with you, too."

I purse my lips, not wanting to return the lie just for courtesy's sake. "I'm sorry they did that to you, Father."

He looks back at the goblet of wine in his hands, saying nothing, but I recognize the remembered loss in his gaze. I've felt it myself.

My room is dark and cold now that night has fallen. The soles of my feet are still sandy from the garden paths and I brush them on the velvet mat inside my doorway. Henbane and Godwin are gone, but as my eyes adjust to the light, I see Neev's slender form on the lounge in the corner of the room. She's asleep with a throw draped over her legs. Her bare, slender feet peek out from beneath it.

I'm humiliated that she waited for me, like I'm a child who needs help undressing for bed. Why didn't she help Dette out of her things instead? That question breeds an unwelcome thought. Perhaps Dette sent her away because Topaz came back with her to her room. But then wouldn't the girl have just gone to her own room, rather than come back to mine?

I close the window and pull the lapis pins from my hair, and with a bit of maneuvering, I manage to unlace my dress and let it fall to the floor in a silken heap. I toss my chemise atop it.

Relieved of the weight of my dress, I let the cool night air wash over me after the heat of the dining hall and the fire in Father's room. Then I drag a comb through my hair and splash water from a basin onto my face, grabbing a cloth to scrub the glitter off my cheeks.

"Your Highness?"

I turn and see Neev sitting up on the lounge, blinking blearily. She swings her legs over the side and the throw slips to the floor.

"If you were going to wait here for me all night, you could've closed the window and lit a fire."

"I'd not presume, Your Highness. And I'm not cold."

She adjusts the flame on an alchemical lamp to light her way out and blanches when she glimpses me in the sickly purple glow and realizes I'm naked. Her eyes linger on my body for a beat before she looks away.

Knowing she might have been looking at me like that for even a second makes heat bloom in my belly, ripe and insistent.

I step toward her. I can't help it. It's like she's the moon, and I'm the tide.

I barely noticed her when Dette's entourage arrived. Next to Henbane and Dette, she's understated and quiet. Dette is like a showy day of early summer filled with vivid flowers and brilliant sky, while Neev is more subtle, a spring raindrop or moonlight on water.

Get a hold of yourself, Thedra. You had too much to drink.

I take a slow breath, trying to calm down before she looks at my face and realizes what I'm thinking. I slip on a robe and tie the sash around my waist, and she regains her composure enough to look at me again. I'm expecting her to leave, but she asks, "How'd the evening go, Your Highness?"

I blink, surprised by her interest. "I survived the nobles, as you see."

"Did the goddess really heed your voice at the tombs?"

I think of the darting movement of Zori's arm as she plunged the stone dagger into my heart, quick and merciless as a striking snake. "She awoke, but I don't think Zori obeys anyone but herself."

"What was she like?"

People have been congratulating me all night, but this is the first time anyone has asked what happened. "Why?"

She shrugs. "When I was a girl, I used to dream of meeting Thorne. I always left little offerings for her on the altars around Zelen. I wanted her favor in case we ever met, so I might ask a gift of her."

"Oh? What would you have asked for?"

"That's a secret for Thorne." There's a playful tilt to Neev's mouth. It feels like she's flirting with me, and a shiver runs down the back of my neck. I haven't had this reaction to another girl since Dette...

I turn my back to her and pour a cup of water from the ewer beside my bed. Beryl refilled the ewer last night, and the water tastes a bit stale, but it's cool and it soothes my wine-parched tongue.

"I hope you meet her one day then," I say, turning back to her. "Thorne, I mean. And I hope she's kinder than Zori."

"Zori was unkind?"

I take another sip of water, considering. "She was fearsome, and she spoke nonsense, as deities do in stories."

Neev shifts slightly and I catch a hint of her perfume over the lingering scent of the burnt-out cinnamon candles on my dresser. She smells of blooming jasmine and sugared rose petals. Light and sweet. It occurs to me that if she doesn't leave, I'm going to ask her to stay for a drink. Or something equally foolish.

"You're free to go," I say again, reconstructing the barrier between us with effort. "I'm sure you're tired."

She takes a few compliant steps back, sensing my change of mood. "Goodnight, Your Highness."

CHAPTER FIVE

I sleep through the ringing of the temple bells for the first time in years, and breakfast after. My sleep is deep and filled with bizarre dreams. When I enter the dining hall, I ask a page to fetch Dette and he informs me she left before first light.

I clench my fists, fighting the urge to curse in front of him. His eyes dart to my hair and he bows before scurrying away. My hair gives away one of the first signs of my power. The growing static makes it float away from my head, which is why I usually keep it bound and held back from my face.

I can't believe Dette left without a word just because we argued. I thought maybe the morning would bring us both perspective on our disagreement. She has never left without telling me goodbye before.

My throat burns as I remember the fiery words I said to her last night. That she never loved me. That I'm glad I didn't marry her. That the crown of Zelen, her crown-to-be, is meaningless. I wince and swallow hard, wishing I could take it all back, wishing she were here so I could tell her I'm sorry.

I gulp down a glass of berry juice, stewing over Dette's departure. If she had stayed, I could have explained myself. I said those things after being stabbed by a goddess and left to bleed out in a dark tomb, and my outburst was influenced by drinking wine on an empty stomach. It doesn't make picking a fight with her during my death ceremony ball any better, but it might make it more understandable.

Dette left hours ago, but her large entourage of horses and litters is sure to move slowly and stop frequently. Maybe I can catch up to them.

I scarf down some fruit, buckwheat soaked in milk, and coffee before heading to the stables. The breeze in the open courtyard brings the scent of roasting mutton from the city streets—peddlers will be selling meat pies and cups of mead for flin'pennies.

My head throbs and I give the path to the Temple of the Dead a loathing glance, running my thumb over the rough patch of tiny scars on the heel of my palm. Three days a week for the past ten years, I rose before dawn to kneel on the temple's stone floor and listen to the priestesses' chants. I bathed corpses in the mortuary, scrubbed the nave, extinguished the candles on the altar, and pricked my palm over the smoking wicks as a blood offering.

And for what? For Zori to insult me, stab me in the heart, and give me some stupid prophecy. The passing of the priestesshood from mother to daughter is a new concept, born of the political choice to make a slayer like my mother High Priestess.

I taste the injustice of it like bile at the back of my throat. To be a princess and not even possess the freedom to choose which god to serve? Given a choice, I could've worshipped the god of wealth and spent my time counting coins and weighing jewels in the Bank of the Triumvir, allocating funds to the poor.

I think of Thorne, the goddess Neev praised last night. Her statues in Thistle always portray her naked, aside from the garlands people drape over them as offerings. I'll bet her proselytes spend their time weaving flower crowns, boiling berries for healing, and giving one another green gowns in meadows.

The whole thing makes me want to rush to the temple and knock the head off the statue of Zori, push the altar over, and denounce her as a worthless goddess. But that would accomplish nothing. The priestesses would probably drag me into the tombs and slit my throat as a blood offering.

I turn my back on the temple and head for the stables. A groom emerges as I approach, rubbing sleep from his eyes.

"Zmaj, my lady?" he says, offering to saddle my horse.

It smells like he and the other hands were gifted a cask of ale to celebrate my confirmation. "Go back to bed," I say. "You're still drunk."

I saddle Zmaj myself. He chuffs at me as I tighten the girth on his saddle and I feed him a handful of grain. Mother sent him to me as a gift for my fifteenth birthday, the last summer Dette and I fostered on Lebed together. He was fierce back then, barely under saddle, and Dette named him Zmaj after the old dragon from one of our favorite legends. Sometimes it seems every happy memory I have involves her on some level.

I lead Zmaj out of the stable and climb into the saddle, turning his head toward the gate. As I nudge his ribs with my heels, I hear a voice behind me, smooth as satin. "Not heading off to do lightning practice without a spotter again, are you, princess?"

A gray stallion trots into my path, blocking my way. The young man astride it has soft, carefully arranged chestnut curls, and rich, golden-brown eyes. It's Agate Mason, one undercaptain in my father's guard, saddled with all the message-bearing, boot-licking, and degrading jokes the position entails. He's one guard who is often sent to follow me.

I lean forward under the pretense of tightening a buckle on my boot. "I was actually thinking of riding after the Empress's entourage and accompanying them to Lebed. Dette invited me," I lie. "But I overslept."

"A long holiday, right before autumn?"

"Why not? Winters here are misery."

Agate studies his nails, his tone nonchalant. "Does King

Thede know you're heading off with no maids or guards in attendance?"

I narrow my eyes. "What do you want, Gate?"

I know he thinks as the king's daughter I should set an example and address him by his title, Undercaptain Mason, not a nickname used among his mates. But his voice doesn't betray him. It remains silken as warm honey, and he flashes me the smile that has half the palace in love with him, both men and women.

"I was thinking we could practice magic together," he says. "You don't really want to go after Dette, do you? Such a tiring journey."

I roll my eyes. I've little desire to let Agate practice his magic on me. Not today. Today I'm angry and I want to stay that way. "I've traveled through Thornewood lots of times."

"Not alone."

Despite knowing to be on my guard around Gate, peaceful waves wash over me, loosening the stubborn set of my shoulders. I think of the tedious, uncomfortable days in the saddle—the lack of a bed or hot bath or decent meal. Sleeping on the hard ground. I don't want that.

I shake myself like a dog coming out of a bath. "Get out of my head, Gate!"

This is why they always send him after me. Naturally occurring power, power like mine, is rare among men in Lazul. Gate was probably taken from his family as a boy and trained to use his. I've always suspected his gift for persuasion is why he was promoted so quickly through the ranks when he's barely older than I am. Sometimes I think his power is stronger than mine.

Lightning might put on a good show, but what defense is there against someone who can put you to sleep or change the very thoughts in your head? The only warning is how foreign it feels, having someone else's will inside your mind. In the hands of a crueler man than him, such influence would be a nightmare. He's lucky it only works on one person at a time, and not for very long.

He puts his hands up, and the blissful waves recede. "Sorry. You know it's my job."

"That doesn't make it any less annoying. I'm not a prisoner. I can follow her if I want and you've no right to stop me."

"King Thede will be displeased."

"He's always displeased."

He grimaces. Agate always seems indignant at how freely I disrespect the king, but I don't bother explaining myself. I don't expect him to understand what it's like to grow up with a lavish monarch and a great warrior as one's father and mother.

Agate's horse prances nervously as I consider. Now that he's stalled me, I'm not sure I do want to go after Dette. But Agate's power isn't the thing that's holding me back; it's my pride.

I pull on my riding gloves. "Fine, we can practice. But

let's go before I change my mind."

Agate spurs his mount as I nudge Zmaj onward. Once we've left the courtyard, I turn Zmaj's head toward the Fallow Dunes, away from the trade road. We stop at a watering place several miles from the palace where a sparse ring of firs encloses a spring fed by a river flowing from the nearby mountains.

As Agate tethers the horses at a safe distance, I uncork the vial at my hip, snapping my fingers. A ripple of lightning snakes into the sky, a white vein standing out in a pale blue arm. Without waiting for Agate to return, I thrust my fist toward the ground and snap my fingers again, twisting my wrist in a downward, corkscrew motion. Lightning flashes in the clear sky and a branch fingers out and spirals to the ground. It strikes ten feet away, turning the sand into molten glass.

Agate yelps at the ear-splitting crack of the lightning hitting the ground and I laugh. No matter how often we do this, there's always a glimmer of fear and admiration in his eyes.

"What's the point of my coming along if you don't wait for me to spot you?" he calls, coming into the clearing.

"I was just flexing. It's been several days."

Agate narrows an eye, cocking his head. "Try that dead fir."

I crook my fingers and curl my hand the way a knitter gathers yarn, snaring a branch of lightning. Once I have hold of it, I cast my arm out before it can burn me, aiming for the tree. The bolt strikes the trunk, spraying bark and sawdust twenty feet into the air. I keep my arm extended, feeding it with my pent-up anger and energy until the entire tree crackles with electricity.

"Gods, Highness," says Agate. There is fear in his voice. "Rein it in before you light up the whole glade."

I withdraw my hand and snap my fingers over my vial. The lightning recoils, spiraling back into its container at my command.

"What made it combust like that?"

My eyes slide to Gate's and back to the blackened fir tree outlined against the backdrop of snowy mountains. "Emotion."

"Aren't you supposed to practice striking *without* emotion?"

I think of my teacher, a wielder with silvery-white lightning scars threaded across her palms and snaking up her arms. If she sensed me using anger or sadness or even joy to feed my power, she disciplined me by restricting my weapons practice to something relatively archaic, like archery or swordplay. Our legends say the gods gifted mortal women power by mating with them, and women passed the powers on to their daughters, and sometimes, but rarely, their sons. In the beginning, many of the children died because they couldn't control the raw energy spiraling through them from a young age. Mortals with power learned to survive by controlling emotions and draining energy.

"Yes," I answer, "but it's not your job to make me obey the rules."

"Actually, it is m—oof." He doubles over as I wedge my elbow into his sternum.

"Just stop," I say. "Leave me to my own devices today. I'm in no mood."

He glares at me, but doesn't argue further. We spend a few hours at the oasis, and I practice with smaller bits of lighting, aiming for rocks and pebbles. Finally, Agate convinces me to let him give me a dream. It's a skill he's still carefully honing because there's money in it if he can do it successfully.

I recline in the cool dirt beneath the spreading branches of a spruce as he puts me to sleep. In the dream he gives me, I swim in a deep, clear mountain lake beneath a massive sky with billowy clouds skimming across it. There's a forest of dead trees at the bottom of the lake, leftover from when it formed. It must have been created by a vast river flooding a gorge. All is still on the water, and the air is sweet, but the spindly black branches of the trees are haunting in their watery grave below my feet.

When I wake up, I ask, "Where was that?"

Agate shrugs. "Nowhere in our world."

I squint at him, baffled by the extent of his power. Not for the first time, I'm glad that even if we're not really friends, we're not enemies either.

The sound of hoofbeats breaks into our tranquility. I stand, my hand hovering over my vial, and Agate draws his crossbow. I hear the jingle of bells and as the rider nears; I see that it's a soldier from the palace.

He spurs his horse into the clearing and yanks recklessly on the reins.

"Don't treat your horse that way, grunt," barks Agate.

The soldier salutes him hurriedly. "I'm sorry, sir. Your Highness, you must come back to the palace quickly. It's Princess Dette."

"Why? What's happened?"

He shakes his head. "I'm not sure. But all's in chaos and I was sent to find you. Please, come."

I force Zmaj into a gallop on the way home, leaving Agate and the guard behind. When I reach Peakstone, I ride into the courtyard faster than I should, but no one notices. He wasn't exaggerating when he said all was in chaos. Part of Akina's and Dette's entourage has returned and is in the courtyard. Stable hands and guards run back and forth, and the horrible sound of a horse screaming echoes from the stable.

I slide out of the saddle, toss the reins to a nearby groom, and rush into the palace. I find Queen Akina seated on the dais at the end of the throne room. Father is huddled off to one side, conferring with one of his advisors.

Although I usually flout them on purpose, my thousands of lessons on palace protocol come back to me like muscle memory, and I stand in the hexagon of colorful tiles in the center of the throne room, waiting to be addressed. Akina slumps on the throne with a vacant expression, clutching a folded linen to her temple. There's a trickle of dried blood on her cheek. Both she and Father seem too preoccupied to notice me.

"What happened?" I demand. "Who attacked you?"

"Something...some horrible creature. It slew my guards with twisted magic, turning their power and weapons against them." She studies her hands as if she's never seen them before. "Most of the horses were transfigured."

My belly clenches with fear. "Where is Dette?" I ask, my voice croaking in apprehension. "What happened to her?"

She meets my gaze. "She was taken."

I take a step back, breathing hard. My fingers hover over the vial at my hip, tingling from the static crackle of the bottled lightning. My ears have been ringing since I left the oasis. "Where, exactly?"

"It flew south with her, across the moors toward Thornewood."

"Then what are you doing here? No one pursued her?"

"I told you, the horses were killed or transfigured. My maid...she died protecting me, and I accidentally turned one of my captains to flint. I was aiming for the fucking bird."

I've never seen her like this. I've certainly never heard her curse. She's trembling, and she traces the velvet trim on the

sleeve of her garnet-hued gown with her free hand.

"Sylphs are born in eggs," she says suddenly, as if telling me something of grave importance. "When they mate with humans, our bodies don't make the shell to protect them at birth. But I risked it for the alliance. When I went into labor, they cut her out so she wouldn't be crushed by the contractions.

"I was so afraid. But she was perfect and strong. She had Cygnus' beauty and my power. One of her wings was slightly crushed when they pulled her out, but it healed itself before the sun had set that day. And now she's—"

"Your Majesty," I interject, recognizing her rambling as a sign of shock. I wonder if her head wound is worse than it looks. "I'll find her."

She gives me a quick, sharp glance, looking like her old self for a moment, and I take her free hand in both of mine and give it a squeeze. "I will," I say firmly.

"You'll do no such thing," says Father, crossing the dais. "I command you to stay here unless otherwise instructed."

Ignoring him, I scan the room for a servant and beckon to a boy hovering in the doorway with wide eyes. "Take the Empress to one of the royal chambers. She's in shock and she's injured, so bring a healer and keep her under heavy guard."

"Yes, Your Highness." He rushes forward and I place Akina's hand in his. She allows herself to be led away, looking dazed.

When they're gone, I find another servant, a page this time.

"Fetch Rothbart. He knows defensive spells, doesn't he?"

"Rothbart is missing." Father lowers himself to the vacant throne, looking pained. "His mage's lair has been abandoned."

"And you think this is a coincidence?" My voice rises nearly to a shriek and Father puts his hand up to calm me.

"Your lightning, Thedra," he says through his teeth. "Be calm. Your hair is standing out from your head."

I can see the tendrils floating about my face and I palm them away, and clasp the vial at my hip until it digs into my hand. The static stings and shocks me, but I don't let go. "I'm not going to lose control of it just because I'm angry," I say. "Let me go after her."

"No. I plan to form a regiment with Akina. You may ride at the head if you wish, but I forbid you to go alone. Whatever took her may take you as well."

"There isn't time!"

Some of our troops were sent to Dendronia to quell an uprising a few weeks ago. Those who aren't stationed all over the Triumvir are here in the city, but there isn't enough to form a formidable army, and Akina's soldiers will have to travel from Thistle to join them. A week's journey, at least.

"There *is* time," says Father firmly. "If Rothbart was behind this, I doubt he'd be foolish enough to assassinate the future empress. He would want something. Ransom, most likely."

He looks away as if the matter is settled. I march out of the throne room and stop in the palace kitchens to sneak some food, which proves to be easy. The return of Akina's caravan six hours after its departure has thrown everything into disarray. I take a loaf of bread, a few apples, a hard biscuit, and some jerky before heading back to my room, where I begin piling supplies for the journey on my bed. I'm shoving a dagger and some bandages into a pack when I hear a rustling coming from inside my closet.

Snatching up the dagger, I take a few cautious steps toward the door and clasp my vial. "Show yourself or I'll strike you!"

A short figure steps out of the closet with their hands up. It takes me a second to realize it's Neev. She has taken off her servant's garb from last night and washed off her makeup. She's wearing breeches, a cloak, riding gloves, and a pair of old, scuffed boots, all of which are mine. Her face is frozen with fear, and I tense, static rippling over my skin. I've trusted no one since my mother's murder, and even less since royal girls started disappearing. She could be here to assassinate me.

"What the hell do you think you're doing?" I demand. "And why are you wearing my clothes?"

"I want to come with you."

"Come where?"

"Aren't you going after her?" she asks. "Princess Dette?"

"That's none of your business. Get your thieving, presumptuous little arse back to the servant wing. You probably can't even ride. You'd only slow me down."

Anger flashes across her face, like a spark flaring to life on a piece of dry wood. "You'll have to travel through Thornewood. Do you know the people who live nearby call it Poison Forest?"

"Why?"

Neev's oval gray eyes are solemn. She's just as pretty without makeup, but in a different way. "It's an old forest, and not always a safe one to travel through, but the locals say it has turned evil and is filled with dark creatures. They don't go in after dark."

"Sounds like superstition and rumors."

"You weren't there. You didn't see...the thing that took her."

I glance around, still worried about being caught. If Father cautioned me not to go alone, that means he's going to have me followed as soon as it dawns on him what I might do.

"What will you do if I refuse to take you with me?"

She meets my gaze. "Steal a horse and follow you."

"What will you do if I tie you to it and send you back to the palace?"

Neev's mouth tightens in a stubborn line. "I'll tell King Thede and Queen Akina where you've gone."

Her voice is still soft and low, but the look on her face is one of pure obstinacy. Servants in Zelen are often hired out when they're little more than infants, so by the time they reach adulthood, they're utterly servile. It's a tradition going back

to the days when Zelen first became a matriarchal society, and the women in power feared rebellion and retribution from male servants. Neev's actions are both reckless and selfish for someone given to servitude in early childhood. The blank servant's expression that was on her face yesterday is gone, replaced by hard determination and a hint of fear. I think I like her better this way, even though she's currently derailing my plans.

This reminds me I was tempted to sleep with her last night. "Look, you're very cute. If you weren't Dette's handmaid, I'd have invited you into my bed last night. But I can't bring you on a journey after goodness knows what. I need a better reason than threats you'll tattle to take you with me."

She looks stunned by my honesty, but she recovers quickly. "It was an owl."

"What was?"

"The thing that took Dette!" She looks irritated by my slowness. "A giant owl the size of an ostrich. Larger, even. Big enough to kill a grown man with its talons and beak. It killed three of the guards and attacked the horses."

My heart goes into my throat. My mother's bird form was a horned owl. She and her two sisters were all shapeshifters recruited for the Dendronian army as teenagers. Her sisters' bird forms were a hawk and an eagle. But they're dead now, all three of them. My two aunts were killed in the giant wars.

It has to be a coincidence. But what if Mother didn't die?

What if she somehow survived and is trapped in her bird form?

Then, I think of something worse. What if it's not her at all? What if it's someone else? *Rothbart is missing. His lair is abandoned.*

"Oh shit," I say under my breath. "You're sure?"

She nods. "I was riding in the litter with her."

"You weren't harmed?"

"I was no threat compared to the guards."

"What sort of owl was it?"

"Horned."

"Great goddess." I tear off the locket that's still around my neck and toss it onto the bed. Why would he give it to me? Is it cursed? Will he use it to track me?

"I know where Dette's father lives," says Neev, breaking into my thoughts.

"King Cygnus?"

She nods. "Have you been to his castle?"

"No, but I know which path to take to get there."

"I went to his palace with her last summer. She always stops to visit him on her way to Lebed. Perhaps he can help you find her, but you'll need to get there before they close the gates for autumn. Once they're closed, they can't be opened until spring, not even—"

"By force or spell. I know. But why would dragging you along help me get there faster? Can you ride?"

She purses her lips. "A bit."

I resume my packing.

"I can do other things." She pushes her hood back from her hair and closes her eyes in concentration until her deep purple hair turns to a mousy ash brown. So, it wasn't dyed after all. It was a glamour. She opens her eyes, and with a snap of her fingers, her hair turns back and one of the apples from my saddle bags is in her hand.

I laugh. "Pickpocket magic. Now I really don't trust you."

"I can glamour people," she says, as if she's saved this for last.

I widen my eyes. "Fine. Help me get out of the palace without getting caught or causing a distraction and maybe you can come along. But if you slow me down, I'll leave you behind."

Chapter Six

Neev helps me finish packing before we sneak out of my room, passing a couple of Dette's ladies-in-waiting in the corridor. Henbane is huddled in an alcove, sobbing onto the shoulder of a scullery maid, and doesn't see us. A wounded guard stretched across our path is being tended by a healer. I pull my hood over my face and we skirt around them quickly.

In the stables, the same hungover groom who greeted me this morning comes out looking grouchy and rumpled. Neev whispers, "You get the horses. I'll see to him."

A change comes over her demeanor as she approaches him. She looks taller and there's a sensuality in the way she moves. I glance at her over my shoulder as I slip into the stables. Her face is completely different. She has full, pouting lips, smoldering eyes, and high cheekbones. Her delicate, ethereal beauty has been replaced by a glamour. She looks like some adolescent boy's fantasy of the perfect woman, but her real self is still underneath, the way you can see the youth in a grown person you've known since childhood. It's one of the most unsettling things I've ever seen.

I quickly saddle Zmaj and find an old, placid horse for Neev since she's an inexperienced rider. I guess at the proper height for her stirrups. I can fix them later if I'm wrong.

She joins me in the courtyard, giving the horse I chose for her a slightly wary glance.

I hold the reins and tilt my head toward the horse, indicating that she should climb on. I want to see what she meant by being able to ride "a bit."

She makes an admirable attempt to swing into the saddle, but her lack of height throws her off and she slithers down the horse's flank. I put my hand on her hip before she can hit the ground in a heap, and she gulps down a soft yelp as I shove her into the saddle.

Not going back on my word, I urge my horse toward the open gate leading out of the courtyard without waiting for her. If she wants to come with me, she'll have to keep up.

The stable hand still looks dazed as I ride past him. In a few moments I'm surprised to hear the clatter of horseshoes on the cobblestones, and when I've made it down the path that winds up to the castle from the lower city and understreets, Neev's managing to keep up with me, albeit a few paces behind. I don't fully relax until we've made our way past the gaggles of kerchiefed housewives gossiping beside dirty puddles and the sellers hawking braised apples and stones with magical properties.

I watch the way Neev sits in the saddle when we reach the trade road. She has a short torso but long legs, and I realize I misjudged the height for her stirrups.

"I'll fix those for you at the first watering hole," I say, gesturing to the stirrups. "I made them too short."

She nods. "Thanks for letting me come along."

I don't say anything to this. "How'd you do that?" I ask. "Changing hair color is one thing. But I've never seen a glamour that good."

"My grandmother taught me. She was said to be part fae."

"Oh?" I glance at her.

Many claim to have fae blood, especially those with elemental power, but I'm more willing to believe it of Neev. She has a preternatural look.

Once we've left the town that surrounds the palace, our route is the trade road to the south, toward lush Zelen, and then east, across the moor toward Thornewood. Dendronia lies north across the Fallow Dunes. It's a land of white-capped peaks and lethal cold, of year-round snow and permafrost; a ground that never thaws. The wind from the north is what brings our harsh winters. I'm glad our way doesn't take us there, but it would be far simpler if it did. That road is less traveled, and now I have a pretty servant girl in tow. She looks as out of place on the back of the old mare I stole for her as I do in a ballroom.

We don't make it any farther than the first watering place outside the city before she attracts attention. It's nothing but a well with a wall of stones built around it, a few troughs, and a small stable for sheltering horses. But a couple of grizzled men are leaning against the stable wall, and I keep the hood of my cloak up.

The mare I chose for Neev is placid but stubborn, and it refuses to walk to the trough. Neev grunts in frustration and tugs at its harness, and the hood of my borrowed cloak slips off her brilliant hair. One of the two men leaning against the wall of the stable nudges his companion, nodding at her. He only has one eye. His companion is younger and looks cunning, in a cruel sort of way.

I mentally kick myself for not telling Neev to remove the glamour that turned her hair purple. Brightly colored hair makes her recognizable as a noble lady's maid.

The younger man eyes us with open curiosity. "You two headed down the trade road alone?"

Clad in my worn traveling clothes, we don't look anything like a noble and her serving girl, so I try to appear casual, but I can hear how curt my voice sounds when I speak. "We're going on a journey. Where and why is none of your business."

He gives me a doubtful look and pushes away from the wall. "What about you, lovely?" he asks Neev. "What do you call that color? Plum? You run off from your mistress?"

She ignores him, keeping her eyes down, so he reaches for

her. His hand gropes in the loose folds of the cloak she wears before his fingers close around her arm.

"Don't touch her."

He ignores me, pulling Neev against him and pinning her arms to her sides. Her eyes grow large with fear as he swings her around.

"Serving girls from the palace," he sneers to his companion. "Run off before their bonds are up, is my guess. Those are palace harnesses on those horses. No bells, but polished and gleaming. Fine silver."

"I warn you," I say. "I'm an elemental, and the newly confirmed Priestess of the Dead. If you don't let her go, I'll decide your fate for you."

He bursts into mocking laughter and nods to his companion. "Hey Flint, grab the Priestess of the Dead."

The one-eyed man pushes away from the stable wall, and I sweep my cloak back with my left hand, reaching toward my hip with my right. As my fingers touch the vial and crackle with energy, there's a flash of blinding light and the man holding Neev lets go of her with a scream. He flails his hands as if he picked up something too hot to touch.

My fingers close around the diamond vial and I pop the cork, snapping my fingers. My lightning strikes the stone lip of the well, sending up a spray of pebbles and silt. One of the rock fragments hits the man headed toward me in the forehead, leaving a cut that oozes blood.

He falls to his knees, stunned. The malice drains from his face, replaced by terror, but the one who grabbed Neev is staring at his hands in enraged horror. Ugly bubbled blisters cover his fingers and palms. Before I have time to process what this means, he rushes Neev again and I swing my arm toward him.

Lightning follows the track of my arm in a sizzling line that strikes him in the chest, knocking him flat. He lies on his back beside the well, his handsome but wicked face frozen in open-mouthed disbelief. The one-eyed man scrambles off his knees and backs away with his hands out.

When I turn to him, he pleads, "Please, priestess, show Zori's mercy!"

I lower my arm. "Go then, quickly. And leave the horse."

He turns and runs down the path toward the trade road without a second glance, leaving his horse tethered to a ring in the stable wall.

Neev is staring at me. Her chest heaves. "You killed him."

I'm shocked at what I've done, but I don't want her to see it. "He would've done the same to either of us. And I doubt it would've been the first time."

She swallows. "Thank you, Your Highness."

"Don't thank me. Stay out of trouble so I won't have to do it again. Change your hair, keep your hood on, and don't talk to anyone."

Her eyes are on the stones set in the well and I study

her. The magic she used to burn the man who attacked her wasn't simple magic, like changing her hair color or taking the apple from my saddlebag. It was complex. Defensive. Now I understand the gloves she wears, and the heat in her touch when she did my hair.

Magic like hers is rare among the daughters of commoners in the Triumvir, because the nobles have spent so long hoarding it for themselves. When it does appear in commoner children, they're taken from their families to be trained and given government, court, or military positions. I wonder why Neev kept her magic hidden.

We check the dead man's clothing and take a small thin knife, waybread, and a few coins. Then I slowly approach the horse left behind by our other attacker, clucking my tongue. He jerks his head away from my touch, unnerved by the static still emanating from my body.

Neev says, "Let me."

To my surprise, the horse whickers when she speaks to it, letting her stroke its velvet nose with the back of her gloved hand.

"It's your voice," I say, reaching to remove the saddle as she continues to pet it. It won't be as easy for someone to steal without the saddle. "Soft and soothing."

She looks at me sidelong. "Oh, is that it?"

I snort. "It can't possibly be the fact that it just saw me kill a man with lightning."

I untie the horse's halter from the iron ring set in the stable wall and smack its flank. It trots off with a whinny, back down the trade road. I'm confident it will return to the public stables. Horses and mules might be stubborn, but they know how to find their way back to food and shelter.

When we stop to camp at sunset, Neev watches me conjure a crackling blue fire with peat and dry sticks. We eat the bread and apples I brought in silence.

Once we've finished, I study her across the campfire. Her hood has slipped down again, and she lets the glamour she put on her hair fade as I told her to, turning it back to plain brown. "How'd you do that?"

"Do what?"

"When you burned the man's hands."

"Oh, that. I didn't do it on purpose. It just happened."

"You mean you're an untrained elemental? Why weren't you selected for training?"

She looks at her hands. "My mother didn't report it. I was her only child, and she didn't want to lose me."

Wielders of fire and heat are particularly powerful and therefore dangerous elementals. Failing to report a child with magical capabilities is a crime punishable by imprisonment in the Triumvir. They're considered far too valuable and dangerous to be kept a secret. My history tutor told me there was an uprising when the laws were passed several hundred years ago, but it was eventually quelled. The truth is, I've always been on the commoners' side. If someone tried to take my child from me, I'd resist too, no matter the reason.

"And where is your mother now?"

"She died."

I'm hit with compassion for her, the unwelcome kinship of having lost a parent, and I frown. "I'm sorry. No one should have to go through that. It's awful."

She merely nods, not meeting my gaze. "After, I turned to begging and doing simple magic tricks for payment." Her voice is low. "That was how Dette found me."

I nod. This sounds too much like Dette to be a lie. She was forever taking in needy, wounded things when we were children.

"Can you control it?"

"Sort of. I mean, I keep it contained, usually. But sometimes it just...leaps out. Especially when I'm in danger. Like today."

"Containment isn't the same as control. If you bottle it up and don't use it, it's bound to injure someone."

"I had to keep it a secret. I couldn't have the royal family finding out one of their servants was an unreported elemental."

"Does Dette know?"

"Yes. But she'd never tell on me."

Dette has never held any qualms about flouting her mother's rules. Usually, when we got into trouble together, it was her idea. The memory of this gives me a pang, and I hope against hope that she's all right.

"Maybe I can teach you to control it," I say. "You've seen my power. Light, fire, heat, lightning—they're all connected."

She hesitates, looking uncertain. She has barely touched the toasted bread, apples, and jerky I set out for us, and I wonder if she's upset about the men attacking us, and the one I killed to protect her. I've never killed anyone before, and I keep thinking of his open mouth and staring eyes. Thoughts flutter through my mind like moths around a torch. *I am High Priestess. It was my divine right. He was going to hurt her, or worse. Dead men can't murder.* This last line was a favorite of my old teacher. She always said it when she taught me to cast a defensive branch of lightning. I consider saying it to Neev, but I doubt it would make her feel any better. It's easy to see she has a tender heart.

"I don't know if you know this," I say, "but my mother was Priestess of the Dead before me. It's normal to be shaken by death. But taking a life is even more traumatic."

Neev doesn't say anything, and I stare into the fire. I always knew I'd find myself in my mother's position one day, taking life instead of giving it. Long before I became an elemental, I knew the path I'd walk, because I saw my mother walk it first. I knew one day I'd be Priestess of the Dead, take the black veil, and wear it under my crown at each Death Day Eve feast to light the candles for Zori. I knew I'd be viewed with awe and dread.

My mother's power was what earned her the coveted place

at my father's side, but in the years after I was born, her role as High Priestess and the expectation to provide a powered heir conflicted with one another. She wasn't allowed to transfigure when she was pregnant because of what it might do to the growing child, but her offspring were affected anyway—the dead babies often had feathers and claws. At night, I would lay in bed and check myself for such horrors—rubbing the back of my neck in search of a prickly ruff, inspecting my fingernails as if they might to turn to talons before my very eyes. But I had nothing to fear. In this way, as in every other, I was ordinary.

But it wasn't only the constraint that plagued Mother. In my early childhood, after a sentencing was carried out, she often spent days alone in her solarium, rooting cuttings and grafting branches, convincing things to bud and bloom bit by bit. I wept and begged her to play with me, but she only brushed my cheek with fingers stained green and resumed her work until my nurse bustled me away.

She told me once when I pleaded with her to return to court with me that a penance must be paid for taking a life. One way or another. I wonder sometimes if hers was paid when she died. Now I wonder how I'll pay mine.

Neev is watching me across the small campfire, her eyes reflecting the fire in twin blue flames. "Thedra? You trailed off."

I shake my head. "Sorry. I was just thinking about my

mother. Something she told me."

"What?"

"That's there's always a price for taking a life."

She regards me solemnly. "Do you believe that?"

"I don't know." I stand up and turn my back to her, surveying the distant, tree-covered hills of Thornewood in the failing light. "Go to sleep. We need energy for tomorrow."

Our journey is blessedly uneventful for the first few days. On the fourth afternoon, we reach the first trading post outside Lazul, stopping to water our horses and stay the night in an inn. The downstairs tavern is crowded, thanks to it being the end of summer and the start of autumn trading season. At least we'll be less conspicuous. I find the proprietor to procure a room and then give one of the kitchen maids a bronze queen for a mug of small beer. Neev doesn't want anything, but she stands by quietly as I drink, making me feel awkward with her large-eyed, silent gaze.

Even though it's late summer, we're many miles from the warmth of Zelen's green hills, and the night is cold. When I've finished the ale, I warm my hands at a brazier of burning coal. Neev follows me like a shadow, although she hangs back from the heat.

"Come closer if you're cold," I say.

"I'm not."

"Then why are you still wearing my cloak?"

Before she can answer, I hear the familiar timbre of a silky, melodic voice over the cacophony of the tavern.

"Two women. One tall and haughty and probably dressed in leathers. She might be in the company of another. Small and pretty, a maidservant—she has bright hair and a Zelenean thief's tattoo on her inner wrist. You must take us to them immediately, by order of the king."

It's Agate Mason, and he's speaking to the proprietor.

Damn it. If I had a flin'penny for every time this happened, I'd be richer than my father. I put my hood up to cover my face and snatch at Neev's sleeve. "He found us!"

She looks frightened, as if she's expecting a villain to jump out of the shadows and grab her. She looks over her shoulder.

"Who did?"

I place one finger along the edge of her jaw and turn her face gently toward me so she doesn't draw their attention with her wide-eyed gaze. "That's Agate Mason, a man from my father's guard. Shit. Don't look again."

Neev disregards me and looks back to where Agate is conferring with the innkeeper. "Oh no. He has Pietr with him, Akina's head of staff."

"I said don't look at them."

"Oh green goddess, Thedra. Do something." Her voice sounds as panicked as I feel, but I don't fail to notice that this is the first time she has called me by my given name.

I grab her by the waist and yank her toward me, pulling her

head down onto my shoulder in an embrace.

We should've gone straight to our room. At least then we could've barred the door and escaped out the window. With the tavern so packed, our best bet is to weave through the crowd and escape through the kitchen and out the back door before Agate and Pietr see us. I stand up, hauling Neev with me, and sidle toward the arch at the back of the room where I've seen servants coming and going with trays of ale and tureens of soup.

I glance over my shoulder several times to make sure they haven't spotted us. But just when I think we've made it, the innkeeper points toward where we were sitting by the large, open fireplace, and I see Agate stride in that direction with Pietr scuttling behind him. I shove Neev into the dark corner near the kitchen door and press my body against hers, putting my hands to either side of her head like a swaggering man attempting to seduce a maid.

"What are you doing?" Her voice is barely a whisper.

"Would he know your face?"

She nods.

"Then keep still. Look."

Her eyes dart over my shoulder, wide with fear.

"Not at them, at me. They can't see you."

Uncertainly, as if she is breaking a rule, she lifts her gaze to mine. This close, her gray eyes have shades of dark slate and pale blue blended together. I reach out and pull the hood forward to cover her face, and she presses her hands against the wall behind her. I lean my forehead on my arm, waiting for Gate and Pietr to pass our darkened corner.

Neev is frantic, her hot breath puffing against my neck like a tiny dragon's.

"Do the glamour," I whisper. "The one you used on the stable hand at the palace."

She shakes her head. "I can't. I'm too nervous. If Pietr finds me, I'll be taken back to the palace. And what if they know about the man at the well?"

She's trembling against my arm and there's a note of hysteria in her voice. I place one finger against her lips to quiet her before she gives us away. "It's all right," I breathe. "I'll get us out of this. Look under my arm, just for a second. Tell me if they've passed."

She ducks down. "No."

A few tense seconds pass, and then she looks again. "They've gone the other way."

"Follow me to the kitchen."

I grab her hand, and we run for the doorway of the hot kitchen. I dodge the cook and a kitchen maid, losing my grip on Neev's hand. I was expecting to pull her behind me, but the instant we're separated she darts off and leaves me behind, scurrying around tables piled with vegetables and strings of hanging onions.

"Have you stolen somethin'?" barks a woman, possibly

the innkeeper's wife.

I dart out the back door into the dirty alley. Neev is a good ten steps ahead of me and we continue to run, skirting oily puddles and piles of refuse.

We weave through the narrow, unpaved streets of the trading post, hearing footsteps close behind us. When Neev veers into the side streets of a nearby slum, I follow her. I run until I feel like my legs will give out and my lungs will burst, but she's so fast I can barely keep up. Several times I nearly lose sight of her among the tightly packed ramshackle houses.

When I can't run anymore, I lean against a wattle and daub wall, holding my aching side. "Neev! Please stop." A scrawny black cat nibbling at a discarded meat skewer eyes me with dislike before running away.

Neev returns silently, edging along with her back to the wall.

"You're fast," I manage, still struggling to catch my breath.

She nods. "I've run for my life more than once."

"I kept them from seeing you and then you left me behind," I say, unable to hide the accusation in my voice.

"The only thing on my mind was escape. If they find me now…"

The consequence of deserting the Empress's service is imprisonment. In some cases, depending on the reason, even death. But perhaps the fact that Neev is on a rescue mission for the princess would be in her favor.

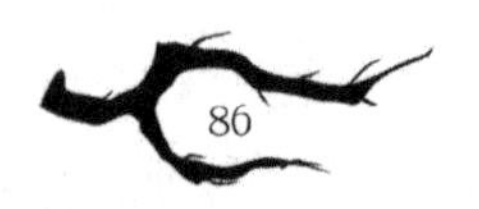

"I understand," I say, "but when I give someone the benefit of the doubt, as I've given you, I appreciate being shown some loyalty."

Neev lowers her head. "Yes, Your Highness."

Just like that, we're back to commoner and princess again, and this time it's my doing. I had to turn queen-bitch on her just because she was faster than me. I drag my hand across my mouth. "Let's find some water and get out of here."

She nods and follows me out of the alley. We fill our skins at a well on the outskirts of town. I hate the thought of leaving Zmaj, of not knowing what will happen to him. I'm afraid he'll be stolen and sold, and then I'll never see him again. But returning to the stables is too risky, so we go on foot, heading onto the rocky moor where we can hide in the rock crevices and the tall heather. We walk for a few hours, then stop to gather kindling before making camp beneath an outcropping.

Neev gathers rocks and places them in a circle and I make a pile of peat and dry sticks in the center.

The rock is tall enough to hide the light from our fire, but it also conceals the view of the open moor, which makes me nervous. We won't be able to see anyone approaching from a distance.

"We should take turns as lookout," I say.

"Pity. I was looking forward to sleeping in a bed."

"Me too. But I'll take first watch. Can you make fire? With your power, I mean."

She gives me a distrustful glance. "Why? You lit the fire last night."

"With a spark. But it's hazardous. Heat is much safer than lightning for creating fire. I just thought you might be able to help."

"I'm sorry, Your Highness. But I can't control it except when I'm in danger."

"Please, you should call me Thedra. My father's court is obsessed with bowing and scraping, but I'm not."

"Oh. All right." She crouches beside the little pile of tinder. As I get the fire going, she produces a packet from within the recesses of my cloak.

"What's that?"

"I did steal something," she says, sounding sheepish. "It's just dried meat, but there's a good amount."

"That's brilliant!"

She brightens at my praise, and we share some of the jerky. It's salt cured and seasoned with herbs and it tastes delicious.

"Does it hurt?" I ask.

"What?"

"Your power. Mine did, when I was young and untrained." I roll up a sleeve to show her the silvery scar branching down my forearm—a painting of lightning in miniature.

I glimpse what looks like remembered pain in her eyes and she looks down at her gloved hands, concealing her gaze. "Not that badly. That was clever, by the way. The way you kept them from seeing us at the inn."

"My father has me followed all the time, ever since my mother died. I've learned how to escape without notice."

She looks curious. "He has you followed? Why? To keep you safe?"

I grimace. "Something like that."

"But that's not how King Thede is portrayed in Zelen. Our political mummers make him out to be decadent and withholding—" She catches herself, placing a hand over her mouth. "I'm so sorry, Your Highness. I didn't mean..."

I laugh at the look of horror on her face. I'm well aware the people of Zelen mock my father for his self-absorption and opulence, just as those in Lazul mock Akina for her haughtiness.

"I promise my father is just as self-indulgent as they say, but I'm his sole heir. Without me, he'll be stuck ruling Lazul until he dies, and he doesn't want that. I'd say it's in his best interest to keep me safe."

"Oh." She places her hands in her lap, and trains her eyes on the ground again, appearing prim and polished, a good maidservant. I don't like it. I want her to act like a regular person again, so I change the subject. "Why have you had to run for your life?"

She blinks at me, not understanding.

"In the alley, you said..."

"Oh, that. I stole a few times when I was a beggar. To eat,

you know?"

I nod, but the truth is, I don't know. I've never known true hunger in my life, aside from the night and day I fasted for my death ceremony. But I can imagine it. The kind of long distance traveling I've done in my life sometimes means long tiring days and cold nights. But I always knew there was a palace and a warm bed awaiting me at the end, whether it was in Thistle, Lazul, or on Lebed. What Neev is talking about—poverty, homelessness, and the fear of starvation—is foreign to me, although I've seen it all my life on the streets of my own city.

⁂

I see nothing during first watch but a lone gray wolf making its way toward our fire, drawn by the warmth and the smell of our food. He's skinny and his eyes have a haunted look to them. They glimmer silver and green in the moonlight. I hate to drive him away, but wolves and wild dogs are dangerous even when they're alone. If I give him something to eat he'll never leave, so I send up a spark and he slinks away. When Neev takes my place, I fall asleep as soon as I lie down. It feels as if she awakens me an instant later.

"Your High—Thedra. Wake up."

My back and hips ache from sleeping on the hard ground, and I groan as I sit up. It's still dark, and the fire has dwindled. I clutch the edges of my cloak over my chest. "What is it?"

"I see a light."

We climb the rock outcropping together, and she points to a flickering pinpoint of light in the far distance. Another campfire.

"Damn it."

"It might just be another traveler." Neev sounds uncertain.

"Maybe. Or it might be Agate and Pietr. And if so, we're on foot, and they're on horseback. We should smother our fire and go."

I'm still exhausted, and it gives my frustration an edge. Agate has always been a pain in my arse, but this is worse. They should've known it wouldn't be like me to wait around for an army to form to rescue Dette. But maybe they think I was kidnapped by her magical little servant.

We cover our campfire with dirt and hide the evidence of our presence, hastily sweeping away our footprints. By sunrise, we've already walked several miles and stopped to eat wild berries and drink from a pool. By dusk, the trees of Thornewood Forest look like we could reach them before dark, but it's an illusion. They're still at least two days away on foot.

Despite our good timing, the light of another campfire appears again tonight, much closer this time. I'm certain now that we're being followed. A small voice tells me they just want Neev. Maybe I should let them have her. She's a raw, untrained elemental, and she left the Empress's service without being released. Though I disobeyed the king, I won't face imprisonment or death for it. I decide that's unfair, so I resist the urge to turn her over to them.

The owners of the distant campfire aren't the only repeat of the night. During my watch, I glimpse the glow of the gray wolf's eyes again. It is growing bolder.

Its fur gives off a strange bioluminescence in the moonlight, and I can hear ragged breaths as it paces in and out of the trees just outside the circle of our fire. It must be starving, cut off from its pack and hunting alone. Against my better judgement, I take a small piece of jerky and place it at the far edge of our campsite.

For a while, nothing happens. Then two glowing paws appear, followed by a snout. The wolf scarfs the meat and withdraws. When I'm sure it's gone, I lie back, pulling my cloak snug around me. The stars are plentiful out on the moors, like chipped mica scattered in thick whorls on black velvet.

Dette loves the stars. I wish she were here beside me, safe. She's always been such a confusing mixture of strength and frailty. Her light bones make her more fragile than a human, but her body can heal itself from most wounds, even breaks and deep cuts, and she has the ability to absorb pain to help others heal faster.

She's one of the only half-sylphans to survive infancy, but the few who lived on in the past were longer lived than mortals, if nothing like the sylphs, who live for centuries. They're also talented greenhealers, like the dryads. Empress Akina thinks

Dette's healing power comes from her sylph heritage.

If whatever it is that took her harms her, maybe she'll be all right. If we can get to her in time. I curse Agate for coming after us and forcing us to leave our horses behind.

When Neev relieves me of my post, I tell her, "We need a plan for tomorrow night."

"Why?"

"They're not going to stop following us, and soon they'll have caught up. I don't know why they haven't already, honestly. But we need to sneak up on them before they can do it to us. In the dark."

Chapter Seven

Neev and I light our fire as always the next night, but we don't stay in the ring of its warmth. We conceal ourselves in the nearby underbrush, watching and listening in cramped stillness. Every time I hear an animal in the undergrowth, my fingertips crackle.

I run my fingertip over the tiny tributary of lightning scars on my right forearm while we wait and wonder about Neev again and the gloves she wears. How has she not set herself or someone else aflame in a moment of rage or terror?

The heath and Thornewood are always cool at night, even in summer, but tonight seems much colder than normal, unnaturally so. I try moving my limbs just enough to keep my blood flowing and to stay awake, but not enough to attract attention. It doesn't work. The cold coming from the nearby forest and the ground seeps into my bones and I start shivering as my body attempts to warm itself. I inch closer to Neev to take advantage of her natural heat.

As soon as Neev's toasty form warms me a bit, sleep steals over me like a thick, cozy cloak. Before I know it, I'm dreaming of being curled in a soft armchair beside a warm fireside in the palace kitchens. The homey crackle of the flames soothes me, and I stretch my toes to the grate. A table at my elbow is laid out with endless, extravagant dishes: capons stuffed with grain and figs, tureens of potatoes swimming in butter and parsley, platters of mushrooms, steaming mugs of hot spiced wine, and cakes packed with candied fruit and crusted in sugar.

I feast on the crisp meat and buttery potatoes, and a cake made of dark chocolate, sour wild cherries, and sweet icing. I shove bites of it into my mouth with both hands while a soft-looking servant girl walks over and massages my shoulders. I'm savoring the gentle pressure of her breasts against my back when someone kicks my ribs.

My eyes fly open. I'm lying on my side near our campfire. My hands and ankles are bound and Neev is in a heap beside me. She's squirming like a caterpillar being attacked by ants—I think she kicked me on accident. I writhe and twist, trying to reach my diamond vial.

"It's not there, princess."

White hot rage courses through me at the silky sound of Agate's voice.

His feet appear at my side and I crane my neck, looking up at him. He's wearing his undercaptain's uniform—high black boots, a white-collared shirt that brushes his chin, and a cloak of brilliant blue trimmed in gold. There's a crossbow slung over his shoulder, and my diamond vial is in his hand.

I'm seriously going to hurt him for this. I don't have time for such nonsense. "How did you catch us?"

"When I saw no one was at your camp, I assumed you were nearby, so I sent out a wave of soporific magic and sensed for your whereabouts," he brags. "Sorry to have done that... Sweet dreams at least?"

I scoff, not wanting to give him the satisfaction. His power is so subtle, based on intuition rather than action. I'm jealous of it sometimes.

A few paces away is a pack with a tinderbox and cooking utensils attached to it. It occurs to me that Gate could be useful to us. He's a trained soldier, used to roughing it in the wild.

"See," he continues, "everyone thought Neev had kidnapped you, Thedra. But I know you too well for that. I assumed it was more complicated, and it seems I was correct. What exactly is going on here? A poorly conceived rescue attempt? An elopement?"

"Goddess below, untie me and maybe I'll tell you, idiot!"

Neev is still huddled at my feet, but she has stopped struggling. "Where's Pietr?"

"I sent him back to the palace with the horses. He'd no experience in tracking. He only came with me because most of Akina's best officers had been killed."

"Liar. What bounty did Father offer to bring us back? I'm

assuming you didn't want to share it with him?"

He just chuckles at this and I roll onto my back with effort and kick out at him, but he sidesteps me.

"Again, my apologies for the restraints."

He doesn't sound apologetic at all. Great goddess, I wish I could punch him. The fractured hand would be worth the feel of my knuckles connecting with his impossibly sharp jaw.

"King Thede has ordered for you to be returned to the palace," drones Agate, as if he's rattling off a practiced speech. "Method of capture irrelevant, so long as you're unharmed. And I assume there will be some reward for returning an escaped serving girl as well." He nods to Neev.

I struggle against the ropes binding my wrists. I'm no longer freezing, but the ropes are tied in expert knots, and they scrape against my skin.

"You're a sneaky, irritating bastard," I say. "And if you don't untie me, I'm going to boil you alive."

Agate chuckles again. "You can't boil anyone without your vial."

I slither sideways. "That's not how elemental magic"—I wrench myself into a sitting position— "works."

I snap my fingers behind my back and the vial shocks Agate through his glove.

He hisses and drops it, clutching his wrist as his fingers curl around his burned palm. "Giant's tits!"

A second later, Neev struggles to her feet with the singed

ends of the rope that bound her hands and feet falling away. She starts to untie me, and her hands are so hot they burn my bare wrists and slice through the ropes in a matter of seconds.

Agate's mouth falls open. "No one told me she could do that."

His head snaps back and forth between me and Neev, as if trying to figure out which of us to disarm and which to sedate. His eyes change as he focuses on Neev, pupils dilating in the firelight, nearly eclipsing his amber brown irises.

"You want to give yourself up to me," he says.

She takes a step toward him, looking dazed, and I grab her arm and give her a slight shake. "Hey! Don't listen to him. Is the money really worth the trouble, Gate? I'll double it if you go away."

He sucks his teeth. "You don't have the authority to give me what I want."

We know one another too well. None of my father's other men would dare to dismiss me like this. Or tie me up, for that matter.

The three of us remain frozen in our little stand-off, none of us wanting to move in case of retribution from the others. I can feel Agate attempting to penetrate my mind with his persuasive magic again, and it's all I can do to keep him out. Fingers of purple and orange are creeping through the sky on the horizon when the wolf paces into our midst. His eyes are pale green in the firelight and his coat has the same luminous glow it had when I saw him last night.

Agate's power doesn't work on animals, and he reaches for his crossbow. Before he can aim, the wolf rises onto shaggy hind legs. His body stretches upward, lengthens, becoming less lupine. Horns like branches sprout from his head and he shoots up like a tree until he is taller than me or Agate.

Before us stands a hulking, humanoid being with eyes of green fire and hair of moss.

I give Neev a horrified glance. Her expression is one of half-terror, half-guilt.

Just as I say, "I fed it," she says, "I gave it some of our meat."

With one stride, the thing we thought was a wolf but clearly isn't grabs Agate around his torso, pinning his arms to his sides. Its hands are huge. They must feel like iron bands tightening around him.

There's a high-pitched wheeze—the sound of the air leaving Agate's lungs.

"Snap him, wolf-friends?" His voice is very deep, with an inhuman rasp.

"Oh," I say in surprise, still shocked by his sudden transformation. "No! No, don't snap him. He's not an enemy. He's—well, it's hard to explain. But just hold him there, if you could? And don't break his bones."

I retrieve my vial and put it back on my belt. Neev edges toward me.

"Princess? What is this...*thing*?" Agate's voice trembles.

"I don't know."

"I think it's a goblin of the forest," says Neev. "I've never seen one, but I've heard stories about them. This one has been with us since we neared the Poison Forest, but we thought it was just a normal wolf. After the second time I fed it, it lay next to me for the night. I thought you'd be angry if you knew."

I study her, chewing my lip, until Agate says, "Your pardon, Highness, but it's still got me!"

I turn to him. "Gate, you must make a decision. Go back without us and accept the consequences of your failure, or help us find Dette and bring her home safely."

Agate's eyes burn at the word *failure*. I'm sure in his ambitious mind neither of these options is acceptable. But he has no other choice, now that Neev and I are free of his spell and the goblin has him.

"A third option, perhaps," I say, addressing the goblin. "Break his neck if the other two options don't suit him."

Agate tenses as one of the goblin's giant hands starts to close around his throat. "Wait! Are you mad? I'm only doing the king's bidding."

"And I promised the High Empress I'd find her daughter. Your power could be useful to us. And arrows are sometimes surer weapons than fire or a lightning branch."

Agate is seething, nostrils flared and eyes burning with

dislike at my triumph over him. "Fine. But make this beast release me. Can't feel my arms."

I nod. "Let him go."

The goblin drops him to the ground in a heap and he rolls over, groaning. I stride to him as he's still getting to his feet and slap him across the face with my open hand as hard as I can.

He staggers backward, gaping at me.

"Good," I say, pleased by the look of shock on his face. "You're speechless for once." I grab him by the collar. "I don't care who ordered you to bring me home. If you ever use one of your stupid sleepy spells on me, or her" —I nod to Neev— "without permission again, I'll kill you. Got it?"

He rubs the reddening mark on his cheek. "Yes. Got it, Highness."

I release him and he tugs at his collar, smoothing it. I turn to the hulking black form of the goblin. The sight of it is fear made flesh. I'd not want to meet such a thing in the forest.

"I'm Thedra." I leave off my cumbersome list of titles. "Thank you for your help."

The creature begins to lose height, shrinking back down onto all fours until it's a regular gray wolf again, except for the glowing green eyes. I move aside and it saunters past the fire and out onto the open moor. If it really is a forest goblin, like Neev said, I wonder what it was doing so far from Thornewood.

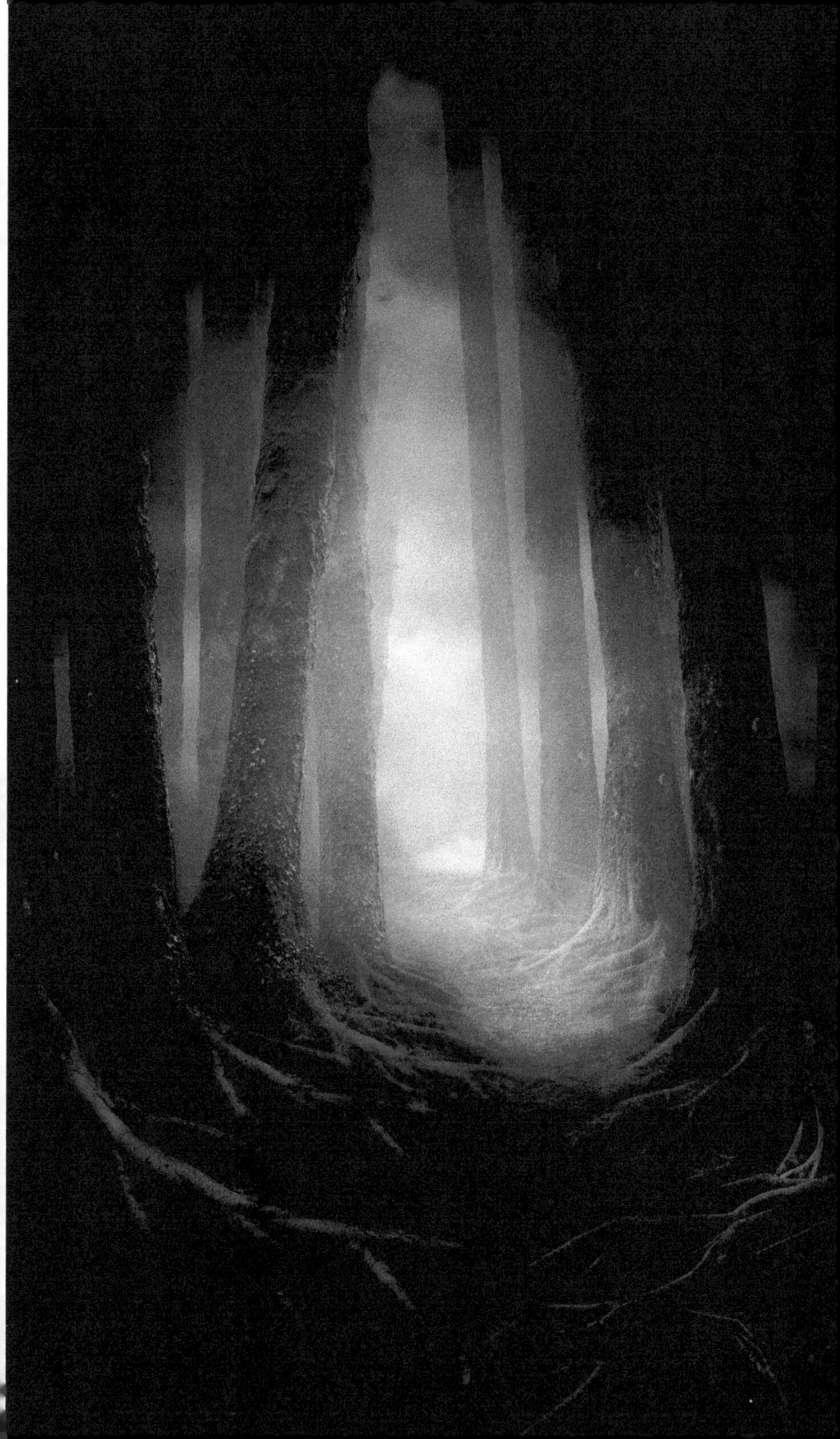

Part Two:
Poison Forest

Cross lavender moor and emerald vale
to linger in Thornewood's hollows and dales.
But tarry past autumn to winter's chill
and lie evermore under glade and hill.

-Old Zelenean Proverb

Chapter Eight

We finally reach Thornewood at dawn. In the gray light, the mist-shrouded fir trees look like ghostly, unwelcoming sentinels. They waver across my line of vision as I try not to think about what might await us.

A stone pillar covered in runes marks the border between Lazul and Zelen. One of the fae folk is seated beside it, in a chair carved from a gnarled tree. Behind him is the entrance to Thornewood, a massive arch made of thickly woven vines. They grow from the ground, coiling round one another in an impenetrable spiral.

We don't have many fae in Lazul. They shun cities and the bitter cold, keeping to forests, lakes, and moors. My guess is this one is a brownie. It wears a pointed cap with a cowslip stuck in the band and is popping mulberries from a basket into its wide mouth with one warty hand and smoking a reed and hickory nut pipe with the other.

"Attention!" Agate begins. "We are Her Royal Highness

of Lazul, Princess Thedramora, daughter of—"

I elbow him in the ribs before he can go any further. "Hush, you overeager wank. It makes no difference to them." I nod to the fae. "Good morning."

It hops off the stump and makes me a gracious bow. The cowslip in its hat bobs. "Greetings, travelers. I am Catkin, a brownie of Zelen's outer lands. 'Tis tasked upon me to require a toll." His mouth is stained purple from the berries and his teeth are plated with gold and silver.

"Oh, great," mutters Gate. "What is it, a riddle?"

"I require gems, food, or coin." He holds out a long-fingered hand.

I rummage through my pack until I find a few coins. The brownie bites a crown, the Lazulian twenty-five-cent piece, and inspects the profile of my great-grandmother's face stamped on it. He counts the pieces out one by one, before nodding and dropping the coins into a pouch at his belt. "Many thanks, good lady. Travel carefully in the Poison Forest. It isn't what it once was."

"And what do you mean by that?" I ask. "This forest has been named Thornewood for millennia, after your goddess Thorne, the Lady of the Wood."

He shakes his head. "It's ailing, festering. There are things in there what shouldn't be."

"Like what?"

"Things," he says again, and I resist the urge to roll my

eyes at his theatrics. "I don't go in anymore, not far. But I'll take more coin and offer provisions in return."

"Do you live nearby?" asks Gate.

He nods and hops off the chair. We follow him about a quarter of a mile into the bracken that skirts the edge of the forest until we reach a little cottage tucked into a glade. The cottage entrance is too low for us to enter, so we stay outside until Catkin returns carrying a basket. He hands it to me and tells Gate, "There's a pile of kindling in back if you want a bundle."

I inspect the little cottage as Gate goes to fetch the firewood. Vines grow along the thatched roof, and the side is painted with clever depictions of mushrooms and dragonflies. I lean forward to look at them closer and the basket over my arm shifts, emitting a rank smell. Cautiously, I lift the lid. Inside is a loaf of moldy bread, several pieces of rotting fruit, and three slimy fish with glazed, staring eyes. A maggot squirms out of a fish's eye, and I shriek and drop the basket. Just then there's a sound behind me, a cross between a grunt and a huff, and I whirl around.

Catkin is clinging to Neev's back like a child wanting a horsey ride, but he's clutching at her shoulder with one long-fingered hand, and with the other he presses a small, sharp blade to her throat, perfectly placed to slash the artery and spill her blood on the ground.

I stand perfectly still. If I move to touch my vial, he could

kill her, and if I strike him, I might hit her too.

"Go," he whispers. "I'll take care of her."

I shake my head. "What do you want? Why are you doing this?"

"She's one of them."

"One of them?"

"*Them*. The broken ones." He says this like I should know what he's talking about.

"The… I don't understand. She's with me. Please, Catkin, put the knife down."

"No. They're no good for anything once they go bad."

"She's *not* bad. She's with me."

I can tell he isn't listening to me, and I start to panic, terrified he's going to kill her. In my peripheral, I catch a glimpse of Agate returning from the woodpile, but I keep my gaze on Catkin, hoping to distract him. Almost imperceptibly, Neev shifts, like she's redistributing his weight, but in the process, she angles her body slightly so that Catkin's back is closer to Agate. A few seconds that feel like eons pass, and I hear the *thwack* of the crossbow.

Catkin goes rigid and his fingers loosen on Neev's shoulder before he tumbles to the ground.

Agate strides to his limp form and rolls him over with a foot. The bolt struck him in the side of the neck and he's clearly dead. "Dark goddess, save us from nutty fucking fae," he mutters.

Neev falls to her knees, putting a hand to the side of her neck, and I run to her in case he somehow managed to slit her throat in the second before Agate's crossbow bolt hit him. When I pull her hand away there's only a small cut where the blade nicked her. I tear a strip off the edge of my shirt and hold it against the cut until the blood stops, squeezing her gloved hand.

"It's alright," I tell her over and over. "You're safe."

She looks up at Agate, her luminous eyes clouded with sadness. "Did you have to kill him?"

"What else should I have done? Let him kill you? He was mad."

I stand and pull Neev to her feet. "Let's get out of here."

"What about the food?" asks Agate.

I shake my head and point to the overturned basket. "Spoiled. Like you said, he was mad. It's a shame, but I don't feel safe here."

We don't waste any time returning to the forest gate. Neev grabs my hand as we cross beneath the arch, and Agate's fingers hover over his crossbow. The air beneath the trees is cold, and there's no wildlife to be seen or heard. Thornewood should be alive with the calls of birds, the buzzing of insects, and the foraging of small creatures at this time of year, but it lies quiet as a crouching panther, watching. Waiting.

As we pass through a clearing a few hours into our hike, I glimpse my first animal. It looks sort of like a deer, but it's an odd shade of green and in place of antlers, branches sprout from its head. It blinks two sets of eyes at me—eyes that are rimmed with moth wings instead of lashes. When I take a step, it turns and disappears into the forest with a flash of white tail, just like a normal deer.

"Have you ever seen anything like that?" I ask Neev. "Was it...natural? I mean, was it fae?"

She shakes her head. "I don't think so. There was something wrong about it."

Catkin's words echo in my ears. *There are things in there what shouldn't be.* Neev warned me too, at Peakstone. I thought she was gullible to believe such folk tales.

"What exactly did you hear about this place?" I ask.

"I only heard about it through servant gossip. They say those who live near the forest have started to leave because the game has gone bad—that it's become aggressive or inedible. And some say children who go into the forest for berries or water don't come back. They're taken by a monster called the Gaunt Man."

A shudder goes down my spine and I shrug it off. This too has the ring of an old folk tale more than truth, surely? Nonetheless, I have a sudden instinct to turn back. It's so intense I taste bile in the back of my throat.

"Sounds made up, doesn't it?" I say lightly. "Like a story to keep children from running off alone."

Neev shrugs. "Maybe. But Catkin..." She bites her lip.

"It's like Gate said, something was wrong with him. He probably went mad being out here alone for so long. Brownies are meant to live on farms or in houses, aren't they?"

"Yes, there was one on the farm where my mother and I lived when I was young," says Neev absently.

My gaze slips to Agate, and his cheerful, conceited expression is gone. He looks somber and scared. I force myself to walk past him, leading the way down the path.

"Let's press on." I try to make my voice sound normal, but it comes out strained. "Several hours of daylight left."

Neev and I make camp in a chilly glade filled with unfamiliar blue flowers while Gate takes his crossbow to hunt for our dinner. Once we've started a fire and set up an A-frame shelter of fir branches, I inspect the flowers and find them covered in a powdery mold that crumbles away at the slightest touch with a puff of sickly-sweet rot.

Neev spins one of the blossoms between her gloved thumb and forefinger. White dust drifts into the air and she lets the flower drop to the forest floor.

"What if this dust is toxic?" I ask.

She shrugs. "I've traveled through Thornewood before and never seen it."

This non-answer irritates me. When Agate returns, I start to tell him about the strange flowers, but before I can, he holds up a pair of small game. "I shot a brace of something, but...I

don't know what they are. I thought they were hares at first, but they're not."

We kneel beside the campfire to look at the animals. They're small, and I can see why he mistook them for hares in the dim light, but they have spines like porcupines. Taking one to the edge of the campsite, I draw my dagger and slit open its gut, careful of the wicked-looking spines. Luminous gray and green entrails spill onto the dirt, releasing an odor like the ferment of the blue flowers.

"Not folk tales, then," says Neev.

Again, I'm hit with the instinct to flee this place. Something really is amiss here, and I don't want to know what it is. I just want to run, to send mages and greenhealers from the Triumvir to work it out.

But that's cowardice. Taking the easy way out. It's not what a real queen would do. Dette would never abandon me because she was afraid of an old forest. I glance at Agate and Neev, not knowing how to tell them what I'm thinking. They both showed up as unwelcome companions at first, but now I seem to have taken on the role of their unelected leader.

"I don't think we should eat them, Agate," says Neev carefully, as if she doesn't want to offend him.

"Yeah, no shit."

"Sorry you went to the trouble," I say, although I'm not entirely.

I'm still angry with him for enchanting me last night, for

putting me to sleep without asking. He's been persuasive with me before, but always for my safety—luring me out of some drinking hovel or convincing me not to sleep among the old tombs when I was feeling implacable. But he's never sedated me or given me a dream without asking for my permission. It felt invasive, and while I know he did it to bring me safely back to Lazul, more than likely for a reward from my father, I trust him less now than I ever have.

Agate shrugs, looking angry with himself. "I shouldn't have shot something I didn't recognize."

I can't read Neev's face like I can Gate's. It's not clear if she's annoyed with me for bringing the two of them here, or just regretting her own decision to come.

"I guess it's hardtack and the berries we picked from the moor, then," I say.

Neev pulls her cloak off the low-hanging branch where she hung it while we built our shelter. "I'll forage something to eat. Won't be the first time."

She throws the cloak over her shoulders and leaves the campsite. Agate and I sit by the fire as we wait for her to return. "Do you think she'll come back?" he asks.

I shake my head, staring at the blue flames. "I don't know."

She could find her way to the path with little trouble and follow it back the way we came. The road from Thornewood to Thistle is more winding than the trade road, but it leads there all the same. I'm relieved when she returns with a spray of pepper grass in her hand. She tosses her cloak next to the fire, and a pile of spongy mushrooms, dark berries, and greens spill out of it.

"Ramps, morels, and mulberry," she says. "I found them in a hollow."

I munch on a spike of pepper grass while she chops the roots and greens on a flat stone with Gate's knife. The pungent weed makes my mouth and nostrils tingle, but it's satisfying after eating nothing but hardtack, jerky, and wild game.

"Here, I'll do that. You'll ruin your gloves." I hold my hand out and she places the knife in my palm.

"Have you ever chopped anything in your life, Princess?" asks Agate.

I slice into one of the long white pepper grass roots. "Yes. The fingers of a man who touched me without asking."

Neev bursts into unexpected laughter, covering her mouth.

Agate exhales noisily. "Is this because I used my power on you? Will you please let it go? I had no choice."

"That's nonsense. You know how I feel about being persuaded without permission. I thought we were..."

I was going to say *friends*, but that's ridiculous. I'm not friends with an undercaptain in my father's guard. He's an errand boy and social climber, and I'm a princess who hates doing what's expected of her. We were lovers for about five seconds after Dette and I didn't work out. Now we're reluctant sparring partners. That's it.

Agate looks at me askance. "I won't do it again," he says. "Unless you expressly ask."

I turn my head and he huffs impatiently at my stubbornness. "Why do you wear gloves all the time, anyway?" he asks Neev, changing the subject. "...I knew someone in training who always wore them. He didn't like to touch people."

"It's not like that."

"How is it, then?"

"None of your business," I say.

He looks between us, his black brows drawn together. He knows we're hiding something, but I don't enlighten him. It's not my secret to tell, and Gate's not exactly a snitch, but I wouldn't put most things past him if they involve coin. I don't want him putting her in danger.

I have two nightmares. In the first, I keep glimpsing something walking through the forest, something pale with an uncanny gait that scrambles from tree to tree on disjointed limbs. I thrash in my sleep as it gets closer and closer, clammy with sweat, but I can't wake up.

That dream fades into another, and I find myself wandering through Peakstone. I walk through the large bronze doors inlaid with lapis and turquoise, and cross the throne room, the feasting hall, and the corridor to the inner chambers. I push open the door to the solarium, which has been left unused since my mother died. It was her sanctum. My heart leaps into my throat, because she's sitting by the window surrounded by the dried, shriveled remnants of her ferns, trees, and succulents.

I go and kneel before her, laying my head in her lap like I did as a young child. Her fingers toy with the dark waves of my hair.

"Everything died," she says. "No one watered them."

I look at her. "We thought *you* were dead."

She shakes her head. "I've been alive all this time."

"But...they told me..."

"They lied."

I rest my head in her lap again, crying burning tears at the injustice of thinking her dead all this time. Her fingers comb through my hair until the nails catch in the strands. When I put my hand back to disentangle them, my fingertips brush sharp claws and prickly feathers instead of smooth skin.

I lift my head to look at her, nearly paralyzed by dread. She has transformed into her bird form, her familiar face changed to that of a giant horned owl, the yellow eyes cold and merciless, the sharp, curved beak the length of my forearm. She blinks at me, once, and opens her maw to swallow my head. My skull crunches like an eggshell as the razor-edges of her beak sever the bones and sinews of my neck.

I jerk awake with a scream trapped in my throat. I lie perfectly still, breathing hard, trying to quiet myself as the thick terror of the dream recedes. It's been a long time since I had a nightmare about my mother.

I was four the first time I heard that she bit off the heads of criminals as executioner. It's where our people got their names for her: the Horned-One. The Devourer.

When I grew older, I understood it from a practical standpoint. She was small, and it was much easier for her to transform into her stronger bird form than swing a heavy ax and worry about doing a shoddy job. Nothing worse than a botched beheading. Not to mention the show of force such a spectacle must have been.

None of that changed how terrified I was at the idea of my mother in her owl form, and what she did while in it.

I wasn't allowed to see an execution until my first menses. She didn't want me to, but the other priestesses and my father's advisors were all in agreement that I must. It was one thing for my mother, a warrior queen, to become executioner. But I could not come to it as a soft, untried girl who had never seen the weight of my forthcoming title.

That morning was cold enough to freeze the blood in one's veins and my nurse dressed me in layers of fur and leather. The pealing of temple bells rung by black-veiled priestesses sliced through the crisp air as I walked to the courtyard, and my breath curled from my lips in white vapor. The man being executed had been arrested for murder and cannibalism. When his head was severed from his neck, the blood steamed in the frigid air and then froze in a wide pool, red as the blood I'd found on my sheets the day before.

When I finally saw what my mother could do with my own eyes, I feared her, but I also understood her. It's no wonder my nightmares about her are always a mixture of comfort and terror.

൭൬

The rotten-smelling powder from the flowers has dusted my face and coated my bedroll as I slept. I sit up, brushing it out of my hair and lashes. That's when I notice Neev. She's sitting on her pallet with the hood of her cloak on and her knees drawn to her chest. Our cooking fire has gone out and the air is so cold I can see her breath.

"Are you alright?" she asks.

"Bad dream." I'm embarrassed that she might have heard me screaming or thrashing around in my sleep. "Did I wake you?"

"No. Couldn't sleep."

I squint, staring through the brush of the A-frame into the branches of the trees above. A light powder drifts down from the tree like snow. I scramble out of the shelter. It's coming from the sea of white blossoms in the tree nearest the tent. They're distorted and swollen. I make a sound of disgust, duck back under the shelter, and shake off my blanket before climbing back under it. "I think this is pollen." I rub some of the powder left on the blanket between my fingertips.

"That's worse."

"Why?"

Neev wraps her arms around her shins more tightly. "Because mold makes sense. Flowers can get diseases. But fermented pollen?"

Agate groans in his sleep. "Should I wake him?"

She shakes her head. "We slept under this tree all night. If it's going to kill us, we're as good as dead already."

I don't know how logical this is, but I'm tired and cold, and I decide to take my chances. Lying back down, I draw my knees to my chest and pull my cloak over my head to block out the sickly sweet smell of the pollen.

When I wake in the morning, my mouth is parched and I reach for my water skin, eager to take a long swallow. When I pick it up, it feels lighter than it did last night. I don't see how this is possible. The water I drank from Thornewood on past journeys is clear, cold, and sweet, but I always ration my water when traveling. It's a trick my mother taught me from the years she spent on military campaigns. Never count on having fresh water. Always conserve.

Agate is gulping from his own canteen, and Neev is preparing the leftovers from last night for breakfast. Asking either of them if they drank my water will only breed bad feeling. It's a poor leader who creates mutiny in a small company, and I imagine Gate will accuse me of being paranoid, so I say nothing. Soon we'll reach the Black Stream, the wide, rushing river that runs through the center of Thornewood, and the other skin in my pack is still full. I tell myself I'm being overly cautious and decide it's better to say nothing.

As we make our way back to the path, I say, "Neev, will you show me where you found those mushrooms last night?"

She nods. "Sure, if I can find them again."

"I think we should gather more, in case any other animals we encounter are..." I clear my throat. I don't want to use the word *deformed*, but I don't know how else to describe them. *Transfigured* comes to mind, but I shrug it away and catch Neev giving me a strange look. "Inedible. It'll be nice to see some healthy trees."

We follow her through a frozen fen, at one point crossing a pond of water lilies encased in solid ice. They're still green and white beneath our boots, like they've been preserved in glass. When we come out of the vale, it's a bit warmer, and I pause to look at a cluster of toadstools growing around the base of a chestnut tree. They're normal toadstools, red speckled with white, but as I study them, they change before my eyes, swelling and growing into bloated, fleshy flowerheads that look like a cross between fungi and flora.

I don't even realize I'm reaching for one until Neev snaps, "Don't touch those! Or the chestnuts. The spines on them are sentient."

Sentient? I frown at her. She can't be serious.

"Good rule of thumb for roughing it," says Agate, giving the chestnut tree a wary glance and nudging one of the toadstools with the toe of his boot. "Don't touch anything unfamiliar."

"And yet you just did," I reply.

He glowers at me and drags the toe of his boot through the carpet of fallen leaves. "There. It's sorted."

"Maybe. Or maybe it'll eat through your boot like acid and turn your toes into writhing worms."

"Won't be much good to you then, will I?"

Neev is listening to our exchange. "Are you finished?" she asks.

"With what?"

"With whatever this is." She motions to me and him. "Or should I leave you two alone?"

Gate scoffs. "Already done that. Three times."

Neev gives me a surprised glance and I feel my cheeks redden. As usual, I could kill him. "An underwhelming experience," I reply. He rolls his eyes.

"Have you forgotten we must reach the gates of Cliff Sedge before they're closed for autumn?" asks Neev.

"That's days from now," says Gate.

"Right. And if the two of you keep distracting me with your bickering, I'm going to lose my way and it'll take us even longer to get there. And once closed, they cannot be opened by force or spell, in case you forgot."

Gate and I clam up like scolded children. Neev turns on her heel and we follow her in silence.

The hollow she leads us to is full of mist, and I'm relieved to find that it smells clean and normal. As the sun burns away the mist, I identify the aroma of sweet timothy grass and lavender. The summer flowers scattered on the carpet of moss are healthy and familiar: bluebells, daises, and nasturtiums. We fill our packs with pungent offshoots—wild onion, garlic, bidens, bloodroot, chickweed, and more of the spicy peppergrass. Neev picks handfuls of the spongy morels and flat, round oyster mushrooms too.

"I don't want to leave," I say, hugging myself. "It feels so safe here."

Neev grunts as she pulls up a stalk of pepper grass. "It'll be all right. I know where we're going, and I trust you to get us there safely."

I wish I shared her confidence.

There's an oak growing in the center of the hollow. It has rough variegated bark and a cap of healthy leaves. I pause beneath it to listen to the wind rustling the branches. There are offerings nestled among the roots: bundles of fragrant herbs, polished stones, fat acorns, and little figures carved from sticks. I crouch to inspect them, and Neev joins me beneath the branches.

"Do you suppose this tree has a dryad, and the offerings are for her?" I ask.

"They're for Thorne. See?" Neev points to a rune shaped vaguely like a woman, carved into the thick trunk. "It's one of the altars I told you about at Peakstone. Her tree is said to have been an oak."

"Was Thorne a dryad?"

"Yes. One of the oldest." She takes a little spray of white bloodroot flowers and adds them to a handful of lavender and springy heather. Binding it all together with a thin stem, she kisses the makeshift bouquet and places it among the roots of the tree with the other leavings.

"Wait," I say as she starts to turn away. "I want to leave something, too."

I cast about for a suitable plant, but I'm not skilled in foraging like Neev, or a greenhealer like Dette. For all I know, I could choose something pretty but poisonous. Finally, I take off the plain silver ring I wear on my thumb. A gift from Dette for my fourteenth birthday. I touch it to my lips and nestle it atop a patch of brilliant green moss.

"Blessed Lady of the Wood," I whisper. "Give me strength to find her." When I meet Neev's eyes, she looks stricken. "What's wrong?"

"Nothing. It's just, you love her."

"Dette? Of course I do."

"You told me you didn't. You said your engagement was political."

I bite my lip. "I barely knew you when I said that. I've known Dette since we were eleven. We were betrothed by our parents, and that was political, but I loved her, always. I can't help it. We had a fight the night of the ball and she said that I've always loved an ideal of her. She was right, in a way. But this isn't about some infatuation. It's about saving her. She's my best and oldest friend."

Neev frowns slightly, nodding. "I see. I understand why you mean so much to one another. Dette talked about you all the time." She looks sad, but I can't tell why. Agate is waiting for us, looking impatient, so we leave the hollow reluctantly.

By late afternoon, the warm, sunny hollow is like a distant memory. It's dark beneath the trees, as if the summer sun can't filter through the branches. By nightfall, the forest is freezing, and I can't stop shivering. As Neev and I build another A-frame with fir branches, I shake so hard my teeth clack together and my muscles start to ache. I can tell Agate is cold, too. Although he holds himself still better than I do, he stamps his feet and beats his arms against his chest.

I go with him to find firewood. We end up walking far from the campsite to find any that's not wet and rotten. I'm so busy searching for fallen branches with the shifting light from my vial that at first I don't even realize I'm alone. I have no idea where he went or how long he's been gone.

"Gate?" I call. "Where are you? Agate!"

I hear footsteps shuffling through the underbrush and turn toward them in irritation. "Don't wander off like that. One of us could get lost."

He doesn't reply, and that's when I realize the footsteps moving toward me aren't heavy enough to be made by his iron-toed soldier's boots. They're mincing, rushing forward and then stopping. My heart jumps into my throat. I tell myself to stay calm and stop being so afraid of everything. But then I make out an odd shape, moving toward me through the trees.

The thing walks on two legs, ambling from behind one tree to another like it doesn't want to be seen. Its body is the color of pale flesh, and its arms are long and disjointed, flapping about as it takes strange steps on short, bowed legs. But perhaps the worst part is that it has no head.

I nearly scream in terror when Gate's hand closes around my upper arm.

"Highness?" His voice is barely a whisper. "Do you see that?"

I nod.

"What is it?"

I swallow with difficulty, unable to answer him. The creature is nearly a stone's throw away now, and it stops its ambling, bow-legged gait.

When it angles its body and flops over into the underbrush, dragging itself forward with long, disjointed arms, I gasp, "Gate? Run."

We run like we're being pursued by a whole horde of horrors instead of just one. When we stop to catch our breath, I make out the sound of the creature's ambling shuffle kicking up leaves from the forest floor. I don't know how it's keeping pace with us. It's almost like we're pulling it along with our terror.

Eventually, we're too tired to run any more, and we turn to face it. Agate draws his crossbow and I wrap my hand around my vial, although I'm not sure physical weapons will have any effect on it. As I stand in the clearing, clutching my aching side, the cursed thing fades before my eyes.

"Fuck's sake," pants Gate. "All that and it disappears?"

I shake my head in disbelief, trembling all over. He frowns at me. "Have you ever seen anything like that before?"

I close my eyes. "Only in nightmares."

"Zori have mercy. What do you think it is? A shade? Have you cast a circle?"

I shake my head. "No. It's worse than that. A shade can be sent to the next-world easily. I think this place is bringing our fears to life."

"That's impossible."

I throw my hands up. "Are any of the things we've seen here possible?"

He doesn't answer.

When we reach the campsite, Neev is wild-eyed. Her gloves are still on, but she's pulling at them and twisting her hands together. I can feel the heat rolling off her, and I resist the urge to stretch out my numb hands like she's a campfire to warm them over.

"Where were you?" she asks. "You were gone forever!"

"Something followed us and we got lost."

"Followed...?"

"We're fine now."

She quivers, her lips and hands and even the ends of her hair vibrating with suppressed energy. A wave of light ripples over her, glowing white-hot beneath her skin.

I blink, and a spot obscures my vision, like I've been staring for too long at the sun. Dark goddess. I've never seen Neev like this. She must have worked herself into a frenzy while we were gone.

I can't believe I once compared her to moonbeams and dewdrops. She's the spark that ignites an inferno, and it's only a matter of time before she goes off. Unharnessed, the godsgift is just another curse.

I wonder if all the wet, rotten shit in this forest will burn if she loses control. A part of me hopes so. Gate and I will, for sure, if we don't get out quickly enough. We'll be incinerated. Nothing but piles of ash.

I stretch my hand to her now, but not to warm it. "Neev," I say softly, "it's all right."

She shakes her head. "I thought you were dead. I imagined being stuck here forever, alone. Or—"

"We're not and you won't be. Try to calm down. Breathe."

She nods, gulping air, but that same ripple of light glows beneath her skin again. "It's not working."

"Should I persuade you?" asks Gate.

I don't know why I didn't think of that. I nod encouragingly. "Let him. This is an exceptional situation."

"All right."

Gate approaches her slowly. "Listen to your heartbeat and the sound of my voice. Nothing else. Close your eyes."

She does, and the tightness in my chest releases a little, but I keep my hand stretched toward her, as if it will make any difference.

"Feel your lungs inflate," Gate continues. "Take slow breaths. You're not made of heat, you're flesh and bone, and this forest is nothing but ice. Let the chill wash over you. You are not a raging fire. You're a river. Slow and cold as a glacier. Old as time. Water runs through your veins, cooling, extinguishing heat and flame."

Gate keeps talking and the tension visibly drains out of Neev. She's not trembling anymore. I've never seen him go this far with anyone else. After a while, you no longer hear what he's saying. Your brain just makes the images he suggests for you.

When Neev's head begins to loll, I touch Gate's shoulder to make him stop talking. He steps back from her and she opens her eyes. All the fire has gone out of them.

"That was brilliant," I say. "How do you feel?"

"Better. I'm so sorry."

"Don't apologize. Without training, I'd be a raging lightning storm, and he'd be a monster who torments the world."

"Damn," interjects Gate. "Missed my chance."

The bit of firewood we salvaged in our mad dash to escape the headless thing is too wet to stay lit, even with my lightning and Gate's military-grade heat spells. We give up on having a fire for the night despite the bitter cold. I shake out my bedroll beneath the A-frame and squirm down into it. In classic soldier fashion, Gate has already bedded down and thrown his cloak over his head. He'll be snoring presently.

Neev doesn't lie down. She hovers, restless, trudging back and forth between the A-frame and the failed campfire. Finally, she wanders over and looks down at me. I'm trembling from head to toe.

"We have a s-saying," I tell her, "for harsh winters in Lazul. *Shivering means life*. And whoever invented it can fuck right off. It's like there's an iron vice b-between my shoulder blades."

"Scoot over."

"What?"

"I'm warm again."

"Good for you."

She rolls her eyes. "No, I'm. Um..." She gestures to herself. "*Warm*. So let me lie down next to you."

Understanding clicks in my cold-addled brain, and I shimmy sideways so she can slide under my blankets. My discomfort eases almost immediately. It's like having a person-sized hot water bottle tucked alongside me. I give a long, involuntary sigh, and Neev giggles. I don't think I've ever heard her giggle before. The sound is out of sync, both with my idea of her and with her behavior from earlier.

"Don't laugh, I can't help it. You're like my own personal five-foot tall furnace."

"So I've been told. I'm not laughing at you." Her voice is soft. "I'm laughing at the situation."

"I fail to see what's funny about it." When she doesn't explain, I say, "Sorry. I always give my father a difficult time for his love of luxury, but discomfort makes me grouchy. I suppose that's the spoilt palace brat coming out in me."

She wriggles, trying to get comfortable, and her thigh slides against mine.

"The night I met you, it appeared you'd just been stabbed in the chest by a goddess," she says, sounding thoughtful. "That or forced to undergo some sort of ritual...? I don't know. I'm not asking you to explain, but you acted like it was nothing. I don't think I'd call you a spoilt palace brat."

"What would you call me?"

"Scary."

The laugh practically leaps out of me, loud and coarse, and Gate snorts in his sleep and rolls over. I turn my head a little, so I can see Neev. There's a slight smile on her lips, but it's not hesitant like it usually is. She must still be relaxed from Gate's magic.

"Thank you," I say. "You didn't have to do this. Warm me up, I mean."

"It's no trouble."

It occurs to me that under different circumstances, this is the moment when I'd kiss her. My cheeks heat as I recall what I said to her several days ago when she insisted on coming with me: that I'd have invited her to my bed if she weren't Dette's lady-in-waiting.

I should never have said that. It was condescending and conceited, though true. I wish she were just someone I met… Where do normal people meet? At the market, or in a tavern? Someone I brought home, not because I needed her help to not freeze to death in an ancient forest, or because I need to survive to rescue my best friend from a shapeshifting sorcerer. But because I think she's lovely and interesting and comfortable to be around.

I'd lace our fingers together and nip her bottom lip as I kissed her, and if she sighed and opened her mouth, I'd slide my tongue into it.

I squeeze my eyes tight, clench my hands, and roll away from her as if I can blot out my sudden desire. "Good night."

Neev stays on her back, and when her soft breathing tells me she's asleep, I lie in the comfortable cave of warmth made by her body and the blankets, thinking of the invisible barrier I imagined I'd built between us the night she saw me naked in my bedroom. The throne of Lazul. Her hidden, illegal magic. My past as Dette's betrothed. Her duty as Dette's servant. Brick on brick, I raise it until we're divided again.

Chapter Nine

Agate and I stand beside the Black Stream, staring into the rushing water. The water's not actually black—it's known for being crystal clear and sweet to drink—but the riverbed is covered in obsidian, making it appear as deep and dark as a slab of jet.

It still runs swift, but now it's brackish and foul-smelling. I can't see any reason for moving water to smell so foul. It makes no sense, just like everything else in this place.

We've been on the trail for five days. My feet ache, my stomach is empty, and my tongue is dry. I might not have known hunger and thirst before I entered Thornewood, but I know them now. I keep having nightmares, too. Always the same ones: first the headless thing with disjointed limbs dragging itself after me through the underbrush, its feet rustling through fallen leaves. Then the one about my mother taking her owl form and crunching my skull like a roasted chestnut.

Lovely.

"Are you even listening, Thedra?" asks Agate.

I blink at him. "Sorry. What did you say?"

"I said we'll have to drink the water from the stream sometime. How long before we reach King Cygnus?"

"Neev says it's several more days. Which makes it over a week before we reach Lebed. We should ration what's in our skins."

My breath puffs in little white clouds as I speak. The deeper we go into the forest, the more the unnatural cold increases. Ten times I've crossed Thornewood Forest on the way to and from Lebed. I've seen it tranquil in the green of summer or glowing with the vivid golden embers of autumn. But I've never seen it like this—the gnarled trees slick and black with rot, the plants encrusted in white frost that leaves them dead.

We've passed clearings of crystalline flowers frozen in ice, and dead, decaying trees. Once, the trail led us through an apple orchard and the smell of rot became so strong it made us retch and vomit. As we drew closer, I saw thousands of windfall apples, putrefied and crawling with worms. This time of year, they should be rosy pink or ocher gold, but they were swollen and black. The smell of ferment and decay was so strong it clung to our clothes for hours after we passed.

We have glimpsed several more animals changed or mutated into unnatural forms. Some are half-plant, half-animal, or a combination of two animals. Some defy explanation.

No wonder Neev says the villagers call it Poison Forest.

There's a spell on this place, there must be. An ugly spell.

I'm afraid the river is enchanted like the rest of the forest, but I don't want to say it out loud. My water supply is also much lower than I want to admit, and I keep questioning myself. I've tried so hard not to drink from it recklessly, and yet it's nearly gone.

Normally, I'd think resting near water would be a good idea, but not this water. It smells as evil as it looks. We walk along the river until we reach the path again and stop at nightfall in a clearing.

I make a small fire, but as usual, the wood we gathered refuses to stay lit. Agate paces from one edge of the clearing to the other. Back and forth, back and forth, like a nervous cat. His blue and gold uniform looks out of place in the drab surroundings.

"Gate, stop. You're making me anxious."

"Can't stop moving. I'll freeze if I do."

I kneel beside Neev, forming an idea. I hate to keep thinking of her in terms of how she can keep me warm, but I'm desperate for a diversion. "I said I'd show you how to control your power."

She gives me an uncertain look. "Here? In the forest?"

I look at the gray, ice-encrusted branches around us. "I don't think any of this wood will burn. It's all wet, frozen, or rotted. Besides, we need something to do."

I take a few dried leaves and place them on a stone. "See if you can burn these like you did the rope when Agate tied you up the other night."

She reaches for the leaves, and I say, "Gloves off."

Neev pauses, her hand in midair. She shakes her head. "No."

"I've seen unregistered elementals before. They showed them to us in training, to make us agree to having our power harnessed. Nothing about your hands could be worse than that."

She bites her lip and gives a small nod. "How does that work?"

"They use something called a siphon to drain your power and contain it within an impenetrable vessel. Like this one." I point to my diamond vial.

"But doesn't it lessen your power?"

"Considerably at first, but it also makes it easier to control and less likely to kill you."

Neev studies my face with wide gray eyes. "Does it hurt?"

I look at the vial in my hand, remembering even though I don't like to. "Yes. But I don't have a siphon and I wouldn't want to try it on you without help if I did. They think that's how my mother died. She was a shapeshifter. You can't draw out their power or bottle it like an elemental's power. It doesn't work. It's too much a part of them. And an adult elemental is similar. Your power is all grown into you now, difficult to remove."

Neev still hasn't removed her gloves, and she smooths her fingers over the back of her hand. "If we can't drain or harness my power, then what's the point?"

"If you can at least learn to control it anytime you want, not just when you're angry or afraid, you're safer. Aren't you?"

She pauses, considering. Finally, she tugs at the fingertips of her right glove until it comes free and slips off. The skin on her hand is bubbled and scored with the glossy white scars of a thousand healed burns. A few of the nails on her dominant hand are blackened, and two are gone, replaced by scar tissue.

"Oh, Neev. You said it didn't hurt."

She cradles her hand to her chest, hiding it. "They used to go away when I was a little girl. But the more it happened, the less they healed. And the older I get, the worse it is if I lose control. Dette used to bathe them for me in a tincture she made. It helped."

This conjures images of Dette stuffing herbs and fragrant blossoms into jars of oil, with sunlight glinting off her sable ringlets. Neev's gaze is on the remnant of rope I placed on the stone for her to ignite, but now that I've seen her scars, I have misgivings about making her use her power, even if it means she'll be safer in the end. Agate has stopped his pacing and is watching us, but he says nothing.

"Maybe try lighting it with your mind, rather than channeling it through your hands?"

She nods, focused on the rope. I remember what it was like

to be an untrained elemental. The way my power intertwined with my emotions—fear and anger and joy and sadness. Before I harnessed it and made it obey me, jumping like a trick pony at the snap of my fingers or a twist of my wrist, it was me, as much a part of me as my hair or lungs, or the rivers of blood in my veins.

Sometimes I dream of wielding my power as I could have if they had not drawn it out of me and condensed it into a diamond cage. I could cast branches from my fingertips, energy streaming from my every pore, my eyes, the ends of my hair. A lightning elemental in a storm is an instrument of incredible power. And of death and destruction. This is why our mages created the siphon, a contraption of glass tubes attached to the fingers that drains an elemental's raging power until they learn to control it.

The pile of leaves still hasn't ignited, and a crease forms between Neev's eyebrows as she refocuses on it.

Nothing happens. She sighs. "It's no use."

"Use some emotion to start. Annoyance, for example."

"It won't work if I'm not touching it. The only time that works is by accident."

"Neev, this journey will be dangerous. *Try again.*"

"No!" Neev's eyes flash at me, and a wave of heat rolls off her body like the air wafting from an open oven door, infinitely comforting in this frigid death-hole of a forest.

"That's more like it," I urge. "It's there, beneath the

surface. But don't use the emotion to control it or you'll lose hold. Keep it in your mind. Make it obey you."

Her lips tremble with repressed emotion and she turns to and looks at the pile of leaves as if she hates it. She holds her hands out, perhaps instinctively, and claps them together before I can stop her. Brilliant white light flashes through the clearing, burning my retinas and knocking me onto my back like the shock wave of an explosion.

When I can see again, Agate is bending over me and Neev is standing at my feet.

"Are you alright?"

I nod feebly. My head aches, and there are spots behind my eyelids when I blink, but at least I'm not blinded. Agate helps me sit up. When I look at Neev, her face is frozen with anger and fear. She crumbles the ashes of the burned leaves into black dust.

"There," she says, as if the matter is settled. "Now leave me alone."

She turns and leaves the clearing and I put my head in my hands. Agate looks amused.

"I see nothing funny."

"No?" He snorts.

"Stop chortling at your future queen. She could have killed us. She still could."

"Exactly. Why didn't you drag her back to the palace the minute you learned she was an untrained elemental? You're

more like your father than you know, Thedra."

My spine stiffens. "What do you mean?"

"Stubborn as a mule until it comes to a pretty face."

I press my lips together. Neev and I have shared my bedroll for the past five nights, and I haven't touched her. Gate's not wrong about my attraction to her, but he's wrong if he thinks I'm abusing my power.

"That's bullshit. I brought her because she threatened to rat me out if I didn't. And how dare you speak to me that way? You think because you've been sent to fetch me a thousand times it makes you someone important? An undercaptain, with your sleepy spells. Licking boots and oiling hinges and sucking—"

"Ha! You think I'm ashamed of what I've done to get ahead?"

I roll my eyes. Most people with power glory in it to some degree, but men fortunate enough to be born with it are often particularly self-aggrandizing. Agate is no different. But despite how irritating I find him, I've never been able to summon hatred for him since he's not malicious.

Neev doesn't return, and I fall asleep waiting for her beneath our brush shelter. Being hit by the wave of her raw magic exhausted me, and the cold doesn't help. I'm tired and sore when I wake up in the morning. Neev's cloak is draped over me and she and Agate are preparing a breakfast of hard biscuit, jerky, and a pile of ramps and wild onion. I wander over to them, rubbing sleep from my eyes, and we greet one another with murmurs and nods.

We eat the plants raw since we have no fire. All I can think about is finding something to drink. I keep recalling the dream I had from Gate's spell the other night, the one with all the delicious food, and my mouth waters. We still have four days of walking left.

As we pack up our supplies, I say, "Neev, I'm sorry for yesterday. I shouldn't have pushed you." I resist the urge to point out that technically, my instruction worked. She did incinerate the rope. She just nearly blinded me in the process.

Her gaze slides to mine, her pale gray eyes no longer hard with anger. "It's all right. Keep my cloak. I mean...it's yours anyway." She shrugs. "And I don't need it."

For the hundredth time, I envy the power that makes her hands like living coals and gives her the ability to withstand the forest's bone-deep cold. A girl of fire and light. But I suspect the poison of Thornewood goes beyond the cold, frost, and blight. I fear it's more insidious, and I don't know how much longer we can stand it before something else goes wrong.

Chapter Ten

We trudge through the endless cold, our feet crunching on hoarfrost. Where once there were fens full of bracken and briars, now there were only frozen bogs and unrecognizable plants encased in ice or crumbled and rotted away. When my feet manage to thaw out beside one of our meager fires, they ache. Even with two cloaks and gloves, my hands are numb, my nose frozen.

I look habitually, even obsessively, at my diamond vial. My lightning is subdued, not sparking or spiraling along the inside like it usually does. The deeper we go into the forest and the closer to Lebed, the more my power is weakening. An elemental's magic is only as powerful as they are, and I feel about as strong as a dried husk. It scares me, and I fear the icy blight on Thornewood has permeated my mind, muddling it with doubt and dark thoughts.

A few times we find a hollow dry enough to make a fire. One night, Agate even burns a few of his arrows, although I tell him not to. He and I start to sleep with Neev between us to share her warmth, with all three of our cloaks and blankets piled on top.

Two days' journey from Shoreana, I wake to soft whispers and Neev's fingers twined in my hair. I normally keep it bound and out of the way, but tonight I left it loose for the added covering on my shoulders. I fell asleep imagining the dark waves had caught fire by the pale white light of Agate's flame. I'm no longer strong enough to make fire. *A cold so evil the thought of burning alive is a comfort*, whispers the nagging voice in my head. *What a wicked magic.*

Neev is stroking my hair, whispering something. I lie still, listening intently so I can make out her words.

Be still, child, and slow.
Look out your window.
See the sky, blue and clean?
Vale so deep, heath so green?
Little lambs are in the dells.
Maids are drawing at the wells.
Be still, child, and sleep.

I see the images in the rhyme unfold like the pages of a child's picture book: sapphire sky and emerald grass peppered with daisies, rivulets of clear water tipping over the edge of a wooden bucket, lambs snuggly with soft gray fleece. Neev's fingers pause, still twined in my hair. She must have sensed that I'm awake.

"What was that?" I ask. "I could see all of it so vividly."

"It's an old Zelenean rhyming charm for children. My mother sang it when I was ill. Sorry if I overstepped. You—you had another nightmare. You were crying out in your sleep, and trembling." She sounds sheepish.

I blow into my hands. "What a pretty charm. If it were from Lazul it would be about stunted crops and wolves at the door, and snow beasts hunting from the north. No one wants to see that playing in their head."

Neev laughs. "Don't forget thieves on the trade road."

"Of course not."

I pull my cloak up to cover my nose and mouth. My legs have gone numb, but I continue to shiver violently. Agate is snoring on the other side of Neev, damn him.

"When I fell asleep, I dreamt of being on fire. Then I had a dream that I fell through ice on the Lake of Tears. I've never even heard of it freezing over. I'm so cold." I've probably said this a million times since we entered the forest. I'm tired of saying it, and I'm sure she is tired of hearing it.

"Here. Take off your gloves."

She removes her gloves too and takes my bare hands beneath the pile of cloaks and blankets. She rubs my fingers and the backs of my hands with her scarred palms until the feeling comes back into them. I don't want her to stop. Heat spreads over my body as I imagine pulling her against me and kissing her. The thought is as natural as the hunger in my belly and the longing for a fire that won't go out.

"I doubt you'd have insisted on coming along had you known you'd be playing nursemaid to me," I say, trying to distract myself.

"This is hardly playing nursemaid."

"No? You were just singing a nursery rhyme to me for fun?"

She grins. "You're so hard on yourself, but this cold is a strong enchantment. And for some reason, it weakens you the most. I think you should go back, Thedra. To Lazul. This place will be the death of you. You may be a corpse-waker, but you can't resurrect yourself."

I frown at being told what to do, but then I think of Zori's words to me in the nextworld. That I'll walk among the dead. "I can't go back. Dette has been gone for a nearly a week. Anything could have happened to her by now. And what about you? I'm afraid you're going to be a living torch by the time we reach Lebed."

"A torch is better than a block of ice."

I stare into the blackness above. The summer constellations were always so bright when I glimpsed them through a clearing here on past travels. My mouth is dry, and I swallow, trying to summon a few drops of saliva, but I drank the last of my water before I went to sleep. When I woke up this morning, my extra water skin had frozen and burst. I sewed it back together, but the water was lost.

Tomorrow, I'll have to brave the water from the Black Stream. I try to remind myself I'm doing this for Dette, but my thoughts keep circling back to Neev and how right it felt to have her arm thrown over my waist.

Maybe it's the sickness of the forest seeping into me, but a part of me hates Dette for leaving the palace without telling me goodbye that day. I never got to take back the harsh words I said to her by the fountain. I'd give almost anything to take them back, but I'd also give anything to get the three of us out of this place. And now Neev and I are traipsing through thick enchantments that could kill us both, all for our love of her.

Chapter Eleven

"May Zori have mercy on us."

I bump the water skin in my hand against Gate's as if we're drinking wine at a wedding, rather than pouring oily, possibly cursed water down our throats. He takes a mouthful first, as agreed, and I watch apprehensively. When he doesn't gag or fall over, clawing at his throat, I drink from my skin.

The water doesn't taste of poison or filth, but it's not sweet either. There's a staleness to it, with a sickly aftertaste. Neev stands several paces away, watching us with a cagey expression.

"Aren't you thirsty?" I ask.

She shakes her head. "One of us should abstain. In case the other two..."

"But what will you drink?"

"I hoarded my water. I had less of a load to carry than you, and I need less. Because of my power."

Gate gulps another mouthful of water and pulls a face of

disgust. "It tastes like the air in a tomb." He caps his canteen and removes a whetstone from his pocket.

"You know," I say cautiously, "the other morning I started to drink, and I swore my waterskin was lighter than the night before."

"You probably took a drink in the middle of the night and forgot." Gate swipes the whetstone down the length of his dagger. "The other skin bursting was just a stroke of bad luck. Not the first we've had on this journey."

I shoot him a perturbed look. That's just the response I imagined when I debated telling them about it. "I'd remember if I had," I say, trying not to sound testy. He shrugs.

We keep to the path, but some hours into the day—I don't know when, for I've lost all sense of time without the movement of the sun—I hear something crying a little way off in the trees. The voice of caution in the back of my head tells me not to look for the source, but there's a strange disconnect between logic and action in my mind now. I pause, peering between the tree trunks. They glisten wet-black like obsidian. There's stillness, and then I glimpse something flitting between two trees and see a flash of white wings.

"Dette!"

Since I drank the lake's water, I've struggled to even remember why I'm here. But now I remember. Dette. I'm going to Cliff Sedge to ask for help to save her. Fearing I'll lose sight of her if I stop to call the others, I step off the path into the frozen bracken, crunching through dead leaves. When I've gone several paces, I hear the sound again, right behind me. Every time I draw close to the tree it seems to come from, it moves.

I run after her, losing and regaining ground, losing all sense of direction. I catch up to her in a small clearing crusted with hoarfrost. When I see her clearly, I realize my mistake. The person I've been chasing isn't Dette at all. They're a small sylph, crouched over and dressed in finery turned to tatters. I can see why I mistook her for Dette, though. She has white wings and stands about Dette's height. But her eyes are dark and large with hunger and sorrow, and her hair is lichen and feathers, not black ringlets like Dette's.

Sylphs often have wings, but hers are stunted and molting, and one twitches and drags on the forest floor like the broken wing of an injured bird.

As I approach, she starts singing a tune with a haunting melody.

Come and eat
Come and eat
Berries and apples
Compote and trifle
Crumbling and savory
Warm and sweet
Come and eat
Come and eat

I recognize it as a snippet of a feast ode sung by the sylphs at summer's end. Dette used to sing it at dinners on Lebed in her clear, lilting voice.

"Are you alright?" I ask her softly. "You're a long way from the realm of your folk."

"What are you?" Her voice is a throaty tremble.

"My name is Thedra. I'm an elemental, and princess of Lazul."

She blinks, studying me with an air of confusion, like a sleepwalker. "Can you help me?" she says at last.

"Yes. I'm going to Shoreana. Let me take you there."

"No!" she hisses. "Not there." She reaches for my wrist and grasps it, her grip surprisingly sure. Her hand is like a bird of prey's claw, bony and grasping with sharp pearlescent talons. "Help," she says again.

She forces my arm down until my hand is just a few inches from my hip. "You're a lightning elemental," she says. "Strike me."

I manage to twist my arm out of her grip, unclip my diamond vial from my belt, and move out of her reach, keeping the vial snug in the palm of my hand. "Why would I do that?"

"The forest got inside me, and I'm..." She retches, and I expect something horrible to come out of her mouth, but she emits a shrill wheezing cry instead, like a grackle startled from its hiding spot in a clump of fern. "Poison and rot. Quick." Her eyes dart to the edge of the clearing. "Do it before he comes back!"

A chill runs down my spine. "Before who comes back?"

"The mage. He brings evil, but you have power." She points to my diamond vial.

"The mage?"

"Yes. The Gaunt Man."

The Gaunt Man. I shudder at the strange name. She reaches for me again, and I side-step her. "Stop! Let me take you to the air folk. They have healers."

Her face changes, distorting into the stubborn scowl of a child denied a plaything. She lunges again, and this time she connects with my arm, her claws sinking through the fabric of my sleeve, deep into my flesh. They're like finely sharpened bone, and she drags them down my arm to my wrist. I gasp in pain, releasing the vial, and before I can stop her, she snatches it and uncorks the stopper, upending it into her mouth as if it's a dose of medicine.

I scream and try to grab her, but it's too late. Strands of energy unravel from her mouth like living threads and creep down her body, sparkling in a blue-white web of electricity. I dare not touch her now, even though the magic is mine. Light pours from her mouth and eyes and her every pore until she is lit up from the inside out.

I turn and run when I realize what's going to happen. I'm thrown to the ground as she implodes and shatters into a million pieces, like a fragile vase dropped on a marble floor.

I stay curled in a ball with my face in my hands, incandescent spots hovering behind my eyelids. When I can see again, nothing is left but a black spot on the forest floor that stretches outward in a starburst of sharp points. Crawling to it on my knees, I find my diamond vial in the center, unharmed. I retrieve it and snap my fingers, and my lightning funnels into its cage like a glittering tornado. I replace the cork and examine the vial. Its contents are no longer blue, white, and purple. There's a greenish tinge to them now, as if my lightning absorbed the sylph's essence.

I don't understand why she did this. Why she refused my offer to help her. I manage to take a bandage from my pack and wrap my arm, beyond caring if I do a thorough job. I stay on the ground until my legs are numb and the gashes on my arm sting, cutting through my reverie.

When I hear footsteps, I think Agate and Neev have found me, but then I see a pair of boots and the edge of a dark cloak.

A man is standing in the clearing. I tense like a rabbit caught in the gaze of a lynx.

"You look sick," he says, his tone concerned. "And you're bleeding. Did that creature hurt you?"

"She wasn't a creature. She was a sylph." I struggle to my feet, keeping my hand at my hip, near my vial. My arm throbs and blood soaks through the makeshift bandage.

"You should never have come here," he says. "The grief growing here will destroy you."

A terrible suspicion is forming in the back of my mind, cutting through my exhaustion, confusion, and pain. "Who are you?"

He tilts his head and then makes me a low bow. "Your Highness," he says. "Don't you know me?"

I know his voice. I've heard it echo across the cobblestones of the courtyard, heard its rich timbre over the laughter of children when he performed magic in the great hall, before I had magic myself.

I've heard it call my mother's name.

"You."

Rothbart comes closer and lowers his hood, revealing his dark eyes and hollow cheeks. *The Gaunt Man*, the sylph girl said.

My thumb hovers over the stopper of my vial. His eyes flicker, following the movement of my hand before returning to my face.

"I wouldn't do that, Thedramora. The forest has weakened you."

I stare at him in disbelief. "What's wrong with this place? With me? What did you mean when you said there was grief growing here?"

His dark eyes dart to mine, and I glimpse something in them. Something cold and calculating that leaps out before he can suppress it. "I'm not sure. But I think perhaps all the twisted things wrought in this forest from your mother's magic are killing you."

"Her magic?" I sound like an idiot, chatting with him beneath the trees like this, but my head is muddled by pain and shock, and I can't think straight.

"Yes." He looks around us at the dying trees, his expression more musing than anything. "This forest is millennia old and has its own ancient magic running through the root systems of the trees. Nothing I transfigured here with Mora's power came out as it should. And then it grew out of control. This toadstool, for instance." He stoops to pluck a mushroom from the loam, and I watch, transfixed. "See the little mutant ones growing from the cap? This variety used to be edible, but if you tried to eat the duplicates, they'd be toxic." He drops the toadstool and brushes his hand across his thigh.

Blinding rage erupts inside me, temporarily blotting out my pain. My mother's radiant power, the terrifying beauty of her transfiguration into the war bird that could pierce a giant's eyes, snap off a man's head in a blink. Her years of study in the temple of the dead; all this, mined for mad experiments in a forest?

"You killed her?"

"She died," he says, as if correcting me.

I stagger toward him, and he sidesteps me deftly.

"*How*?" I don't want to know the answer, but I can't stop myself from asking. "They found only ash and a few feathers in the palace and they thought she'd combusted. A spell gone

wrong."

"A feather and some ash? That wasn't Mora. That was just our first failed attempt. I took her with me. This—" He gestures widely at the forest. "—is Mora. I buried her body among the roots of a great ash that grew into the root systems of all the other trees centuries ago."

I think about the cloying smell of rot pervading the forest, the decaying apples, the pollen I thought was mold, the strange grotesques. "What did you do to her?"

"She wanted to share her power with me, but it went wrong."

I speak through clenched teeth, clutching my vial so hard the beveled edges cut into my hand. "Went wrong *how*?"

He licks his lips. "Once, when we first met, I complimented her flawless transfiguration. And she said, 'I'd share it, if I could. But it can't be taught except to those with the talent.' All those hours we spent in my lair, trying to find a way to transfer elemental power to a regular mortal... She wanted it, too."

I'm shaking, and I open my vial even though I know I shouldn't. Maybe he's right. Maybe I am too weak to use my magic. I can barely grasp its static crackle. *An elemental's power is only as strong as they are*. But I don't care. I snap my fingers without another thought, pointing to him. A lightning branch leaps obediently, but my wounded arm makes me miss, and it strikes the ground near his boot instead of my target.

My eyes are dazzled, and Rothbart throws up an arm to shield his face. I advance on him, snapping again, but he extends his palm and sends my lightning back at me. It hits me, but I absorb it as I learned to do in training, letting it strengthen me.

The next time I try to strike him, he puts both hands over his head and brings them around in the shape of a sphere, and the lightning spreads into a shield in a sparkling web.

He smiles at me through the glittering dome. "Your power has grown since you were a child, Thedra. But so has mine."

The electricity spins and swirls in a blinding white column as it flows from my hands, spreading like the roots of a tree as it hits the shield. My strength begins to waver as I funnel all my power toward him. "Are you the one who took Dette?"

My arms tremble and I pant from exertion, but I keep forcing my lightning toward him.

"Forget Dette," he says, still resisting me easily. A non-powered mortal shouldn't be able to resist the full force of my power like this. Not even a skilled magician like Rothbart. I hoped he was bluffing, but it's clear he wasn't.

"Go home," he continues. "Back to Thede's sad little kingdom where you belong. Mora loved you. She wouldn't want you to die here."

The raw, open cuts on my arm are sizzling with electricity now. They sting like fresh burns and my eyes water. "What have you...done with Dette?"

"I've made good use of her."

"Is she still alive?"

He smiles at me like he has a secret he can hardly bear to keep. "She is. Have you forgotten she has the power to heal?"

I surge forward, forcing him back a step. "I *will* find her."

He laughs. "Perhaps. But make sure you shore your defenses ere we meet again."

With a thrust of his hands, he pushes me with his magic, taking back the ground he lost. Then he shoves me backward with the invisible shield like a knight staving off a swordsman. I stumble, and Rothbart vanishes. What energy I had left drains out of me in his wake, and the clearing goes blessedly dark.

I lie unconscious until Agate and Neev find me and shake me awake.

"What happened?" demands Agate. "Why did you leave us?"

"I followed something."

Neev is crouched beside me, looking worried. "Are you hurt?"

I nod listlessly, and she looks at Agate. "She's bleeding."

"Will you give me a dream, Gate? Like the one by the fire that night? But gentler. Something warm and..." I can't say any more. My throat aches; I don't want to cry in front of him. That's no behavior for a future queen. My mother would never have cried before an undercaptain.

"Yes," he says, his voice kinder than before. "I'll give you a dream. But we have to return to the path first, if we can find

it."

"You wandered quite a distance," explains Neev. "One minute you were there and the next, gone. It's lucky Agate is such a good tracker."

I can't stop shaking and she scans my face, looking worried. "What happened?"

Through jarring teeth, I stutter, "S-sylph girl...killed herself with my power. And I saw him."

"Saw who?"

"Rothbart."

Her brow furrows and her gaze darts to Gate, who is inspecting my cuts. He pours water from his skin onto my arm to wash away the blood and I try to jerk my arm free of his grasp.

"Please," I beg, "not that water."

"Help me hold her," he says to Neev, his voice tense.

They clean the cuts with the water from the lake despite my struggles and Agate stitches the deepest wounds with sutures from his pack. Neev smears them with some sort of pungent ointment and wraps my arm in a strip of linen. The wound aches and stings, no matter what position I hold my arm in.

When we stop to make camp for the night, I hear them talking about me. "She's in shock," whispers Neev. "She thinks she saw the sorcerer. The one who stole Dette."

"I think she's hallucinating from the water."

"But you're not hallucinating," says Neev, a hint of

suspicion in her tone.

Gate's tone is quarrelsome. "No, but I'm not injured either. I wish you two hadn't forced me into coming to this goddess-forsaken forest. I hate it."

He continues to grouse, but he puts me to sleep as promised, with a dream about sleeping on a soft pallet in a sylphan platform in the treetops. It feels like the height of summer—stars sparkle overhead, crickets chirp, and I can smell honeyed mead and ambrosia. But a chill wind makes me shiver and there's a gnawing dread in the back of my mind—the sky isn't a sky at all, I think, but a shroud, and the stars are the glowing pinpricks of many waiting eyes.

My arm is worse when I wake up. It feels like the scratches have festered under the stitches, and it hurts so much I can barely stand up straight. I can't stop thinking about the sylph girl. I hate myself for letting her die. It was weak to let her take my vial just because she attacked me. She clearly wasn't in her right mind.

Nor will you be, by the end, says the nagging voice in my head. *You will never leave Thornewood, just like her. Like your mother.*

Disjointed thoughts flit through my mind. *Fuck, what did he do to her? How long did she suffer? Why did he admit to killing her? He must pay for what he's done.*

When we stop to rest and drink water, I peel back the

bandage on my arm. Green pus oozes from the slashes, which are crusted with black scabs.

"How's it feel?" asks Gate.

I tuck the bandage back in place before he can see it. "Fine, I guess," I say shakily. "Sore."

"We should go. If you're too tired to walk, we can carry you."

I give him a disgusted look. "I can walk."

I trudge after him and Neev. When I drink from my water skin my tongue tastes of copper, and my ears ring until my skull is buzzing like a hive of angry bees.

After Neev and Agate have left me behind half a dozen times, they take turns letting me lean on them to walk. "Make them stop," I say to Neev at some point.

"Make who stop?"

"The voices. They won't stop jabbering in my ears."

Neev looks frightened. "Thedra...the only one speaking is you. You've been whispering about—

"Don't," Gate cuts her off. "Telling her won't make any difference."

"Telling me what? What are you hiding from me?"

"Nothing."

I pull my arm from the warm crook of Neev's elbow. "I don't want to walk anymore. Let me lie down. I wish we were back in that sunny hollow."

"Thedra, we have to get you to the sylphs," pleads Neev.

"You're not well."

When I look at her and Gate now, I hardly recognize them. Their faces are the same, but my mind won't confirm who they are. They look hazy, like the face of a dead loved one in a dream. Like the sylph girl, and the way I thought she was Dette at first. Was she even real? Or just another one of my nightmares taking form? I'm realizing nothing in this forest is what it seems.

My arm throbs beneath the bandages, and I stop in the middle of the path and sink to my knees, my fingers grasping at the dirt. My skull throbs like it's going to burst into a thousand pieces. I've never wanted anything more than I want to lay my head on the mossy ground and never pick it up again.

The next time I'm aware of my surroundings, Gate is carrying me, grunting and panting from my weight. I'm not petite like Neev—I have a good appetite and muscles from riding and wielding. He'll lord this over me later.

We stop for the night, and Gate lays me down beside the campfire they've started, but I can't stop trembling.

They bring me food, but my teeth are chattering too violently to eat, and I roll onto my side. Neev lies down beside me and I clutch at her hands, shivering even more from her warmth. Sweat trickles from her forehead even though I'm eaten up by chills. "Help me," I beg her. "Tell Gate to help me. It's inside me, inside my head."

"What is?"

"The forest," I say, as if she should know what I'm talking about, but I'm nattering like a lunatic. "She said it was inside her, and now it's inside me. And he was waiting for me..."

"Thedra, there was no one else there when we found you. You're ill."

I don't answer her. The mage, I want to say, but they don't believe me, and suddenly I can't remember his name. The scratches on my arm are flames licking across my skin and I snatch my sleeve up and claw at the bandage, tearing it off to show them my festered arm. "See? It's poison. It's all poison."

Her eyes go huge at the sight of my oozing arm, and she gets up. I can hear her talking to Gate as if from a far distance.

"We've got to get her to the healers. Her arm is infected."

I think I see them leering at me. *They're talking about me behind my back. Saying I'm mad. That I've led them on a useless quest through a deadly forest that will kill us all.*

I close my eyes so I can't see them anymore, until Neev's gloved hand lands on my shoulder. She handles my arm gingerly, but even a light touch feels horrible. I groan as she bathes the scratches with an herb tincture. She salves and re-bandages them, but my fever doesn't go away. My arm still pulses with agony, and my head pounds.

"I'm so sorry, Thedra," Neev whispers. I don't have the strength to tell her it's not her fault, but when she asks, "Shall I say a prayer for you?" I nod feebly.

"Tell me which goddess. Zori?"

I shake my head. "Not Zori. I told her to fuck off."

I hear a smile in Neev's voice as she says, "Somehow that doesn't surprise me. I'll pray to Thorne for you, then. She's a robust goddess, full of healing growth. Perhaps she has some to spare."

I nod, unable to form a reply. Despite my blasphemy, I whisper a prayer of my own, anyway. *Zori, please. I'm so sick. Help me.*

But Zori doesn't come. Her body is in her tomb in Lazul, her spirit in the next-world. Why would she come to me now?

At last, I give myself up to the darkness, my consciousness ebbing.

When I come to, green tendrils have curled about my wrists and ankles, rooting me to the ground. They're growing from beneath the feet of a woman standing nearby. When she kneels beside me in the loam, I realize she's not human.

Her body is woman-shaped, with a round, soft belly and wide hips, and she has the dark, dark skin of a Zelener, but her eyes are the large, gentle brown of a rabbit's, and stag horns sprout from her head. There are feathers at her wrists, her nails are sharp and pearlescent, and beneath her flaxen robes her chest is covered in a fan of iridescent lizard scales.

"Thorne?"

"Some have called me by that name," she says, taking my hand. "But you don't have to."

"Are you here to end my suffering?"

She looks amused by this dramatic question. "Not the way you think. Have you come to stay the hand of the one who changed my forest?"

I shake my head. "I tried to. He said grief was growing here. That it would kill me. And he was right. Zori said I stink of it."

Her hand roves over the deep scratches on my forearm, making me hiss in pain. "Lies. What is grief? An aching scar where a limb once was. But you are not defined by what you have lost, Thedra of Lazul."

But I am, I want to say. It clings to me like a demon. Spreads like gangrene. Grief is the thing following me through the forest, skulking and scrambling beneath the trees like a pale, bloated spider.

When I met Zori, I felt nothing but cold. But the power coming from Thorne pulses like the heat in a summer meadow. I want to clasp her to my breast and absorb it, drink it up. But it's not mine to take.

As if she has read my mind, she says, "Let me help you."

I only stare at her. I'm sworn to Zori. How can a consort of death be healed by a goddess of life?

Her patient brown eyes search my face. "When Lazulians pay me tribute, they usually do it with the bones of animals, or with spilled blood. Because Zori craves those things. But you left me an object of devotion. You are more than loss and death. You must meet Zori again one day, as all mortals do. But Thornewood is my domain, and I grant you relief."

With that, she squeezes my arm until stinging tears come to my eyes. My chest heaves and I sob huge, choking sobs. Something sharp and rough snakes up my arm and pierces the flesh, funneling and unfurling inside me. Green sap seeps from the wound in my arm, and vines sprout from my eyes and nose and curl around my organs and bones until they burst and splinter.

When I open my mouth to scream, Thorne murmurs, "That's it, out with it," and the vines climb up my throat, crowding it with leaves and blocking out my cries. Black, rotted bile spills out of my mouth and seeps into the ground. I lie still, a hollowed-out shell that used to be a girl. I am one with Thornewood at last.

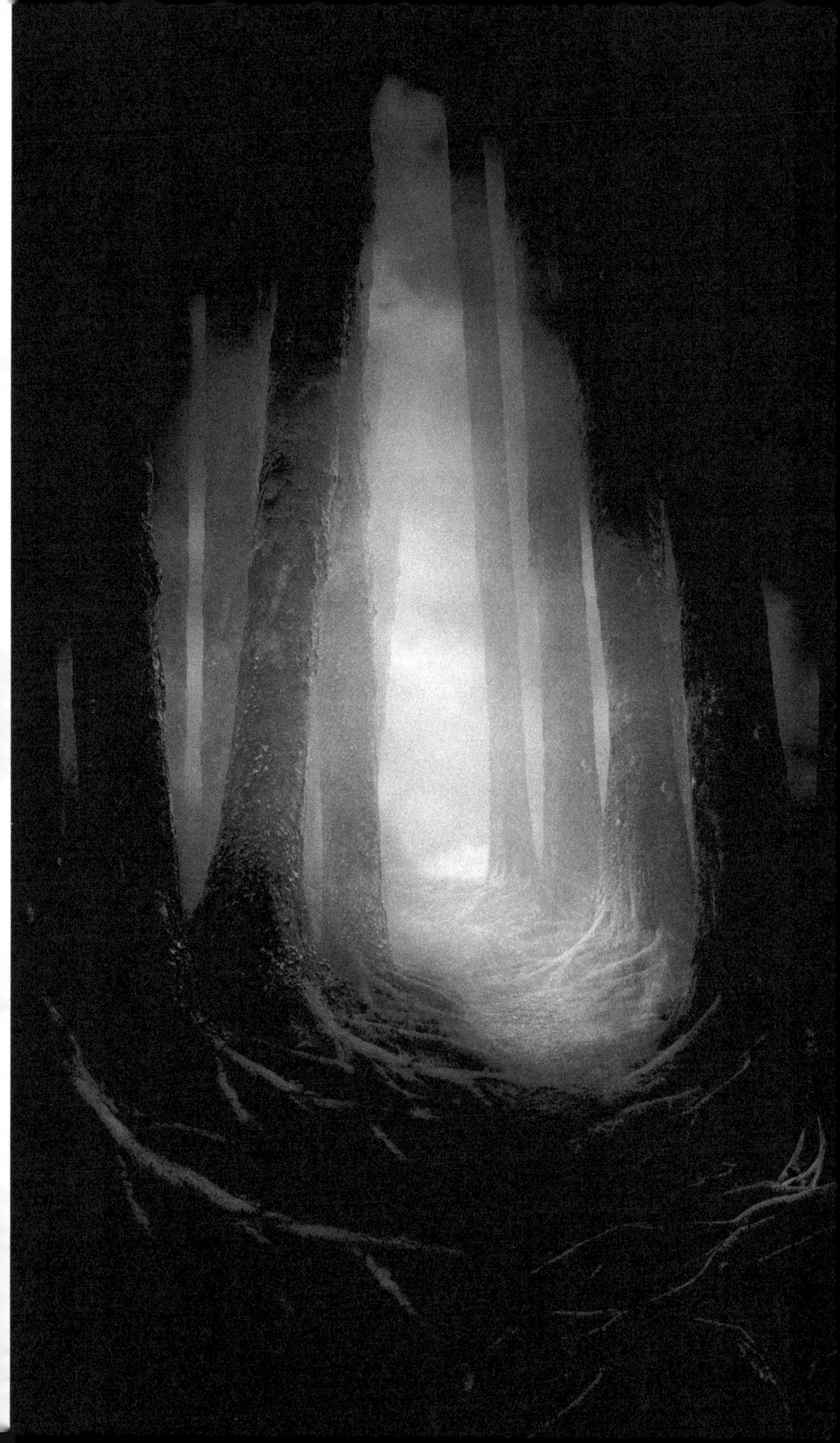

Part Three: Respite

Beyond the trees, above the sky,

Flew golden Shorea

To join the Sun, her lover.

O shining one, o winged one,

Bless us, the gentle sylphs, your children.

-Sylphan Hymn

Chapter Twelve

My consciousness returns slowly. It's less like waking up than swimming from the bottom of a deep pool back into open air. I dream of lying on soft sheets, of being tended by people with melodic, throaty voices who feed me broth and medicine and cool water. I'll never have enough water again.

Then I'm awake. Really awake. I'm reclined in a warm bath in an airy, sun-filled room. There's a slight ache in my head, but it's comfortable here. I can hear the crackle of a fire, and greenery is visible through the window. Ferns with long, twisting tendrils hang from hooks in the ceiling, and the warm water smells of scented oil and herbs. There are round red berries floating on the surface like lingonberries in a forest pool.

After so many days trudging through the bone-chilling cold of Poison Forest, I think I must be dreaming. Perhaps Gate has used his magic on me again. If so, this is good magic. Very good. Not like what dogged us on the path through the woods or lurked in the dark water. Not like the green sap that burst from my arm in my dream of Thorne. I touch my mouth, almost expecting my fingers to brush against leaves and vines, forcing their way past my teeth.

I catch a whiff of something savory, and a fae woman in a robe enters the room and places a tray beneath the window. She's a hamadryad, a tree nymph with skin of gray-brown bark and hair like weeds decorated with acorns. She hobbles and I realize she only has one leg, that the other is a wooden prosthetic.

I try to sit up, but pain sears across my arm. I look down at the four slashes cutting across my flesh. The stitches have been removed, and the infection cleaned out. The bath I'm lying in seems to have helped draw out the poison. The cuts are no longer seeping green pus or black around the edges.

The dryad sees me moving and rushes to the side of the tub, surprisingly quick.

She touches my forehead. "Praise Thorne, you're awake."

I blink at her. "Where am I?"

"You made it to Cliff Sedge, the home of King Cygnus."

"Who are you?"

"My name is Oakroot. I was summoned here from my tree to heal you. How do you feel?"

"Better." I give her what I know must be a frightened look. "Is your tree in Thornewood?"

She shakes her head. "It's kind of you to ask, but no. My

sister's was, though. She escaped, but when her tree died, she perished with it."

"I'm so sorry."

She nods, her face placid as a forest pool. Hamadryads are slow and quiet, and difficult to disturb. Long years of sleep inside their trees teach them to keep their emotions buried deep.

"Where is the girl who was with me, Neev?" I ask, suddenly frightened. I don't remember how I got here. "And the young man, Agate?"

"Agate is in a healing room of his own, and Neev is resting. She'll come in to help you dress for the early autumn feast tonight."

The sylphs have more than one feast per season. They're in tune with every nuance of time.

"It didn't feel like late summer in the forest. It was so cold."

"The spell the sorcerer cast over Thornewood hasn't touched us. Our greenhealers have kept it off, healing the trees each time it starts to creep in, casting spells of protection and renewal."

Just the mention of the forest makes me shiver, but she misinterprets it. "Here, you've grown cold." She unfolds a towel and helps me out of the bath. My joints creak and my muscles protest, but I'm no longer cold, and that's something to be grateful for. My mind seems to have cleared as well.

"How long have I been asleep?"

"A few days. We feared you might not wake at all, but I let your arm soak in the healing baths every day, and they seem to have revived you. Now, let's see."

She gestures for me to hold out my hand and inspects the gashes in my forearm. Giving a nod of satisfaction, she smears my arm with a balm that smells of green leaves and clean, moving water. When I close my eyes, it gently tingles, soothing the pain.

"New skin will grow soon," she says. "It's already improved from when you arrived. Just rest until it does. Eat—regain your strength."

I let her bandage my arm and help me into a white tunic and a pair of soft, woven breeches. This close, she smells like raindrops on grass and fresh-turned forest earth. The food she left beneath the window for me is the best I've ever eaten—crusty bread, soft-boiled eggs with fresh fruit, and porridge made of ground, boiled tree nuts. I eat slowly. My stomach feels like a cavern, but I haven't eaten enough to fill it in over a week, and I don't want it rebelling against the food.

Cliff Sedge is built into one of the crags of the mountain called Frostmead, and my window looks out over the forest below. I study the colors of autumn beginning to turn the canopy of trees from green to red and gold, as they should. But farther out, past the border of Shoreana, I can see fingers of darkness, like ink spilled across a page of beautiful

illustrations. I shudder and hug myself.

Neev's room is connected to mine and I go in when I'm finished eating. I find her lying beneath a linen coverlet on a canopied bed. She stirs at the sound of my footsteps and sits up to stretch.

"Thedra, you're awake!" She swings her legs over the side of the bed, but I motion for her to stay and sit down beside her. Her wide gray eyes search my face with concern. "How are you?"

"Not normal, but better."

She nods, chewing at her lip. "We were very worried."

"I remember." I give her a half-smile. "You offered to pray to Zori for me. And then Thorne."

She looks embarrassed. "I just wanted to help you feel safe if you were..."

"Dying?"

She nods. It's strange, being from a country where death is always on everyone's mind. Zeleners speak of it like something forbidden.

"What happened after we drank the water from the lake?" I ask. "Everything is hazy and I'm not sure what was real and what wasn't." I think of Thorne's rabbit eyes and stag horns.

"You wandered off, and we spent hours following the trail, trying to find you. Finally, we heard a sound, like an explosion. When we found you, you had that wound, and you were...confused. Gate kept trying to calm you, help your mind

clear. But the fever made it worse. The water affected Gate, too. Made him irritable."

I laugh softly. "Are you sure it wasn't just his regular mood?"

She smiles. "It was difficult to tell. It wasn't as bad for him as you. But you were already so sick."

Neev pulls the blanket back and pats the bed beside her, as if assuring me everything is all right. I snuggle down beside her under the soft, woven spread, enjoying the smoothness of the sheets on my bare feet.

"It's so nice to be warm." I have a pang of guilt for what I must have put them through. I wonder how she got us both here in one piece, but I'm not sure I want to know the answer. "Is Gate all right?"

She nods. "He's in one of the fortifying baths. He was drained from trying to keep you calm that last day. But he helped me get you here safely."

I shake my head. It's so strange that I don't remember. I get up and walk around the room, inspecting the fiber-made tapestries and the plants hanging in woven baskets.

"Sylph magic must be awfully strong to have resisted such a horrible enchantment."

Neev nods in agreement. "They say it's older than the alliance of the Triumvir."

"Of course. *The sun begot the sylphs, the gods the elementals. The sylphs taught the greenhealers, the elementals taught the mages.*"

Children from all the kingdoms learn this saying in school with their letters, but I remember too late that Neev's mother kept her at home to hide her magic and she won't be familiar with it.

"There's a festival tonight," she says. "With music and dancing. The first of the autumn feasts. Summer fled while we were in the forest. I can do your hair if you like, help you get ready? They brought those for you this morning, in case you woke up."

She points to a tray where a variety of sylphan hair ornaments are laid out—combs of chestnut and alder carved into the shapes of leaves and ferns, pins of bone, and tiny river stones polished smooth and strung on a circlet of silver. The shimmering powders and dark lip tints so loved in Lazul are conspicuously absent.

I kneel beside the tray, and she joins me. Picking up one of the combs, I run my fingers over the delicate carving and the design of leaf-veins burned into its surface.

"I'll do my own hair today. I think I'll wear the circlet of stones, but this comb is perfect for you."

I tuck the comb into the short, glossy brown tresses above her ear. Her cheeks flush, rosy-sweet against her fair skin.

"Should I glamour my hair?" she asks. "Purple, maybe? Or blue?"

I shake my head. "Deep green, or orange and red for

autumn. But only if you want to. It seems like the sylphs favor natural beauty."

"Dette always liked me to look my best when we were here."

I arch a brow at her. "I'm not Dette, and the sylphs don't keep servants. You were only mine for two days, anyway. During which, you plotted to steal my clothes and force me into taking you on a journey. I know you came because you wanted to find Dette, but thank the goddess you deceived me. I'd be dead otherwise."

Neev's eyes are on her gloved hands, clasped decorously in her lap, but she raises her head and meets my gaze. "I wanted to find Dette in the beginning. I still do. But I also..."

Before either of us can change our minds, I take her hand. She's still looking at me, and I know I'm going to kiss her. Because I'll regret it if I don't. And I hate living with regrets. Even if it's the only time, even if we're both dead by the end of this journey, or if she goes with Dette instead of me, I have to let her know how I feel. But before I can, a sylph comes in through the open door.

"Princess Thedra!"

"What?" I say irritably.

"Your other companion is asking for you."

Agate is tucked up in bed, cramming food from a tray into his mouth.

"Good morning," I greet him. "You survived."

He shoves a wad of bread into his cheek with his tongue so he can talk. "Yeah, no thanks to you, Thedra, wandering off, refusing to walk, accusing me of all manner of deceit and treachery."

Neev laughs at him and he shoots her a grin that shows a flash of his white teeth. His brown eyes are warm with liking for her, and I'm hit with a stab of jealousy that makes me wonder if there's something between them. But we're not in the forest anymore, and I can't let its clinging black thoughts back into my head.

Neev and I lounge on the bed as Gate eats his way through half a loaf of bread dipped in broth, soft-boiled eggs, and the same kind of porridge I had this morning. It's nice not to be walking endlessly, to have nothing to do except lay about. Still, I have to tell them what happened.

"If you're done cramming food down your gullet, I'll tell you what I saw."

He rolls his eyes. "Oh, really? Now that we're safe, you've finally decided to tell us what you saw?"

"Gate." Neev's tone is reproachful. "She wasn't herself. She was sick and confused."

"Don't have to tell me. I'm the one who had my best riding boots puked on."

I don't remember this either, and I feel my cheeks redden. Not very queenly of me, vomiting on my subordinate's boots.

"You're the one who wore your best boots on a journey through a forest," I say, trying to cover my embarrassment. "If you glamoured me to get me back to Lazul, don't see why you couldn't do it for this."

"Oh, believe me, I tried, even if you did threaten to kill me for it before." He nods to Neev. "She did it in the end."

"How?"

"She asked if you were going to let a stupid forest get the better of you. Something like that. Apparently, your pride is even stronger than your need for comfort."

I press my lips together, secretly touched that Neev knows me well enough to say such a thing. Gate takes a long swig from his mug of barley beer. "Well?"

"I saw Rothbart. My mother's chief sorcerer. He admitted to killing her."

Neev's eyes widen with horror. "Killing her? I thought they were lovers."

"They were."

"Then why would he kill her?"

"For her power. And he took Dette as well."

Neev goes white to the lips, and I put my hand on her arm, not sure if she's upset from recalling the terrible day Dette was taken, or something else. "What's wrong?"

"N-nothing."

"Why didn't you tell us this in the forest?" asks Gate.

"Like you just said, I wasn't myself. I didn't even know

what was real or not by then."

I tell them about the sylph girl, the one who reminded me of Dette at first glance, and what happened to her.

"She drank your magic?" Gate looks ill. "I've never even heard of such a thing."

"Neither have I. But it killed her. That's not the most important bit, though. I think he has Dette." I explain the rest of my encounter with Rothbart. "He promised me safe passage out of the forest if I return home."

"Maybe you should." Gate stretches his long legs under the coverlet, putting his hands behind his head. "You recall, I only came on this journey because you threatened me. It's ill-fated."

"No. That bastard has Dette, and whatever he did to my mother, he will do to her. He told me to shore my defenses. He's not afraid of a confrontation. He was powerful." I pause, my stomach churning at the memory of how he bested me. "More powerful than me," I admit with revulsion. "Much as I never want to set foot back in that accursed forest, I need to get to Lebed. The sylphs have a shortcut, and if it means defeating Rothbart, King Cygnus might give me aid."

Gate eyes me warily. "Do you even have a plan for how to rescue her?"

"I have some ideas. Will you be coming with me? The two of you?"

Gate's brow furrows in contemplation, and Neev's face is

still white. She's silent.

Gate sighs. "The king told me to bring you home safely. Haven't done that yet."

I think of the sad-eyed sylph girl whose name I never even got to ask, and the terrible way she died, and I'm frightened for him. For all of us. *You're not likely to, sleepy-spell boy.*

Chapter Thirteen

As the shadows deepen into the afternoon, a palace attendant brings an armful of finery for me and Neev to choose from for the feast. In Lazul, a handmaid would be here to dress us, but things are done more independently here, and I'm glad it means I won't be primped and fussed over the way I was at my death ceremony ball. I select a gray brocade tunic and silk leggings. Neev wears a white, draped gown that flows all around her in shimmery folds. I put out a hesitant finger to touch it as the sylph attendant helps her pin the sleeve over her shoulder.

"That fabric feels like a whisper."

"It's woven of gossamer by moonlight," says the sylph.

I let my hair down and comb out the tangles, placing the circlet of stones on my head, and Neev glamours her hair to an emerald green as I suggested. It makes the carved comb of pale wood more visible.

I try not to stare at her as we walk to the feast hall, but

it's hard not to. Her beauty is exquisite, like a necklace of finely wrought silver only made lovelier by its simplicity. I hang back a few steps, letting her enter the room ahead of me. Even in a hall full of sylphs, who are known for their noble features and showy plumage, many eyes linger on her. A sylph lord bows to her with an elegant sweep of feathers, and she pauses for a moment, looking taken aback before recovering and dipping into a slight curtsy.

A servant with a tray pauses at her elbow and offers her a goblet of pale mead. "Refreshment, my lady?"

She takes the goblet with less hesitation than she returned the bow, tilting it to her lips.

When I catch up to her, she's standing with an air of quiet elegance, but her eyes spark with repressed delight. "Do they think I'm a noblewoman?"

This reminds me she's never been here as an equal, never been shown into the throne room dressed in finery or offered refreshments.

"You look more noble than I do," I say.

The hall is an open room, with soaring arches and a balustrade overlooking the glen below. I turn away from the breathtaking view, not wanting to see the darkness on the edges.

Gate is already here, dressed in his soldier's uniform. He looks dashing, even though the uniform is a bit worse for wear. He's talking to a long-legged sylph with downy wings of brilliant blue, and abalone shells in their hair. They wear a wooden breastplate over a velvet doublet, and the straps of a bow and quiver crisscross over their chest .

King Cygnus is seated on a low throne at the back of the room. The sylphs don't put themselves on pedestals above one another the way humans do. The throne is wide, with arches carved into the back for his wings, which spread behind him like a feathery gray fan. His snow-white hair is long and soft, and his eyes are solid black from sclera to pupil.

I approach and he nods at me.

"Welcome to Cliff Sedge, Princess Thedra. You're better, I trust."

"I am. Thank you for your hospitality." My hand goes to my bandaged arm. "Your healers saved my life. The forest..."

His welcoming look turns to a frown. "We don't speak of the forest on feast days. Not anymore."

"But I must speak to you. We don't have time to waste."

He waves this away. "Tonight, we make merry."

"But in the forest, I saw—"

"We *don't* speak of the forest today. Whatever you have to say can wait. My first duty is to my people and our traditions. And you're not fully healed." He gestures to my bandaged arm.

I chafe at the thought of waiting to tell him what I saw in the forest. Lazul is responsible for Rothbart and the evil he wrought on Thornewood. Whether they meant to or not, my parents gave him a place to thrive, let him hide away in the lair my mother had built for him so he could tinker with his transfiguration experiments. I'm sickened by the thought, but maybe my mother knew some of his plans. She was closer to him than anyone. How could she not have known what he was? But if I learned anything from my father, it's that respecting the customs of other realms is tantamount to diplomacy, so I turn away, hiding my anger.

A sylph boy mounts a stool in the center of the room and begins to sing, signaling the start of the feast. The opening notes of his song sound familiar, and a chill goes down my spine.

Come and eat
Berries and apples
Compote and trifle
Crumbling and savory
Warm and sweet

Diplomacy be damned.

"I've heard this song before," I say, turning back to the king. Cygnus has been listening with his head tilted to one side, and he scowls at me for talking over the bard's lilting voice. "I met one of your people in Thornewood, and she was singing it. She was sick. The forest had gotten into her, and her wings, and..."

He stands up before I can finish and pulls me aside. His talons hurt my arm as he clutches it. "Be quiet before someone hears you. Come with me."

He ushers me down a corridor where we are alone, and I launch into an explanation. "The girl was small and dark-eyed. Her skin was gold-green, and she had lichen for hair. A tree sylph. And she...she died. I tried to save her, but..." I swallow hard, unable to bring myself to explain the manner of her death. "She was dressed in finery. Has one of the children of your lords been taken?"

"One?" His eyes are hollow. "Many children were taken by the Gaunt Man. Both common and noble. From the trees and the rivers and the heights. She could have been any of them. I've tried to keep it as quiet as I can. If I don't, it will mean war. My people will revolt against him and more will die. Maybe all of them."

A weight like a stone settles in my belly. King Cygnus thinks Rothbart is this powerful? "You know of him?"

He nods. "There have been sightings. Whispers that he's the one who enchanted the forest. He is often seen before a blight."

"I think he's the one who took Dette."

"How can you know that?" he asks severely, as if there will be consequences if I'm wrong.

"Because I know who he is. His name is Rothbart, and he was my mother's chief sorcerer. He murdered her and took her power. She was a shapeshifter."

I see his chest heave with suppressed emotion. "Two weeks ago," he says raggedly, "a patrol was attacked on the pass to Frostmead by a giant owl. Was that your mother's form?"

I nod. "Can I speak to someone who saw it?"

"They're all dead, save one. He was stricken mute, but he drew us a map. I'll send you to the pass with a guide when you've healed."

"We don't have time to wait for that. We'll stay for tonight's festivities, but tomorrow we leave."

We return to the feast. There's no long central table as there would be at a Lazulian banquet. Instead, benches are laid out along the balustrade and chairs are tucked into the little alcoves clustered around the room. There are cozy cushions by the two hearths at opposite ends of the room for those seeking warmth away from autumn's chill. I decide to sit by one, as my bones still seem to recall the cold of Thornewood even if my body has recovered from it, but Neev moves to the balustrade to let the wind billow her filmy gown.

We're served a salad of purslane, seeds, and cattail shoots, with clear spring water to drink. After that come platters of oysters in the shell, roasted hazelnuts, and tiny eggs. We crack the shells of the hazelnuts and eggs to pick out the meat and slurp the oysters from their shells.

For dessert, there are berry preserves and candied figs, and

more of the pale mead sipped from bowls with white blossoms floating on the liquid's surface. I place one on my tongue. It tastes like spun sugar.

"Honeysuckle mead."

A young sylph man seated on a cushion nearby puts his plate aside and holds his hands to the fire. He has a beaked nose like a bird of prey, and powerful shoulders. There's a simple pale gold band around his muscled upper arm, and it glints, contrasting with the white and brown feathers that grow in a fan-shaped pattern across his chest and shoulders. "Don't eat too many," he says. "They're like candy, and give the room color, but they'll run away with you."

"The food feels magical here," I say. "We have magic in Lazul, but our food is quite ordinary."

"Like what?"

"Spitted lizards and goat cheese." I wrinkle my nose.

He smiles at me again. "This is nothing. Imagine a trifle taller than you are, a fountain of punch, and little cakes dripping with icing so sweet..." He trails off and licks his lips in recollection. "But we don't venture to trade in Lazul for the sugar anymore. Once, we would have had a great rainbow carp for everyone to share, but we don't eat fish from the Black Stream anymore either."

I don't need him to explain, but he tells me, his voice low, "The fish and mollusks from the river cause some to have an illness of the mind. It leads to dissension and quarrelling."

I nod. “I’m not surprised. I journeyed through Thornewood on my way here. My companion and I drank the water.”

His dark eyes swoop down on mine with alarmed distrust when I name the forest.

“Don’t worry,” I say quickly. “We’re getting better.”

He relaxes fractionally, but seems wary of me now. We only talk a bit more before he moves away. I can’t blame him. He has no reason to believe I’m telling the truth.

Now that the main courses have been served, musicians begin playing lilting music on flutes and lyres, and several sylphs take to the dance floor. Dancing in Shoreana is much more complex than in the human realms. The average sylph’s build of lightweight bones and strong wings lends them a buoyancy and grace most humans don’t possess.

Neev is standing near the dancing sylphs and she clasps her hands in front of her, losing the air of cautious confidence she had earlier. Several of the sylphs have spoken to her with admiring glances, both male and female, and I wouldn’t be surprised if one of them asks her to dance. She seems to have the same thought because she starts to back away.

Maybe it’s the honeysuckle mead, or maybe it’s the way she looks in the draped, filmy gown that moves like whispering moonlight, but I stand with sudden resolve and skirt the dance floor until I reach her. “Would you like to dance with me before someone else asks? Someone over there is eyeing you.”

Neev glances nervously in the direction of a towering

sylph with massive wings of blue, green, and gold. The sylph's feathers grow over its forehead all the way to its broad nose, making it appear less humanoid than some of the others. "Are they male or female?"

I smile. "Does it matter? They're gorgeous and at least six and a half feet tall."

"I'll have to say no and risk offense. I don't know how to dance. Not like this, anyway."

I hold my hand out to her. "It's okay. I know the lead parts. I used to help Dette practice. And no one can dance like a sylph except another sylph."

Dette could, very nearly, but I don't say that. She was always delighted when her wings aided her in the midair twists and pirouettes popular in her father's court. She used to practice them when we were together on Lebed while my tutor taught me traditional Lazulian contra dances.

Neev slips her hand into mine and I lead her onto the floor. I put my hands on her waist and lift her several inches off the floor in unison with the sylph couples, turning slowly. Even though she has no wings to help me, she must weigh less than a hundred pounds, so it's not much of a challenge. The sylphs finish the move by arching their backs and bending one leg until their heads nearly touch their heel, but Neev doesn't have the core strength for it.

I lower her carefully and we attempt to keep time with the difficult steps, hiding our laughter.

"Put your left arm out straight and point your toe. That's right."

I spin her around and she holds the pose this time. She's laughing when she faces me again, her features lit by pearly moonlight and candleflame. I want to kiss her. Lately, it seems I always want to kiss her.

When the dance ends and we return to the alcove where I was sitting, she says, "I saw you talking to that sylph lord."

"How do you know he was a lord?"

She hangs back from the fire as I stretch my hands toward it. "His armband. Only their royalty wear jewelry that's not made of wood or bone."

I nod, still bothered by the sylph lord's aversion. "You should've seen his face when I told him I drank from the Black Stream. It was like he thought I was contagion itself."

She takes my hand. "Don't talk like that. You're out of the forest, Thedra. Don't think those dark thoughts anymore."

I meet her gaze and wait for her to look away, but she doesn't. She's so kind, and so soft, and so—

"Sorry to interrupt."

Neev and I both jump as if we've been caught in an act of thievery and I let go of her hand. It's Gate. The sylph with fluffy wings he was talking to earlier is with him

"This is Plover, one of the guards who will be leading us to the pass where Princess Odette was taken."

Plover has a sharp jaw, pointed nose, and soulful, long-

lashed eyes of blue-gray.

I extend a hand. "I'm Thedra, and this is Neev, my...um, traveling companion." Plover's name does nothing to enlighten me on their gender, and I know some clans can change theirs at will for reproductive purposes or personal preference, so I ask, "What are your pronouns?"

"He and him, for always." He smiles at me but doesn't shake my hand. "Lovely to meet you." It's strange not being addressed as Your Highness, but I like it. Plover blinks, looking dazed. "Do you see the shifting colors? The fire is green as a katydid."

His voice is dreamy, and the fire doesn't appear green at all when I glance at it.

Seeing my frown, Gate says, "He had three cups of mead and ate most of the flowers."

Plover sags a bit and leans a feathered cheek against Gate's shoulder. Gate clears his throat uncomfortably. "He's off duty tonight, and I think I should take him home...while he can still stand. He lives in a hollow tree outside the palace."

"Gentlemanly of you," says Neev. There's no hidden meaning in her tone, but Gate turns his back to us stiffly.

I think how silly I was to be jealous of his friendship with Neev. She might tease him, but she hardly ever teases me. A part of me wishes she would, but I'm not the sort of person people mock to their face. Unless they're interminably stupid. I don't suppose I'd tease someone who knows the word to wake the dead and has a vial of lightning on their belt, either. But I hate feeling cut off, remote from everyone else. Maybe that's why I fell in love with Dette so easily. Aside from the fact that everyone loves Dette. She never behaved as if I were strange or different, or deferred to me, because she was a princess too, and not just that, but the future High Empress.

The dancers leave the floor and the bard returns to his seat near the king's throne and begins to sing again in a high voice. This time his song's not one of merriment, or drink and food. It's about a sylph whose lover's wings were frozen by a killing frost on an early spring night turned unexpectedly cold. The sylph laments that the two of them will never fly together again, and that the lover's wound sent them to an early grave.

I drink a bit more of the mead, careful not to swallow too many of the white blossoms.

The bard is singing, "*Once my heart rose with yours like an evening star, but now it falls like snow*."

His voice is pure as clear water, and so beautiful it makes my throat ache, but the song is long even for a lament and after a while the sadness of it seems to be filling me up, replacing the lightheartedness of my dance with Neev.

I'm gulping back unwelcome tears when her silky, gloved fingers slip into mine. "Come with me. You rescued me, and now I'm rescuing you. I know of a room here you'll like."

"We can't wander the palace alone," I say, feigning horror. "How rude."

"It's what Dette would do."

With that, I follow her out of the feast hall and down one tiled corridor after another, our footsteps echoing on the flags as her shimmery gown swishes around her ankles. We pass sitting rooms with cushioned lounges and gurgling fountains, and a room with a towering ceiling and a tree growing at its center. There are seats in the branches, too high for us to reach.

We go up a winding staircase and climb a ladder made of sturdy, polished branches. The ladder leads to a trapdoor with an open room at the top. There's a domed ceiling with panels of clear mica for star and moon-gazing. Sharp, crystal-cut stars glitter overhead in the inky black sky of a new moon.

I clamber through the opening in the floor and stand up, tilting my head back to look at the stars. It's the first time I've seen them since we entered Thornewood. They're clear here, as they should be, and I can see the early autumn constellations.

Neev touches my arm. "Look."

I survey my surroundings. The room's walls are lined with books bound in hemp and cornhusk instead of leather, and there are cloches containing forests in miniature, and puzzles and baubles and tiny worlds carved into seed husks and chestnuts. There are hanging tapestries too, but they don't show scenes like ours—they're woven of dried plant fibers, dandelion tufts, and feathers in a thousand hues.

"Sylphs use their own fallen feathers to weave art for their lovers," says Neev, stroking her gloved hand along the silken down of a tapestry. "It's like giving a lock of hair."

A glass cloche hanging from the ceiling catches her attention and she wanders over to it. It's full of fluttering white moths. She touches it and the moths cluster against the glass, flocking to the heat of her fingertips.

I pick up a sphere from a nearby shelf and turn it over, inspecting it carefully. It's made of thousands of tiny, interlocking twigs, and it springs apart in my hands, expanding to five times its size to reveal a tiny nest. Nestled within are two eggs of pale blue stone and a bird with sapphire eyes that shrieks at me before the sphere closes back on itself.

Neev laughs at my startled face. "Nothing in here will hurt you. They're just tomes and trinkets to be touched and marveled over."

I laugh too, feeling ridiculous for being threatened by a bauble.

A pair of heavy drapes hang on the opposite wall. Chill air drifts from beneath them, and I loosen the sash and push them aside, expecting a window. Instead, I'm met by an arch that looks out on open air and darkness. The polished floor stretches to a small stone balcony without a railing, and the drop-off is only a few steps away.

"Careful." Neev clutches my tunic with one hand, gripping my forearm with the other. "There's no banister since sylphs have wings."

Even though it's not our first touch tonight, my heart

hammers like it's trying to get out of my chest. I'm terrified to turn around, but finally, I do. She's right behind me, so close the gauzy hem of her gown floats across the tops of my feet. She tilts her chin a bit so she can look into my eyes.

The wind hits my back and I shiver. Her arms are bare.

"Aren't you cold?"

She shakes her head. Of course not.

Even though I've wanted to kiss her all day, I begin to lose my nerve. Suddenly, I'm terrified. I'm afraid she didn't bring me up here for this at all. That she can see on my face exactly how attracted I am to her and how much I care for her, and that she doesn't feel the same way. I'm afraid she won't kiss me back. I'm afraid she will.

When she puts her hands on my waist, I say, "Yes," and she stretches up on her toes until our lips touch.

I cup her face with my hand, and she kisses me with gentle little kisses that turn meltingly slow and deep. Her lips are mead-flavored: sweet, soft, and fiery. I pull her closer, clasping her narrow shoulders with my hands, and her arms tighten around my waist.

When we part, I say her name like it's a prayer, terrified and exultant at the same time. "If you let me go now, I'll fall."

She whispers, "I've got you," and I kiss her again. I don't think I'll ever get tired of kissing her.

This time when we stop to catch our breath, her eyes move over my features in frantic repetition, from my mouth to my eyes and forehead, as if she's memorizing a complex map or a long equation.

"What's wrong?"

"Nothing," she whispers. "Just now, nothing at all. But I wish we could stay tucked away here. That everything else would disappear."

I wish this too, but there are still so many things left to do. I promise myself that one day Neev will be safe. After the things she's told me of her childhood, she strikes me as someone who craves safety, and I'll find some way to give it to her.

I can imagine Father's snide indignation at my bringing home a commoner as my first official lover. But I'll only need to mention his own curly-headed paramour to put an end to it. If I give him what he wants, let him abdicate the throne. There's no reason why he shouldn't let me have real affection. I'm to be queen, after all. And for the first time, it's not an unwelcome thought. With her by my side, maybe it could even be wonderful. My people will love her because she's gentle, kind, and lovely. Having magic has never gone to her head because it was never used to advance her social status, and her perspective on poverty can only help end Lazul's cycle of greed and ignorance.

෴

We meet Agate back in the feast hall, just returned from walking Plover home. He looks like someone poured a

bucketful of starlight over his head and it nettles me, even though I probably looked the same way less than half an hour ago.

"What happened to you?" asks Neev casually.

"Nothing, and don't imply anything did. You know he was drunk."

"And?" I ask. "You look punch drunk yourself."

Gate clears his throat. "He tried to kiss me, but I put him to bed. Doubt he'll even remember it in the morning. Oh, look! They're bringing out more seed cakes and mead."

"No more for you," I say. "We three are going to bed."

"Why do you have to be such a killjoy, Your Highness?"

"*Because*, Gate. We have a task that's more important than you getting drunk and eating too much. We barely escaped the forest three days ago and we leave soon. We need to rest."

He sighs. "Fine. I'll go to bed. But I hope sylphs like boar bacon for breakfast. I'm tired of nuts and berries."

We see him to his door and head to our adjoining rooms. Neev takes a step toward her door and I reach for her hand. "Go into yours," I whisper, even though there's no one around to hear. "But you can meet me in mine. If you want."

I go into my room, take off the circlet of river stones, and strip down to the simple muslin underclothes provided by the sylphs before climbing into bed. I'm beginning to think Neev isn't coming when she enters the room. She has exchanged the shimmery gown she wore to the feast for a plain white robe.

I pull back the woven quilt and she climbs in beside me.

"This is familiar," I say.

"Sharing a bed?" Her smile is shy and playful at once. "But it's already plenty warm in here."

"I don't want you to feel pressured," I say. "Because I'm..."

"Royal?"

"Yes."

She takes my hand and kisses my fingertips, one by one. "Never. I want this. With you."

I let my hand find the gentle curve of her waist beneath the coverlet and then her hip. Her mouth is on mine, warm and insistent. Tonight, I don't think of our differences, of noble and commoner, or servant and princess. I only think of her burning hands on my body, and her soft skin beneath my lips. I don't think of the invisible barrier I used to imagine between us, and when she wakes me in the morning with soft kisses and a sylph brings us breakfast in bed without batting an eye, I hope we've finally torn it down. I don't realize my hope is so bright that it's blinding me.

CHAPTER FOURTEEN

WHEN Neev has gone back to her room, I bathe and dress and explore the palace, this time alone.

I wander through echoing corridors and rooms of trees filled with chattering sylphan courtiers who nod and regard me curiously as I pass them before returning to their storytelling or singing or feasting. When I stray into a library piled floor to ceiling with precarious towers of leather and canvas bound books, scrolls, and maps, I'm surprised to find Gate there, visiting with Plover again. Gate's seated sideways in a high-backed chair with his cloak draped over one armrest, looking up at Plover, who is perched on the high back.

They look so comfortable together that I'm slightly taken aback. Gate wears the same expression I've seen on his face when he flirts with servants and palace guards back home. I sigh and start to turn away, leaving him to it, but he stands up. "Wait, Highness! I need to talk to you."

I put my hands behind my back as I approach. "Good

morning. How do you feel, Plover? Gate said you had too much to drink last night."

Plover grins, showing his sharp canines. "I'm well, thank you. Sylphs aren't affected like humans when we imbibe, unless we've had gallons and gallons."

"That's lucky."

He shrugs. "I should be going. My family will want me to spend second feast day with them. But I'll see you both soon."

He touches Gate's arm with a familiar air before he leaves and I widen my eyes, but Gate says, "Don't."

"Why? I've teased you for flirting a hundred times back home. What's different this time?"

"What's different is he's not human. I don't know their customs. For all I know, if I kiss him, I'll have entered a marriage contract for a thousand years."

I laugh. "Sylph culture isn't that different. And some clans have laws against intermarrying with humans, so there's that."

"But Empress Akina and King Cygnus..."

"I know. They took a risk for power. What did you want to talk to me about? Not sylph marriage customs, surely."

He rolls his eyes. "No, definitely not that. There's something I need to tell you about the night we came here. I assume you don't remember."

I shake my head. I can't remember anything after I passed out in Thornewood and had the dream—vision?—of Thorne. It's strange to have such a huge gap in my memory, and I don't want to talk about it. It makes me feel weak. "What about it?"

"It's about how Neev got us in. When we arrived, they'd already closed the gates for autumn."

"But if they were closed, how'd we get in?"

"That's just the thing. I don't know. It was late and the guards couldn't hear us calling. But Neev, she just...opened them. She walked through and I followed her, carrying you."

"You must be mistaken. No human can open the sylphan gates."

"Right. No human."

I place my hands on my hips. "Gate, if you're thinking something, why don't you just say it?"

"I don't know what I'm thinking. It was strange, that's all. You should be wary of her."

"Because you can't tell the difference between a locked and unlocked gate?"

"It was lock—" He cuts off halfway through the word and puts his head back, growling in frustration.

"Don't sow enmity just because you don't understand something that happened after you drank from a cursed river in an enchanted forest."

Gate throws his hands up, looking away from me. "Typical."

"You already told me you were all in for this, so stop questioning my decisions. Neev is trustworthy."

"Because you slept with her last night? Too bad that grace

doesn't extend to me."

"Stop it." I force myself to speak at a normal register, even though I want to scream at him. "Why are you always so rude and insubordinate?"

Gate shoots out of his chair and gets in my face. "Because I don't care how nice you want me to be! I don't *need* you, future queen. Have your father dismiss me, see if I care. I can make my own way, with my own power."

I stand my ground, my lips trembling with fury. "Then *why* are you still here?"

"Because you promised to pay me double what your father offered. A princely sum, by the way."

The urge to shove him is so unbearable I take a step back rather than give in to it. "Wonderful. I'm in love with my left hand and bound to my right by coin alone. Perfect."

"You're responsible for this, Thedra. Own it."

"I *am* owning it. Get in line or go home, Agate. I don't care anymore."

He swipes his cloak from the chair he was sitting in and throws it around his shoulders with a flourish, dripping with attitude. "I'll see you when we leave."

He departs with a thump of boots and a flash of blue and gold, and I collapse into the vacant chair, surrounded by ancient books and scrolls. I bury my face in my hands. One night. I had one happy night with the girl I like, and I'm plunged back into uncertainty and conflict. If I survive this journey, if I take the throne of Lazul, is this what the rest of my life will be? Questioning everything, trusting no one?

Gate has to be wrong. Never mind that I'm so sure of this because I can't bear to have no one in my corner, no one in whom I can truly trust or confide. I can't bear the thought of being all alone with my duties, like my mother, who had a treacherous lover, and only her plants for company.

The second of the two sylphan guards leading us to the pass behaves in a cross, wary manner, even though the corruption of Poison Forest doesn't reach this far. His name is Ibis. He's brawny for a sylph, and both he and Plover are armed with bows and arrows and daggers. He keeps eyeing my diamond vial until I tell him it has nothing to do with raising the dead.

Necromancy is purely mortal magic, the work of mages and corpse-wielders. They can be mortally wounded, but sylphs naturally live many lifetimes longer than we do. Although they use greenhealing for illness, it's easier for them to accept their mortality. Besides that, they don't worship a goddess of death.

Neev and I walk beside one another, holding hands. The clothes she stole from me back in Lazul were ruined by the time we left the forest, but she still has on my second pair of well-worn riding boots, and the sylphs outfitted her with new gloves of tanned hart hide, breeches, and a light summer cloak.

Plover doesn't share his companion's fear. He slogs on

with cheerful purpose, fully recovered from his night of too much honeysuckle mead. When he launches into a walking song, Ibis cuffs him playfully. "No one wants to hear that. There's a reason you're an archer and not a bard."

"May I ask you something?" I say.

"Of course."

"Why are you named Plover, instead of...I don't know, Bunting, or Grosbeak? Plovers are gray and white, but your wings are such a brilliant indigo." I hope this isn't a rude question. Suddenly I regret not paying better attention to my lessons in sylphan culture.

Thankfully, Plover doesn't look offended. "My mother grew up near the sea. She says when I was a baby, my long legs and fuzzy feathers reminded her of a plover chick." He brushes one of the tufts of his thick, soft wings. "Tell me," he asks, nodding to Agate, who is striding ahead of us with the hem of his dark blue cape swirling about his ankles. "Does he always cut such an impressive figure?"

I roll my eyes. "Unfortunately for his ego and my patience, yes."

Plover only smiles. He and Ibis walk together for a while, talking to one another in their tongue. It's been four years since I had lessons, and my Zelenean is better, but I manage to decipher that Ibis is afraid and wishes he hadn't volunteered. But he and Plover are flight partners, whatever that means.

The pass is less than two days' journey from the palace,

and we stop to camp in the canopy of a towering pine. When Agate sees the tree's height, his face pales.

I can't help taunting him a bit after our blow up back at the palace. "Don't look so scared, Gate. It's like the dream you gave me the first night I was so sick."

"Yes, *your* dream, Highness. I'll stay on the ground. Keep a lookout."

Plover laughs. "You don't have to *climb* it. We'll fly you up there, secure you in a harnessed platform. We don't expect you to sleep in trees the same way we do."

Gate shakes his head. "I'm not ashamed to say I'm afraid. It's madness to sleep so high. Mortals aren't meant for it."

Both guards laugh at him this time, twittering. Plover has been eyeing him when he's not looking, and judging by the warmth in his eyes, he's not put off by Gate's fear. He only thinks it's cute.

"What's madness is staying on the ground," says Ibis gruffly. "That's where night things with sharp claws and tearing teeth hunt creatures like us. Come."

Without further ado, they each take one of his arms and launch into the air, leaving the ground far behind in the space of a few wingbeats.

We sit next to one another on a sturdy branch as we watch the sylphs assemble the platforms and tents. I can see Neev foraging a short distance from camp. The branch we're seated on is stout enough to serve as the central beam for a great hall, but Gate is still white as a sheet, and he puts his head between his knees with every breath of wind.

The platforms are made from mats of lightweight wood that interlock and unroll into a solid base. Canvas sides are attached and the whole apparatus is secured with a series of intricately woven knots and ropes. There are even windows that can be rolled up, if one fancies looking out over the edge of a precipice or a towering tree. It's a far cry from our cold and hungry nights in Thornewood.

"Finished." Plover clutches the tree trunk, wedging his foot into the notch of a narrow branch. "Don't worry. We've done this a thousand times."

"But...they move," says Gate.

"Better they sway with the tree's dance than catch the wind and break or blow away."

Gate moans into his knees, his voice muffled. "Ohhhh, Zori, dark goddess, spare me."

Neev and I sleep on one platform, and Gate stays in the other, lower one. Ibis and Plover perch comfortably on two sturdy branches between us, wings fluffed for warmth and balance. They are playing a game that looks similar to one we call Wolf and Sheep in Lazul, but their white figures are chicks and the black piece is a kestrel.

Gate whimpers every time the wind gusts, and Neev and I can barely stifle our giggles at him. She rolls up our window and peers out of it.

"Give yourself a sleepy spell," she calls down to him.

"Yes," I say brightly, "one with cake and pretty boys."

"Useless," he returns. It sounds like he's going to be sick.

Plover flies down to him, and I hear him speaking gently. "Eat this. It will calm you. Do you want me to stay with you?"

Neev's warm hand slips into mine, and I nestle my face against her shoulder. "The sylphs where I grew up don't sleep in trees," she says. "They live in caves and burrows."

"Tell me more about where you grew up."

"There were cows and workers threshing grain in autumn. My mother fed me sweet cream and strawberries in summer. And I swam in the springs and millponds."

"Was the water warm?"

"Yes." There's a smile in her voice.

"What was your mother like?"

"Kind. And clever. She deserved better."

"Did she have power, like you?"

"No." She rolls onto her side to look at me. "Enough questions about me. What about you? Everyone knows your mother was Queen Mora, powerful shapeshifter, corpse-waker. But what was she like?"

"She was..." *Tragic. Principled. Impossible to live up to.* "Formidable. Her critics called her a haughty shrew, but she protected Lazul in the frost giant uprising. When I was six, my father's cousin Gentian tried to have me killed because I hadn't shown signs of being powered, and she thought I was a liability. And because she wanted the throne for her son.

"My mother uncovered the plot and had her stripped of her title and thrown in an oubliette until her execution. She was executed before all the court." I grow quiet, dwelling on how someone like my mother could have been taken in by a man as deceitful and traitorous as Rothbart. But they all were, not just her.

"Did you know your father at all?" I ask, changing the subject.

"No. He left before I was born."

Her voice has changed now. I prop myself up on my elbow to look at her, but she turns her face to the tent wall and grows quiet. Soon she's asleep, but I lie awake looking at the stars through the window flap, thinking of the song the bard sung at the autumn feast. The one that made my throat ache.

I sleep in Neev's arms with her head on my shoulder, and wake to her fingers stroking my hair. I blink at her sleepily, surprised when she kisses me on the lips.

"Good morning," I say, wishing I could stay cozy beneath the blankets with her. *We could wake like this every morning if...*

"Sleep well?" she asks.

"Yes, when I finally dropped off. You?"

Her brow furrows. "Not really. The wind. I could hear things howling."

"I heard nothing except Gate and Plover blathering and cackling like blue jays. Seems they hit it off."

A covey of quail flies overhead as we're washing in the stream. I'd love a roast quail for breakfast after eating sylphan food for a week, but the sylphs worship birds and some of their deities are avian, so when I see Agate reach for his crossbow, I stop him. Instead, we breakfast on boiled porridge, bread thick with seeds and dried fruit, and a coffee made of ground nutshells. Despite my cozy morning, I'm grateful to have my feet back on solid ground. Like Gate, I'd almost rather take my chances on the ground than sleep in a tree.

Gate passes me as we begin to ascend Frostmead to the pass. I whisper, "The tent wasn't so bad after all, eh?"

He gives me a startled look, and I wish we had the easy camaraderie he and Neev have. "I was afraid," he admits, "and it was a welcome distraction. He's a better talker than some people I've been stuck traveling with the past weeks. You're the ones who spent half the night talking about your parents, of all things. How romantic."

"Plover's nice," I say, ignoring his meaningless jibes. "And a soldier, like you. Plus, he likes you."

"He's friendly. With all due respect, Your Highness, it's madness for someone as frightened of heights as I am to fall in love with a sylph."

"Don't put yourself down, Gate," says Neev, linking her

arm through mine. "Lots of people hate heights. Anyone would be lucky to have you."

"Ugh, don't encourage him."

"Did I or did I not save your life in Poison Forest?"

"I don't remember," I say honestly.

Gate throws his head back, groaning.

Frostmead rises around us slowly as we hike, an avenue of snow-capped peaks leading toward the basin that holds the Lake of Tears and Lebed, its lone isle. We reach the pass at midday. It's high and narrow, and we carefully survey the rock face and the edge of the cliff, looking for signs of struggle, but wind and rain have washed away any trace of blood.

"I know this is where it happened," says Ibis. "They burned the more mangled corpses here and took the rest back to Zelen for burial."

"Here!" Neev comes out from behind a stack of rocks. "There's a pile of ashes, and I think this is a cairn."

Using a stick, I draw a large circle that encompasses both the ash and the cairn. Lighting a lantern, I speak the secret word beneath my breath. "By Zori's power, I summon one of those who lies buried here. Awaken and speak."

Nothing happens. Ibis is giving me a doubtful look, but Plover looks amused.

"I thought you passed the test, Your Highness," says Gate, miffed.

"Believe me, I passed." I think of the scar across my left

breast, and how cold seeped through me as my blood flowed out onto the stone floor of the crypt. I can see the otherworldly brilliance of the shore beyond the world, on the other side of the Endless Sea.

Frigid cold falls within the circle, and the lantern's flame snuffs out. My breath curls in little white wisps. Of course. That's the key. Not just knowing the secret word, or the rituals. Anyone can do that. The true secret is having been dead one's self.

Something begins to take shape at the far end of the circle, near the cairn. I hardly know what to expect. When I woke Zori in her tomb, it was too dark to see. I clasp my diamond vial, more from habit than for protection. Lightning is no weapon against a shade.

The body of a sylphan guard takes shape. His form is foggy and immaterial, like a miasma hanging over a body of water on an early morning. The shade blinks, looking around in confusion. The wind blows my hair and my cloak, but his don't stir. He takes a few steps toward me, and I hear Ibis hiss. Behind me, I sense Plover has nocked an arrow—I can hear the stretch of the hart's sinew as Plover pulls it taut and anchors the string. I put my hand up, motioning for him to stand down.

The shade's gaze is on mine now. "Why did you call me? What do you want?"

"I am Thedramora, High Priestess of the Dead. Tell me

how you died and what you saw."

"The sorcerer—the mage. He came in the shape of a great bird, like an owl, but far larger and more fearsome. He set upon us with hooked beak and talons, then changed into a man. The horses were wild with terror, and they killed two of us. The mage transfigured them into monstrosities, and they died writhing."

"Was there a young woman with him?"

"Yes. Half-sylphan. Brown-skinned."

"Was she hurt?"

"I don't know. I was one of the last he killed, but I was distracted. I stood raining arrows down on him from the rock, but he sent them back at me. I saw him go before I died. He changed into the bird again and took the woman, like an owl takes a vole. There." He points beyond the pass, to the basin between the peaks that holds the Isle of Lebed.

"Thank you." I put my hand out, palm up. "Return to your rest."

When the guard's shade is gone, I look toward the crater lake where Lebed lies and give a cry of frustration. It's another two days away, and we've lost so much time. My power seethes through me, making my hair crackle, my skin tingle. It feels useless. What I need is swiftness. Instant transport.

Disconsolate, I give the lantern to Neev and smudge the circle I drew with the toe of my boot, making sure nothing can follow us from the realm of the dead.

Chapter Fifteen

"How will we keep him from killing us the same way he killed them?" asks Gate.

Neev turns away to stare out over the valley below the mountain pass. I shake my head because I truly don't know. The sylphs had no one with them with my power, or Gate's. But it's possible we lost the element of surprise when I encountered Rothbart in Thornewood. I set out on this quest so recklessly, just because I thought I could save Dette on my own and felt guilty for how things ended between us.

"I need to think."

We find a sturdy tree off the main road to sleep in, sheltering against the wind beneath a rocky overhang. When a fire is going, the sylphs boil their porridge and toast bread, and Gate carries water from a nearby stream. I'm sick of sylphan food, but I eat it without complaint and drink lots of water, grateful it's clean and not enchanted.

"Ibis will be returning on the morrow as agreed," says

Plover, "but I plan to continue on with you."

Agate looks up at him in surprise but says nothing.

I frown. "Are you sure? You could die."

"The shade said the sorcerer came as an owl. I have wings as well. And my arrows are swift and sure."

"We'll be glad to have you, then."

Ibis takes his leave of Plover with obvious reluctance. He catches Plover's forearm and pulls him into a firm embrace, flexing his shoulders until their wingtips touch, blue against white, surrounding them in a feathery fortress.

When they part, he says gravely, "May there always be wind for your wings, brother," and clasps the back of Plover's head.

"And may you fly as swiftly as your arrows," Plover says with a smile.

Agate snorts a little under his breath at this farewell and I kick his ankle, although I know he barely feels it through his boot.

Ibis scarcely gives us a backward glance. I think he's among those sylphs who believe that humans and sylphs are better off not meddling in one another's affairs. I would almost agree with him, if only because sylphs maintain their small realm with relatively little intrigue or conflict. But Dette's abduction and the danger presented to them by Rothbart make the point moot.

Our campsite is the highest point we've camped at thus far.

The air is cool but thin and everyone except Plover is easily winded. He says we're only a day's hike from the summit of the pass and will reach Lebed by nightfall the following day.

Even though we teased Gate about Plover earlier, Neev and I spend half the night awake, not talking. I taste her lips as we caress one another with roving hands. She removes her gloves and holds my face in her bare hands as she kisses me. Her fingertips run lightly over my palms, and she skims the backs of her fingers along my arms and the insides of my wrists with a naked tenderness that makes me feel like I'll fall apart. But lovemaking within earshot of others isn't something that appeals to me and when I can't control my ragged breaths, I make her stop. I lie awake for a long time after she falls asleep, reveling in the warmth of her body next to mine, aching for her.

I have my first nightmare since leaving Thornewood. I dream of Dette. She's in a dark, slimy dungeon. The kind that was outlawed in the Triumvir ages ago. She's chained to the wall, and she begs me to free her. *You forgot me*. She says it over and over as black tears stream down her cheeks.

I jerk awake, my heart pounding with panic from the dream. Something feels wrong. Terribly wrong. I pat around blindly until my hands find Neev's slim body. She's lying on top of the coverings, her breaths soft and shallow with sleep.

A low, trilling whistle comes from the ground below and

Plover stirs in his roost above us.

I peer out the window of our platform. It's so very, very dark, and I can hardly see anything, but something is on the ground below our tree. I can hear its labored breathing. There's a grating rasp, and whatever it is places its hands on the tree trunk.

Plover stands and the branch creaks beneath his weight.

"Don't," I hiss. "You don't know what that is."

"It's Ibis. He used the guard's secret whistle." Plover launches himself from the tree branch with a rustle of his wings. A few seconds later, he lands lightly on the ground and I hear him cry out.

"Gate! Neev, wake up!" I shake Neev and Gate grunts in his sleep below us. Fuck all. This is the worst time for him to be such a deep sleeper. I toss the rope ladder out the window of the platform. I want to rush down it, to look down and see what's happening on the ground, but to do either would be a death wish. I descend slowly and carefully, clinging to the rope in the dark.

There's a sound of scuffling below me.

I keep going, hand after hand, foot after foot. When I'm close enough to drop to the ground, I let go, landing in a crouch and grabbing my vial. Plover is kneeling on the ground beside a prone figure.

"What is it?"

"I told you, it's Ibis." His voice is choked with anguish. I find one of the sylphan torches near the campfire and manage to light it with shaking fingers. It glows with a slowly growing green light and in its partial illumination, I see why Plover is crying.

Ibis is full of arrows. One protrudes from his thigh, another from his belly, and a third is lodged beneath his ribs, stuck straight through his breastplate. There's even one piercing his wing, which explains why he was on the ground. A dark trickle of blood leaks from his nostril and the corner of his mouth.

I kneel on his other side. Plover doesn't try to disturb the arrows, and I assume he knows the wounds will be fatal. He has Ibis' hand in both of his, and is speaking to him in the chirruping, sibilant sylphan tongue. All I catch are a few words of comfort.

"Ask him what happened," I say softly. "Please."

Plover gives me a pained look, but he leans over and utters a high, interrogatory note. Ibis replies with difficulty, his voice harsh with torment as he struggles to speak through the blood in his throat.

"He says it was the mage. It followed him as an owl, then transformed. Much like the shade said. He tried to kill it, but it sent his arrows back at him."

After that, the only sound is Ibis' battle to breathe. Every now and then he convulses and dark blood gushes from his mouth.

Plover weeps loudly. I'm afraid he's going to draw the

attention of any nearby predators, but I can't bring myself to quiet him. Finally, he slides the dagger at his waist from its sheath, crying harder.

I reach across Ibis to put my hand on his arm. "Don't. You'll only torture him more. It—I don't think it will be long."

"It's our code," he sobs. "He came back to me so I could end his suffering."

I watch him from across Ibis' body. His realm has been peaceful for so long, he's probably never seen bloodshed like this. He might be a soldier, but he's a gentle, cheerful one, with no stomach for violence. I hold out my hand. "Give it to me. I'll do it."

He shakes his head. "It has to be me. I took an oath. He is my brother in flight."

I nod in understanding, and Plover reaches to open Ibis' doublet. But there's no need. Ibis is still, his pale blue eyes staring sightlessly into the sky.

Gate and Neev have both descended from the tree by now, and we huddle off to one side as Plover mourns.

"It was Rothbart," I tell them.

"No," whispers Neev, her voice filled with horror. "Ibis was afraid of him. He wanted no part of this."

"I know."

"We're not going to survive this, are we?" asks Gate. I'm shocked at how resigned he sounds.

"He was alone," I remind him. "He didn't have my

lightning, or your persuasion, or Neev's fire."

Neev shakes her head. "You know I can't control it."

"You knocked me on my ass the last time I tried to train you."

"It was an accident! I was angry."

"You can't summon some anger over this?" I throw my arm out toward Ibis' dead body. "For the dead guards on the pass? For the girl I saw in the forest? For *Dette*?"

She blanches in the torchlight, and I'm instantly sorry for shouting at her, but I'm also enraged by her fear, by my inability to help her control her magic or keep her safe. By Rothbart's seemingly unstoppable power. The fact that he killed my mother would be enough to send me after him, but this is beyond the pale. I've seen enough of his evil to last two lifetimes, and I despise it, and him.

We bury Ibis at first light and pile rocks from the mountain over the grave to keep out any animals.

"He was brave," says Plover softly, "because he faced what frightened him head-on. He planned to marry his lover of twelve winters at the Feast of Snow. I'd sing a lament for him but" —he laughs softly— "he never liked my voice."

"Would it offend you," I ask, "if I said something? I don't have to, but in Lazul it's an honor for the Priestess of the Dead to speak at a funeral."

Plover nods and I step forward. The traditional Lazulian death rite is, *may they find their rest on the Far Shore*, but it

doesn't fit with sylph mythology, so I amend it. "May he find his rest on the far horizon, in the Land of the Sun, beyond the clouds."

⁂

"Do sylphs stay with one mate for their entire lives?" Gate asks Plover later, when we're eating lunch beside the trail. "You said Ibis had been with his lover twelve years."

"No, not all of us. But Ibis was of clan Crane. His people choose a lover when they're young and stay with them for many years to make sure they'll be happy as mates, because they mate for life. Twelve years was considered a swift courtship, but they loved one another."

"And what clan are you from?" asks Gate. I glance sideways at him, but his eyes are on Plover.

"Clan Swallow. We're not so choosy." He crunches on a beetle wing. "We intermarry with fae or humans, or find mates amongst our own kind, usually several. Our breeding years are spaced quite far apart, thankfully, or we'd have overpopulated the Triumvir by now. I have six siblings from my father alone, but I don't care for females of any race, so I've no danger of a prolific lineage."

"Interesting," says Gate. He offers a bite of the pear he's slicing to Plover, who accepts it with a grateful expression.

"I'm so very sorry for your loss," says Neev, her voice breaking. She sounds grief-stricken, and I'm taken aback by her level of mourning for someone she barely knew. "How

long did you know one another?"

"Since we were fledglings."

"And um, how old are you now?" asks Gate.

"Less than quarter life in sylph years," says Plover, evading the question deftly. "Humans tend to find our age discomfiting when measured in theirs. You?"

Gate looks surprised by the question. "Nineteen," he says.

"And I'm seventeen," I say, "and Neev is—"

"Sixteen."

"Good, now we all know one another better," I say briskly. "We should go. The sun is moving."

Gate gives me a wounded look. It's not that I want to be rude by interrupting their conversation, but I'm impatient to continue. We've already been set back by burying Ibis.

Chapter Sixteen

PLOVER offers to secure one of the platforms in a tree for us again tonight, but the three of us elect to stay together on the ground. I'm too disturbed by the memory of waking up and hearing something below us but not knowing or being able to see what it was to ever sleep in a tree again.

I'm too tired for nightmares. Instead, I'm awakened from a deep sleep by something sharp stabbing my arm. Half-asleep, I try to brush it off, thinking a twig or pine needle is in my bedding. Whatever it is only embeds itself deeper into my forearm. Then I feel something scuttling up my leg, and there are three more sharp pricks. I grab at it when it reaches my thigh and something punctures my palm, sharp as a pinprick. I hope I'm wrong, but it feels like an insect roughly the size of a rat, with lots of sharp, jointed legs.

I'm fully awake now. I shoot up from my bedroll, frantically scrabbling at whatever has attached itself to me. I manage to tear it free and throw it as hard as I can toward the bracken away from the campsite.

My struggle wakes Neev, and Plover flies down from the tree where he was sleeping.

"Be careful. Something was on me. Bring a light!"

I've hardly spoken when more tiny pinpricks brush my skin. There's something crawling up my leg. I swat at it before it can embed itself in my skin. A strangled sound comes from Gate's pallet a few feet away. Plover lights a torch and I see Gate struggling. Something large and spindly is attached to his face.

I sprint to him, but Plover gets there first. In the torch's ghastly glow, I catch a clearer glimpse of a creature like the one that tried to attach itself to my arm. It looks like a cross between a spider and a squid, but with many more legs, all jointed and ending in sharp points instead of feet or claws. It's trying to stab Gate in the eye with one of its needled appendages, but he's holding it off with both hands. Blood runs from what looks like at least a dozen punctures in his palms.

I pull on one of my riding gloves and snatch the thing off Gate's face, ignoring the pain when it momentarily focuses its assault on me.

Plover thrusts the torch into my free hand and uses the point of a pearlescent talon to impale the thing and pitch it to the ground. I stamp on it with the heel of my boot repeatedly until it crunches to bits.

Gate lies trembling on his pallet. Droplets of blood well up from four perforations in his face, appearing emerald black in the green light. "F-fuck this place."

Plover kneels to inspect Gate's wounded hands, which received more of the assault than his face, while I circle the campsite to make sure there are no more of the creatures waiting to attack. When I've skirted the perimeter twice, I see another of the spider-squid creatures scuttling toward me. It looks like something out of a nightmare. I raise my boot to crush it, but it springs upward and embeds itself into the leather toe with needle-like legs. I shake my foot in a mild panic, managing to dislodge it.

One of Plover's arrows whizzes past me and pins the creature to the ground. It struggles for a moment and then lies still.

I turn and look at him in awe. "How did you see well enough to shoot something that small in the dark?"

"I'm a sylph. Where is Neev?"

"I don't know. Sorry, I was a bit distracted by having my arm impaled by a giant bug."

We wander around the campsite, calling for Neev, but she doesn't answer.

"Go and look for her," says Plover. "I'll see to Agate. But first we should light a fire, hopefully keep the rest of those things away."

The thought of encountering any more of them in the dark

is awful, but so is lingering by the fire with Neev missing. It's too dark to track her, even with a light. I'm just as likely to walk off a cliff as to find her, so I settle for walking a few feet into the surrounding trees and calling her name.

I haven't gone far when I begin to feel lightheaded. There's a metallic taste in my mouth, and the spots on my arm and hand where the thing stabbed me burn and itch.

"Shit!" I strip off my glove and tear open my sleeve to suck on the punctures in my arm, spitting out the blood and venom.

When I've done the same thing to my hand, I stumble back to the campsite. Gate is retching over the side of his pallet.

I groan, holding my churning stomach.

Plover looks up at me, wide-eyed.

"Help me suck the venom from his hands and face," I say. "Quick!"

We each grab one of Gate's hands and begin sucking out the salty, iron-tasting blood and spitting it onto the ground. When I'm done, I hesitate for a moment before beginning on his facial wounds and he takes the opportunity to push me away.

"Not you, him."

I get up so Plover can take my place. It didn't even occur to me how awkward it might be, but I'm glad to be spared the job. Plover hesitates for a second, but Gate's face is already swelling, and he crouches in the same place where I was kneeling.

"Sorry," he says, before bending over and placing his mouth to Gate's cheek.

When we're done, I vomit into the undergrowth, but I can't tell if it's from the venom or the general horror of the night.

"You should lie down," says Plover.

"What about Neev?"

"You can't do anything for her until morning."

I'm already down on one knee beside my pallet, and I collapse onto it sideways as the stars above me spin in a spiral of twisting light.

All night I lie in a stupor that's interrupted only by tremors and vomiting. Gate is worse, since he received more of the venom. Plover gives us purple berries like the ones that were floating in the bath I had in the palace—a sylph antidote for poison and curses. They help with the pain, but they work slowly, and the venom courses through my veins for several more hours, making me woozy and nauseated.

Neev reappears some time near dawn. There's a bundle of plants in her arms. They have tiny, star-shaped leaves and are covered in white blossoms.

I push up onto one elbow to glare at her. "Where in Zori's name have you been? I thought you were carried away by those things."

"I went to find a plant that draws out poison and calms the stomach."

"'Thedra,'" I say, mimicking Neev's soft voice, "'I'm going to gather healing herbs. I haven't been carried off by spiders or an owl-wizard.' That's all you had to say."

"Being ill makes you so grouchy," she replies. "Lie down."

I collapse back onto my pallet. My stomach muscles hurt from vomiting all night, and I'm trembling from the effort of sitting up. Neev places the leaves in one of the cooking pots and uses a rock as a mortar to crush them. She mixes the green goo with water to make a paste, smears it on our stings, and brews the blossoms of the plant into a tea along with some of the purple berries.

I feel better after the first few sips of tea. It takes Gate longer to rally, and the spots where the quill spider stung him stand out like droplets of dark purple wine on his face. His hands are still swollen, grotesque in the daylight.

It's too late to pack up and move, so we stay where we are. But as the sun sets, we light torches and keep the fire going. It might draw other predators, but the thought of the quill spiders is too horrifying for us to ignore.

Neev makes the healing tea for me and Gate again, and we sit by the fire, sipping the bitter brew. Plover is quiet tonight. After a while, he takes out the game that looks like Wolves and Sheep, unrolling a square of canvas with an embroidered cross-shaped grid. He dumps the bag of carved wooden pieces onto it, one black and fifteen white, and arranges the chicks along one arm of the cross. He places the kestrel in the center and takes a coin from the pouch around his waist. "Anyone want to play?"

Gate's hands are still too swollen to hold the figures, and I've never liked the game, so I shake my head.

"I will," says Neev.

"We toss for who is Kestrel."

"Tails."

Plover flicks the coin into the air and catches it, turning it onto the back of his other hand. He smiles. "You win."

Neev moves the kestrel cleverly for a beginner, but he hems her in every time. He beats her three times in a row.

"I'm tired," she says finally, pushing away from the board.

Plover puts the game away and sits down behind Gate on his pallet, folding his long limbs in a way that reminds me of a wading bird and makes me think perhaps his name is fitting after all.

"Will you tell us a story or sing a rhyme?" he asks Neev. "One from Zelen."

"She's been telling me tales of Zelen for weeks," I say apologetically, because I can see she really is tired and in no mood to entertain. "Why don't you tell us a sylph tale? If you're up to it."

"Our tales are too long for human patience. They take hours and hours. Sometimes days."

"Like your laments?" I try to catch Neev's glance, but she is staring into the fire.

"Will you give us a sampling, Plover?" she asks. "Just the prologue of something beautiful."

Plover studies her. I have the feeling that if I'd asked again, he'd have declined just to show he's not subject to my supposed sovereignty. But he nods to her.

"Once, long ago, all the Trees were still awake, not just those tended by dryads. The Winds had faces and voices, and the Waters teemed with nymphs and merrows. In those days, the fae folk were many. It came to pass that the dryad of an ancient, towering tree fell in love with the Sun. And because she was tall and wild, and had locks of golden flowers, he loved her in return.

"He warmed her face when she slept in the meadows and shone rays where she ran in the forest, so that flowers sprang up in her footprints. Seeing how he made everything grow green and fair, she longed to be his lover. Learning how the birds flew to and fro in the skies, she built a boat of branches and feathers, and begged the East Wind to give her a breeze for a fair journey. But the East Wind said she must give something in return—a promise. If the Sun should take her as his wife, their firstborn daughter would be of both earth and sky.

"She promised, so the Wind gave her a breeze to bear her boat upon the sky.

"The journey she made is too long to recount in one tale, but when at last she reached the Sun, his love for her became so great that he made her his bride and gifted her with the wings of a bird, so she might fly from sky to earth and back again. When their first child was born, the dryad kept her promise to the East Wind, and reared her in both earth and air. She is our goddess, Shorea, and the sylphs are her children. Shoreana is named for her."

We sit quietly, letting his beautiful words sink in. Neev sniffs. She's crying.

Plover has tears in his eyes as well, but I suspect they're for Ibis. I have no idea why Neev is crying. I liked the tale of Shorea, but it doesn't strike me as particularly sad.

Plover claps his hands together. "I told you a tale, and now one of you owes me one in return. It's our custom. Thedra, tell us of your power. Not the lightning—the way you raised the dead on the pass."

I sip the herb tea and cough into my sleeve, shuddering at the acrid flavor that sticks to my tongue. "That's a secret older than the Triumvir."

Plover says nothing, waiting. I take a deep breath and let it out. What difference does it make? We're not likely to survive this journey, anyway. "I can't tell you how it works because no one knows for certain. But our lore says the god you call the Sun had a sister."

Plover nods. "Thorne, goddess of earth, Zelen's green lady of wood and vale."

"Yes. I had a vision of her once, in Thornewood. She was lovely and terrible. Legend says she had two sons sired by the river god. One loved all the same things she did. Cultivation, copulation, growth and light." I pause. I'm not as good a storyteller as Plover, but he nudges my knee, urging me on.

"But the other loved moonlight and darkness," I continue. "He loved to walk in tombs full of bones, to learn how things could be unmade, what caused them to decay and rot. He even renamed himself Death, and no one living recalls his true name. He studied how mortals could be brought back, using the power Thorne had granted him over earth to return its dead to life. Until Thorne forbid him from using it. He fled north, and there he fell in love and took his bride, Zori, who learned his ways, and stole his secret words. She is Lazul's chosen goddess."

"May she show us mercy," murmurs Gate instinctively.

I cover and uncover my eyes, more for his benefit than my own.

"Well done," says Plover. "Go on."

"Eventually, Thorne grew tired of Death and Zori gathering the non-living to themselves and banished them across the Endless Sea, to rule over their realm in seclusion, so the dead might not harass the living. That's why there are so many rules to be followed by a corpse-waker."

"And do they?" asks Plover. "Rule over the dead?"

I resist the urge to touch the scar on my chest. "Zori does. Death, I couldn't say. Some say Zori destroyed him. I've never seen him, so I couldn't tell you." *Death's mark was on you before I ever touched you.*

"So, your death deity is different than ours, then?" Gate asks Plover.

"We don't worship death or fear it," says Plover. "Birth and death are two ends of a circle meeting as it closes."

Easy for him to say, when sylphs live for hundreds of years.

"Here," says Plover. "We should go to bed. Let our wounded sleep." He pats Gate's shoulder. "I'll construct a platform for you."

Gate groans. "Noooo. No more trees. No more bugs. Who's to say those things can't climb?"

"Of course they can," says Neev absently. I motion for her to be quiet.

"I never thought I'd sleep in a tree again either," I say. "But we're not sleeping on the ground after last night."

As Plover constructs the tent with Gate watching, Neev wanders to where her pallet was thrown in the melee last night. She shakes sand out of it, and I sidle over to her. "You okay?"

"I'm fine."

She's been so unlike herself since she got back that I don't believe her. I can't help thinking of the time I went missing for a night, and what it meant. "Did you meet something foul in the woods?"

"No."

"It took you all night to find a few plants?"

"They're not as plentiful at this altitude, and it was dark." Her excuse is valid, but it doesn't explain her attitude. Maybe she's just thinking of what could go wrong on Lebed. If that's the case, she's in good company.

I start to turn away, not wanting to pester her when she's clearly in a bad mood, but her hand snakes around my wrist. I let her tug me toward her and my lips find hers in the firelight. Her kisses aren't like they were in the stargazing tower, or the other night in the tree. There's no deliberate slowness, no melting sweetness. She kisses me roughly, her mouth hard and desperate, her tongue questing into my mouth.

I stop returning her kisses long before I want to. Instead, I hug her until she relaxes against me. My face is crushed against her hair, which smells like campfire and chill mountain air. "I want to talk to you. Be with you," I whisper. "I wish we were alone."

"I don't," she replies softly. "I don't need another reason to care for you."

I tense. I can't understand why she'd say such a thing. It's the first time either of us has put a name to our feelings for one another, and she sounds as if she regrets it.

"Don't say that," I say finally. "When we find Dette, you can return to Lazul with me."

"And do what? Don't you have to take the throne?"

"It would please my father if I did. He could retire in his southerly home near the Sapphire Sea with his lover."

"Where would that leave me?"

I pause. Suddenly I'm finding it difficult to breathe. "As queen consort, if you wished."

She pulls away from me. "Thedra ..."

"Neev."

I reach for her hand, but she keeps it behind her back. "An untrained, unregistered elemental as queen consort?"

"I would pardon you, and have you trained. A woman who helped save the future High Empress? Who is the queen's beloved? I don't think anyone will object."

I see her lips start to tremble at the word *beloved*. "No one has been saved yet."

I swallow, hard. "I offer you my kingdom, and you scoff and air your doubts?"

She gives me a small, sober smile in the firelight. "That's the pride of your noble blood speaking, Thedra. You hardly know me."

"My father hardly knew my mother, but he made her the head of his army after seeing her in battle."

"From what I've heard, your father likes men."

"They were partners, not lovers. We could be both."

She doesn't acknowledge this. "You should go back."

"Why are you changing the subject?" My voice goes up an octave, sharp with impatience. "The forest made me ill because the enchantment there was influenced by my mother's death. Why, by the gods, would you come this far with me and then suggest I go back?"

"Because, Thedra, it's a death wish! Go home to Lazul and amass your forces."

"I've come too far to go back. I'll stand against Rothbart if it's the last thing I do. And if you can't stomach that, then you're the one who should go back."

Neev brings her hand down in a gesture of defiance and walks away, putting distance between us. It's not as if I planned this. I feel she forced my hand by practically saying she loved me and then insisting I outline what would happen if she went back to Lazul with me. Her suggestion that I give up the quest only jumbles things further.

Neev makes the healing tea for us again before bed. Gate sleeps between us tonight with his sword and crossbow on his chest like some ancient soldier being laid to rest, and I fall asleep with my diamond vial clutched in my hand.

When I awaken at dawn, Neev's fingers aren't toying with my hair as they were a few mornings ago. She's already up making breakfast with Plover. I sit up blearily, jostling Gate, who groans and rolls over.

"Good morning," I say.

"Mmf." He ruffles his hair. "No spiders last night."

"Nope. Your face still looks like a pincushion, though."

"So does your heart."

"What?" I give him a sharp look.

"Beg pardon, Your Highness. I'm not fully awake."

"No, stop that. I want to know what you meant."

He looks regretful. "I overheard your conversation last night."

"You overheard?"

"You were ten steps away!"

I draw my knees up to my chest. Neev saying no to my offer to make her a figurehead through marriage was a disappointment, but it didn't occur to me until just now that it might mean the end for us. We've barely even begun. If I take the throne and she's not seen as my equal, she'll never be viewed by the people as more than my paramour. I wouldn't wish that for her to be a decorative plaything lolling about the palace in silks. But the truth is, I've never asked what she wants out of life. It's not a question I'm accustomed to asking, since no one's ever asked it of me.

My future has always been decided for me. Study to become Priestess of the Dead. Take the throne as Queen of Lazul, second co-chair of the Triumvir. Marry a prince or princess or the child of a noble with valuable resources. And, once my power showed itself, train as a lightning elemental. Even my hobbies—horses, lightning-wielding, and swordplay—had to do with their value to the crown.

"I'm sure it seemed impulsive to you," I say. "Me asking her to marry me when I've known her for less than a month."

Gate chuckles. "Do you forget I'm the one they send to find you when you wander off on some scheme? The undercaptains in King Thede's army call you Thedra the Impetuous. But I know you better than them. The cogs are always turning. And you know when your mind's made up."

I chew a nail. "Queen Thedra the Impetuous. I don't hate that, but it's not what I'd call an admirable moniker."

"When we return, don't have their heads chopped off for it. *If* we return."

I roll my eyes. I've been thinking about asking Gate to be commander of my army when I'm crowned, but I'm too vulnerable to say it now.

When I've washed and rinsed my mouth at the stream, I find Neev stirring a simmering mixture of porridge and potherbs with the purple berries. I'd like to kiss her cheek and say good morning, but I don't know where our conversation last night left us. I picture hugging her from behind while she stirs the forest stew, my chin on her shoulder, my arms about her trim waist. I'd kiss her neck and her soft cheek, and we'd toast bread and drink hot tea together.

It's such a homey image, and so unlike anything I've ever imagined for myself, that it makes my chest ache. I used to imagine Dette and I in our respective chambers in the palace of Zelen, meeting at night after dinner for wine, and then waking to have breakfast together on the terrace overlooking Thistle's main avenue, which is lined with trees that blossom pink and red in spring. But I never imagined anything like this. Simple and unpretentious, and *whole*. The problem is, both are fantasies.

"Morning," I say tentatively. "May I talk to you?"

She gives a small nod, covering the pot with a lid. We walk to the stream, out of earshot of Plover and Gate.

"I'm sorry about last night," I say. "I sprung the offer on you. I see that now."

She closes her eyes. "Don't apologize."

"No, let me say this. Everything in my life has been planned for me. Setting out to rescue Dette and asking you to be my queen consort are two of the only things I've done for myself, and I did them impulsively. But I don't want to rush anything, to get in the way of...this." I gesture to myself and her. "Because this is good. Neev, I—

"I know," she interjects.

"I want to hug you."

"Then do."

I put my arms around her. I can't keep my hands out of the tufts of her short hair, or my mouth from kissing her. She squeezes me back tight enough to make me breathless. My arms encircle her, and I place my cheek on the top of her head. Her hair smells of wood smoke and sweat and sweet mountain grass. Even now, after promising to take things slower, my insides are in turmoil. I want to kiss her until my lips are raw. I want to lie down in the grass with her. I want to offer her a home, jewels, a closetful of clothes, a life with me. The wants could go on forever, but I force them down, force myself to reign in my desires.

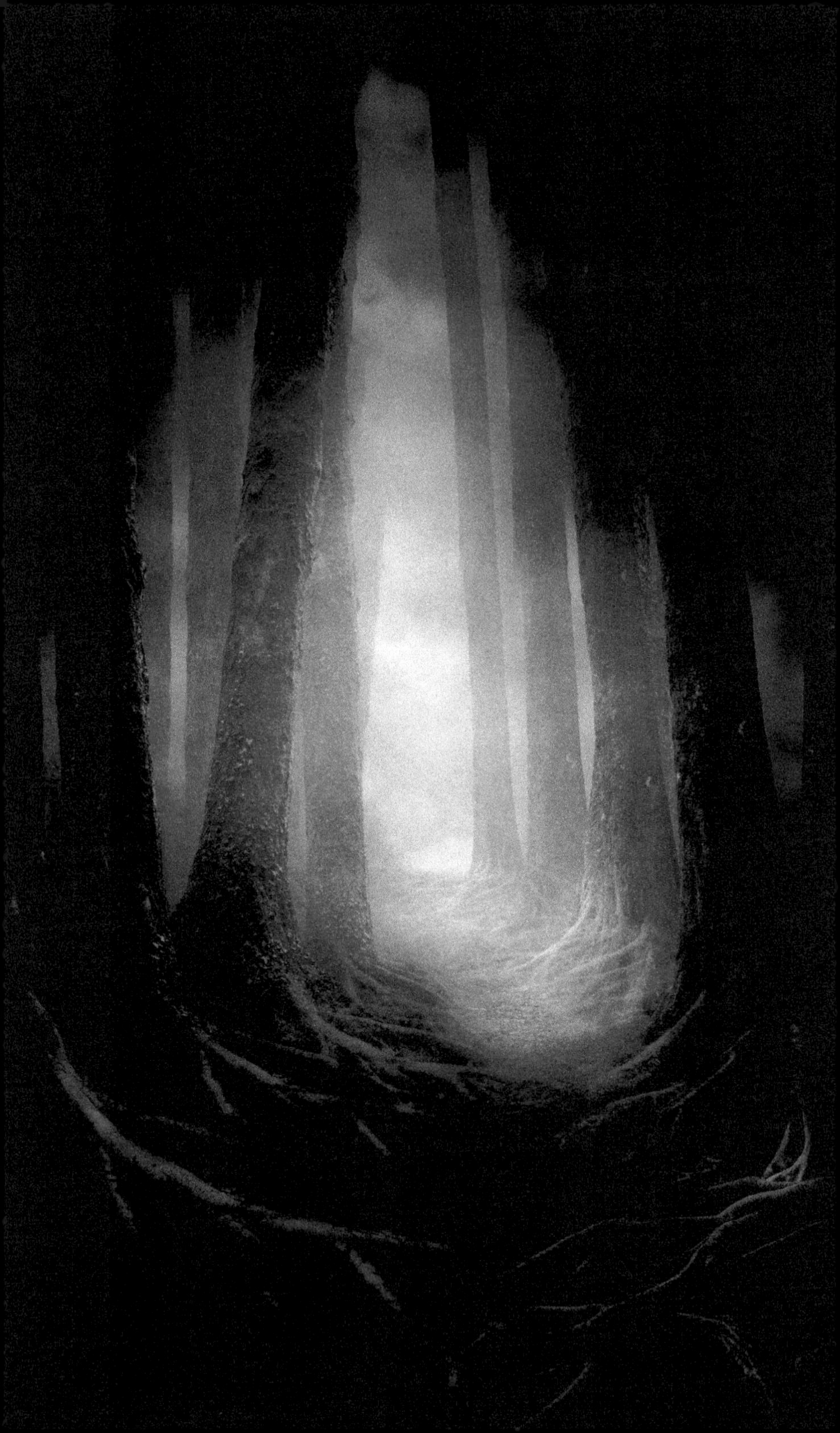

Part Four: Lebed

If the world is divided into seeing and not seeing,

Marya thought, I shall always choose to see.

-Catherynne M. Valente, *Deathless*

Chapter Seventeen

We near the summit of Frostmead before midday. The deep basin on the other side that holds the Lake of Tears is now visible. The lake is as wide and deep as a small sea, and it glimmers blue as cut sapphire in the summer sun. The Isle of Lebed is a green jewel in its center, surmounted by the castle known as Alder Tower.

My heart swells on instinct at the sight of its turrets, the Bell Tower and the Lookout, even though I know only danger waits for me there. But I can't help it; I spent so many summers on Lebed, riding Zmaj on the grounds, practicing fencing and archery, my court manners and my magic. And, of course, getting into mischief with Dette by plaguing the stable hands or sneaking off to swim in the lake, or having a picnic in the green woods with food stolen from the kitchen.

I spare a glance for Neev, who stands silently at the summit. She has her arms outstretched, letting the wind wash over her. It whips the cloak backward and away from her shoulders, molding the loose shirt she wears to the soft curves of her body.

"Neev."

She turns her head to look at me over her shoulder.

"You know I'm going ahead. But if you have any doubts at all...about going on, or using your power, or anything else, then you don't have to come with me."

She bites her lip so hard it turns white, but shakes her head. "If you're going on, so am I."

Despite the certainty of her words, her face is a mask of doubt.

"If you must use your power, remember what we practiced. I know it didn't go well, but if you focus it on him, using emotion, I think you could do as well as you did that night you knocked me down. Better, even."

Neev nods and moves away from the windy summit, back toward the path. I tighten my boot laces and stride after her.

The closer we get to the lake, the more anxious I become. Finally, we reach the glade at the edge of Frostmead. It's less than an hour to shore, but darkness is coming.

"We should make camp here," says Plover. He doesn't like to travel by night after what happened to Ibis.

"No. We'll make our way to the quay and take one of the boats moored there. It's better if we approach under cover of darkness. No one has ever tried to take the tower by daylight.

In ancient times, warring armies always came by night using muffled oars."

"They carried boats over the mountain?"

"I didn't say it was a good strategy, but all methods of approach are visible from the Lookout. Once we're on the island, I know a secret entrance to the castle. A tunnel that was an old servant's entrance. Dette and I used it to get out of our lessons sometimes."

We find an old skiff with a high, pointed prow moored to the quay. Gate and Plover muffle the oars with strips of cloth and the four of us clamber into it. I hide my vial inside my cloak so the light doesn't give us away.

Plover sits at the front of the boat, searching for obstacles with his keen eyes in the perfect darkness. I sit aft, steering the rudder as Gate and Neev row. There is little wind and the muffled oars make no sound in the water.

We ground the boat on the sandy beach and Plover stows it beneath a crag.

It takes me a while to find the place I'm seeking in the dark. It's an old stone cottage with a water wheel hidden in a glade, overrun by ivy. I know the entrance to the tunnel is at the back of the cottage, hidden beneath a clump of aster.

"We should light a torch," grumbles Gate.

"We're not lighting anything," I reply, my teeth clenched.

We spend almost an hour casting about fruitlessly in the underbrush. Beside me, Gate grunts and garbles a muffled oath and I assume he has met with the business end of a bramble. I can tell he's beyond annoyed with me, but it has been years since I last used the tunnel, and I can't be expected to find it in record time on a night this black. I ignore him.

My foot catches against a stone lip. I put my hand out and feel around beneath the shrub until my knuckles bump into something hard and cold. "Ow!"

It's the rounded edge of the tunnel. I lead the way inside and wait until all four of us are present to bring out my lightning vial, brushing my fingers over it to awaken the rotating strands of crackling energy within. The light glints off the wet stones in glittering hues of deep purple, turquoise, and brilliant blue, like sunlight awakening a raw slab of fluorspar.

The tunnel was built as an escape route in case of siege, because of its close access to the beach, but it was blocked by a pile of stones when Dette and I found it. We cleared them without telling anyone and used it as a place to nap on hot days or escape to the cool of the forest and the lake.

The tunnel is cold but clammy. Moisture beads on the low ceiling and drips into my hair and down the back of my tunic. My boots splash in shallow puddles and a soft whispering accompanies our footfalls as we walk—the sound of Plover's wingtips brushing along the cobbled floor.

The walls are close, and I can hear Neev's every breath, every echo as Gate nervously clears his throat. The tunnel was always a place of coolness and peace and secret delight, but now it closes in on me, like a dream of being trapped in a suffocating womb. I wish I could abandon them and run ahead, or at least scream at them to be quiet.

I do neither. I bite my knuckle and squeeze my diamond vial until it hurts.

At last, we reach the door at the end of the tunnel. It leads into a secluded corner of the walled courtyard and it's stuck from years of disuse. Gate wedges his shoulder against it and helps me shove it open, and I claw my way through a curtain of ivy into the brisk air of the courtyard.

Neev follows with Plover on her heels, gasping as if the tunnel deprived him of air.

"Are you alright?" Gate places a tentative hand on his shoulder.

"I will be. Just let me breathe for a moment before we go in." He nods to the looming castle to our left.

I put my vial back into the folds of my cloak. The ragged lace on my boot has come loose again. I bend to tighten it and hear Plover draw and nock an arrow.

Crouching and whirling to where he is aiming in the darkness, I see a lone figure clad in white walking slowly through the shadows of the ivy-covered wall.

Gate quickly mirrors Plover, aiming his crossbow.

"Should we loose, Your Highness?"

"No. Wait."

I crouch in silence, watching as the figure glides closer.

The heavy clouds part to reveal the bright sickle moon hanging low over the lake, revealing a woman with wild black hair and white wings trailing over the grass.

I gasp. "It's Dette."

"What if it's not?" asks Gate. "What if it's her shade? Or the mage taking her form? The things we saw in Poison Forest..."

I think about my theory that Rothbart takes on the powers of his victims, and that he stole my mother's gift for transfiguration. But Rothbart's attempts to steal her power went wrong. Poison Forest is proof of that.

"I don't think it is," I say, "but if I'm wrong, I'll bear the weight of my mistake. Stay here."

Sweeping back the hood of my cloak, I stand and leave the seclusion of the corner where we're hidden. I'm halfway to Dette when she sees me and stops. In the moonlight, her light brown skin looks opalescent, her eyes wide and startled.

"Dette. Is it you?"

"Yes."

I clutch her hands when I reach her, feeling the fragile bones beneath my fingers. She holds herself as regally as ever, and she's whole, not visibly sick or maimed. But when she speaks, her voice is a hollow shell. And she's thinner, her cheekbones sharper than before. There are dark circles beneath her eyes.

"You're all right."

"Thedra, why did you come here?"

"I had to." My throat is thick with tears. "I couldn't just leave you to possibly die! And the way we left things ..."

"You must go," she whispers. She glances around the courtyard. "Now, before he sees you."

"I came all this way for you."

She shakes her head. "I can't go with you."

"Don't be thickheaded."

"Thedra, listen. He is powerful. Cunning. If you made it this far, it's because he wanted you to."

I stare at her, thinking her captivity and fear of Rothbart have made her imagine him to be more powerful than he is. He may be a great mage, but he doesn't have the ability to see inside my mind. Not yet, anyway.

"Dette, come now and tell me everything later. We came through the secret tunnel. Remember it?"

"Of course."

I wonder why she didn't use it to escape, but I don't have time to ask the question before she answers it.

"I can't go beyond the lake. If I do, I'll...change. I've tried. The further I get from Lebed, the weaker I become. He's harnessed my magic. Now go back. Quickly." She looks over her shoulder at the Lookout—the pinnacle of Alder Tower. "He sleeps a few hours after moonrise, but he can see us from there if he wakes up."

Her hand clutches my arm, long nails digging into my

flesh. I'm reminded of the sylph girl again and I want to grab Dette and drag her to the tunnel entrance, but reason tells me to hear her out. I don't understand what she means about changing, but if she doesn't want to come with me, there's a valid reason.

"You've been betrayed," she whispers. "Someone in your company helped you get here."

"That's impossible. We nearly died in Thornewood and were attacked on the way to the pass. Everyone is trustworthy." I turn back to look at Plover and Gate, hidden in the shadows.

That's when I realize Neev is gone.

I stride back to them. "Where is Neev? She was with us when we came out of the tunnel."

Gate turns in a circle, searching our surroundings. "She was right behind me."

"Neev?" Dette looks puzzled. "My lady-in-waiting?"

"She came with me to help free you. She insisted."

Dette's nut-brown eyes darken to black in the moonlight. "She's gone to him."

I shake my head. "That's impossible," I say again. "Not Neev. She—she loves me."

The look Dette gives me sinks deep into the pit of my stomach like a knife. It's the same look I've had on my face a hundred times when trying to understand how Rothbart fooled my mother so easily. How he fooled all of us.

"Quick," she whispers. "Follow me into the castle. If she

knows you came in through the secret entrance, she'll lead him there, but I can sneak you through the servant's quarters into the back garden."

Gate has lowered his crossbow, but Plover's is still trained on Dette. "Why should we follow you? Neev accompanied us from your father's palace and showed only fealty to Princess Thedra, but we don't even know if you're who you appear to be."

Dette's brow furrows. Even here, as a captive, she is still the High Empress's daughter, and all peoples of the realm owe her their allegiance. "We haven't time to debate whether or not I am Odette," she says. "Believe what I say and come with me or flee the way you came. The choice is yours."

"I'm not going anywhere without you," I say. "Plover and Gate can go back if they want to."

Without another word, she turns and strides across the courtyard toward Alder Tower, and I follow her. When I look back, Gate and Plover are following us at a cautious distance, crossbows drawn. Neev is still nowhere to be found.

Chapter Eighteen

I remember the inside of Alder Tower as a castle of gleaming, polished wood and greenery. The oak and alder rooms were filled with trees in ornate pots, enormous ferns grafted into the walls, and reliefs of carefully arranged lichens in many colors and textures. The floors were covered in woven rugs, and candelabras of bright gold and silver lit the rooms. The blooming green and red crest of Zelen was emblazoned upon countless doors and surfaces, embroidered on tapestries, and painted on shields and suits of arms, a constant reminder that I was the ward from a lesser kingdom, subservient to Zelen's military might and lush crops. There to learn magic and combat and riding from teachers superior to our own, and to foster goodwill between our countries.

None of that mattered to Dette and me. We were just two young girls. All we cared about was our friendship. I once thought marrying her would continue our equal footing, uniting our two kingdoms, as my father loved to say, under one common banner.

Rothbart destroyed that hope when he killed my mother. It took the heart right out of me. My thoughts of spending days training elementals while Dette saw to matters of state were replaced by ones of sadness and retribution. Akina feared my dogged one-mindedness would interfere with my ability to rule.

Maybe that's one reason I want to kill Rothbart. Not only did he kill my mother, he ruined my carefully laid plans for my future. Is my motivation that selfish? Am I that much like my father, who I've always judged for being too self-interested? Sometimes, going by history books, it seems an egotistical, reluctant ruler is worse than a tyrannical one, and that's another reason I'm reluctant to take the throne of Lazul. I don't want to fail.

The entrance hall is dark and cool. Dead vines and fronds crunch under the soles of my boots. The clean scent of heartwood and plants I recall from my summers here has been replaced by stale, musty air. Dette pulls a torch out of a wall sconce and we follow her through the hall into a side room, and then another, through the many doors and rooms winding toward the servant quarters and the large kitchen, our escape route.

My mind races with the futility of it all. The weeks spent traveling here in the slowest way imaginable, putting ourselves in harm's way again and again. Neev's disappearance. Trying to take Dette with us without killing Rothbart first when I want to rid the kingdom of his scourge once and for all.

"Stop." I put my hand on Dette's arm, and where there should be fine hairs, I feel soft downy feathers. "Is the only way to break the spell to kill him?"

"I know of no other. I've tried. At night, sometimes, I sneak into the library and look for cures."

"And you found nothing to rid one of a transfiguration spell?"

She shakes her head. "It's not just a simple reversal spell. It's...part of me. It's connected to my own being."

"I don't understand."

She runs her hand along the smooth column of her neck and touches the planes of her face. "If you're here when the sun rises, you will."

"I won't be, and neither will you."

"We don't have time to argue."

"Dette, I didn't survive Thornewood, an infected wound, and an attack by quill spiders to leave you in the clutches of the madman who killed my mother!"

Dette's lips tremble, but I can't tell if it's from anger or an effort to hold back tears.

"I knew this would happen." She sounds relieved and angry at once. "I *knew* you'd come for me, and that you'd be pigheaded and foolish when I told you to leave!"

She steps forward and I think she's going to fly at me in a

rage, but she throws herself into my arms, clutching me in a hug so tight it hurts. I hug her back. Her embrace is soft and familiar, like the memory of a childhood summer. I don't want to leave her here. I can't.

She pulls away first. Her eyes are glassy with tears, but her face is like stone. "I know I am lost, Thedra. I can accept my fate if it means you'll go free. But if you *can* return one day, promise me you'll kill him."

She squares her shoulders, tilting her chin, and the Dette of our childhood who was in my arms only a moment ago vanishes before my eyes. Now she is every inch a queen. The kind I can never be. One who would willingly, not begrudgingly, give all for her people. In her place, I might do the same, but only for a loved one. When it comes to an entire kingdom, I think I'd want to save my own skin long before I gave it up for someone else. Just like Thede the Opulent.

"She's right," says Gate.

I whirl to him, stung by this betrayal. "No, she isn't!"

He groans. "Is it always like this? If you two spend any more time fighting, the mage is going to show up and turn us all to rot and ice. Hurry!"

Dette leads the way into the kitchen, which has been barred from the inside. I wonder why Rothbart didn't take more precautions to keep her locked up before remembering he doesn't need to.

She unbars the door and turns a brass key to unlock it,

but just as her fingers lift the latch, the key turns in the lock, clicking back into place. The latch slams down with such force that Dette throws herself backward, and I know that if her hand had been anywhere near it when it closed, she'd have lost a finger.

I realize I can see the fading pattern on the traveling gown she wears and the mosaic in the center of the tiled floor. The light in the kitchen is pale gray now, and it's coming from the curtained windows, not the torch.

"It can't be dawn," whispers Dette. "Not yet."

Gate's head snaps toward the shaded windows. "Whatever you do, don't open the shades," says Dette.

A massive, brindled cat with long legs and tufted ears saunters into the kitchen, its large, velvet paws nearly silent on the tiles. It rubs itself against one of the table legs before padding over to Dette. It wears a silver collar and reaches the height of her hip, and it nudges her skirts with its head as if wanting a pat, but she looks at it with unveiled dislike.

The cat has a knowing face, so thoughtful and cunning I'm barely surprised when it speaks. "Time to go back to your cage, little bird," it purrs.

With a leisurely stretch, it sits back on its haunches and licks a paw before standing up on its hind legs. Its long body lengthens and stretches, like the wolf when he turned into his goblin form. In a trice, the thing standing before us is no longer a cat, but a creature of shadow with a grinning feline face filled with too many sharp teeth and round gleaming eyes devoid of kindness.

"Step back," it hisses at me, and I retreat from the door because I'm unsure what it will do to me if I don't.

It turns at the sound of Plover's bowstring being drawn and laughs sibilantly. "Arrows can't kill me, bird-boy. I'm not made of bones that crack or feathers that snap."

It clearly finds joy in enunciating the words *crack* and *snap*. I can hear Plover's frightened breaths, and the bow and arrow are quivering in his hands. It's the first time I've seen him truly terrified, and I force myself to laugh, scorning the goblin's fear mongering.

"Don't listen to it, Plover. A being of smoke and shadow."

"And claws and teeth," whispers the cat-thing. "I'm living death. I'll suck out your every breath."

He reaches out a clawed hand with fingers of tawny fog and sweeps away the dusty window hangings, letting in the morning light. Dette groans and bends at the waist as if she has a cramp in her belly. The sunlight dapples over her body and she throws her head back and arches her spine so far in the wrong direction I fear it will snap like a twig. Her spine stretches and ripples, lengthening her neck. The feathers I felt when I touched her arm begin to lengthen, sprouting from her hands and fingertips, bloody and wet.

She screams, quaking as her arms and wings join and grow into one another, and her legs shrivel and gnarl into bony stalks. The scream becomes a grating, strangled keening until it dies in her throat, a sound I know will haunt me forever.

She is still Dette, but she is something else now, too. Before, she was half-woman, half-sylph, but now she is more bird than either, a massive swanlike thing with hulking white wings and spindly legs. Rothbart has turned her into something gorgeous but wrong. She's not maimed like the sylph-girl, but the hands she so often used to heal are now wing tips. Her mouth can't speak human words, and her eyes are full of pain. I didn't believe it possible to hate Rothbart any more than I did, but I think for the thousandth time since I set out on the trade road that I will gladly kill him for this.

The cat-thing moves like mist dispersed by the wind, coiling itself around Dette's body in a binding black and gilded spiral.

"It's horribly painful, transfiguration. Not for the faint of heart. I prefer watching it to doing it myself." Rothbart is leaning in the doorway. "I always admired Mora's stoicism over the agony. You're so like her, Thedra. Of course, you lack some of her finer qualities."

He enters the room elegantly, with the manner of a man pretending to behave humbly at a party thrown in his honor. Plover looses an arrow without waiting a beat. It goes straight toward Rothbart's heart, and for one triumphant moment I think it will hit its mark, but Rothbart puts up a hand and waves it away.

The arrow stops, thrumming in midair as if it has hit an invisible wall before turning in a graceful arc. The arrow flies at Plover, striking him in the wing. He staggers backward into the wall, and Gate grabs him, supporting him under his arms so he doesn't slump to the ground.

"Discernment, for instance," continues Rothbart. "You'd be halfway to the shore of Swan Lake by now, if you hadn't hung back trying to be valiant."

No one was more valiant than my mother, and I want to take his bait so badly, but I don't.

"I've come here for Princess Dette. You must release her from this enchantment."

"Of course, there's a difference between bravery and stupidity," muses Rothbart, ignoring me. "You have a willful sort of blindness and poor judgement." He beckons to the open door and says in a different voice, as if speaking to someone in another room, "Stop being shy, my dear."

Neev steps into the kitchen. He extends his hand to her, and she goes to him, slowly. He embraces her, turning her until I can see her face in the early morning light that's making the room brighter every moment.

"I believe you know my daughter."

Neev won't look at me. Her face is a blank slate. I've never seen her so closed off, unreadable. It makes me question all I thought I'd come to know of her. Of myself.

I can't seem to wrap my mind around this. I can't fathom

how the gentle, kind girl I've come to love so quickly could also be a cold-blooded traitor. "Why?" I ask her. "How?"

She doesn't answer me.

"Ironic, isn't it?" says Rothbart. "My sister a powerful water elemental, and my daughter a heat-wielder, although untrained. Yet I was born with no power myself."

I watch him, hearing the deep resentment in his words. I don't know how I never realized it before, how bitter he is. It drips from him like poison from an adder's fangs.

"She was supposed to either mislead you in Thornewood and leave you to die," he continues, "or seduce you into marrying her instead of Dette. In King Cygnus' palace, she had the chance to kill you, but didn't. Instead, she brought you here to me. So now I have three women with power." He strokes one of the short locks of hair beside Neev's rounded cheek, but there's no affection in the gesture. Only possessiveness. It makes me sick. *Not her, too*, I think. *Not everyone I love.*

"I didn't ask you," I say. "I asked her. She owes me an explanation. Because she's either the greatest actress to ever live, or one of us has been deceived."

"It's you who was deceived, Thedra. The explanation is simple."

"That's enough talking," says Gate. "You are going to let us go now."

Rothbart appears to consider this for a moment, then casts out an open hand. Something like a web of silver appears,

sparkling in the air above his palm. He makes a throwing motion and the web glides through the air and lands on Gate's mouth, rapidly thickening into a solid mass as he tries to pry it off with his fingers.

"That's better. Now. Give me your vial, Thedra. I know it's hidden in your palm. Your fist has been clenched since I came into the room."

The vial is actually hidden in the toe of my boot. My fist is clenched because I've been watching everything proceed but am powerless to stop it, frozen like a spectator in a nightmare. It's like being back in Poison Forest, wandering through cold and darkness with no chance of escape.

I keep my fist in a tight ball. Let him think I'm clutching the vial, that I'm about to unleash my power and fry him and everyone in the room to a crisp.

"Take it from me," I challenge him.

Rothbart sucks his teeth at me. "This would all be so much easier if you'd just give it to me."

"She may have submitted to you" —I nod to Neev— "but I'm not that easily led."

"Oh, Thedra, don't think you're being noble. Neev has made the wiser choice. Think what I said about you being like Mora. You may not be fair, or cunning for that matter, but your magic is strong, and even bottled, it's wild and potent. Join me and—"

"You don't understand women at all, do you?" I interrupt,

realizing his meaning. "You think we all want power, like you? We want *room*. The safety to be ourselves. And when the gods give some of us the power to take it, men like you still find a way to steal it."

He clucks his tongue and laughs. "The godsgift. They gifted my sister with power. And she was my father's favorite for it. A poor man like him, with no magic in his bloodline, siring a powerful water elemental. It didn't matter that they took her away, and I was the one who stayed behind. Next to her, I was nothing. Not worthy of love, or even decency." His eyes grow dark. "I killed him, so he never knew I joined the court at Lazul, but I doubt even that would have gained his approval."

"Your solution for being born without power is to steal it?"

"The hoarding of magical power among the women and nobles in the Triumvir is unjust. Do you know your history, Thedra? In the beginning, for every four women born with elemental power, there was one man born with it. But then they bred them, one powered man with two or three women. Then they killed the male children until it was outlawed. And even then, sometimes, they did it in secret. Because they were afraid."

"Why do you think they were afraid?" I ask. There's no justifying what was done in Zelen a thousand years ago, but he needs to understand why.

"Because women always are," he answers.

I shake my head. “They were afraid because of how often men use strength for evil. But...maybe we can change it.”

I can’t believe I’m saying this. I came here to kill him for using my mother and kidnapping Dette. But it’s so obvious now what led him here. If he thinks I’ll give him what he wants, compromise with him, he might agree to come with us.

“Perhaps we can come to a new understanding,” I say. “I’m meant to take my father’s throne, and I know the laws are unjust. They’re said to protect everyone, but they only benefit a few.”

He studies me. “Then you can see the only solution is to take back power, as I have done. I’m an opportunist, Thedra. Are you?”

“Not like this. You’d have to let us go for me to consider your propositions.”

He shrugs, brushing off my refusal. “I don’t have to do anything.” He claps his palms together and then draws them away from one another, extending his arms to their full width. When his hands come apart, a silver thread like the web he silenced Gate with is strung between his palms, glittering in the sunlight.

“Fen, bring the princess to a room in the north wing. But first, find and take the vial she carries.”

The goblin obediently uncoils itself from Dette and Rothbart tosses the thread to him. I snap my fingers and a branch of lightning snakes from my boot, but it passes right through the goblin's body.

He grapples with me and I fight him, but he is twice my height and overpowers me easily. His body, half solid, half vapor, covers my face and head like a pall. I smell wild cat and forest, and I taste silver. The last sound I hear is Gate's muffled moaning as he tries to get the web off his mouth and Plover's weeping.

൭൭

When I come to, my hands are bound behind my back with a heavy chain. When I try to force open the door of the room where I'm trapped, it gives just a little, but I hear the clink of a chain on the other side.

I sit on the floor with my heels together, thinking. I go over my companions in my mind and their possible whereabouts, skipping over Neev like a bad tooth. If I think about her now, I'll cry, and I don't have time for that. I can wallow in sadness over her betrayal later.

The last glimpse I had of Gate was him bending over Plover's wounded body, comforting him.

I wonder if they are both dead by now. Alder Tower is a small holding, but it's vast enough I wouldn't be able to hear them being tortured in a different wing. The fact that they both willingly accompanied me into danger doesn't make me any less ashamed of botching the plan.

I sit on my chained hands and scoot them under my bottom, maneuvering my legs so my clasped hands are in front of me.

The latch on the window is made of wood, and I kick it until it breaks and shove my shoulder against it to open it. The chill wind from an impending autumn storm gusts into the room, ruffling my hair.

The low clouds over the lake are churning, laced with lightning. Dette is there, swimming on the lake beneath the darkening sky. She glides on the water easily in her strange half-swan, half-sylphan body, a contrast to the jerky movements she made when she tried to walk in the kitchen. She always loved the water.

Fen stalks along the shore in his cat form—a dedicated jailer.

I reach toward the sky with my bound hands, focusing my whirling thoughts, curling my fingers like claws. A finger of electricity obeys my summons, stretching from the sky toward my palms. I grab hold of it. Then I hear the chains on the outside of the door clanking and sliding as they're removed, and I lose my grip on the lightning.

I turn to face the door as Neev slides into the room, closing and bolting the door behind her. She rushes to my side and runs her hands all over me, as if searching for injuries. "Did he hurt you?"

I wrench away from her. "What are you doing here?"

"I came to make sure you're all right."

"Untie me, then."

She stays where she is and I sneer at her hesitation and

snap the fingers of both hands, forming them into fists. The static in the room grows until energy crackles across my skin and Neev's hair floats away from her head. A glistening web of electricity grows between my palms. It's just a spark at first, but I feed it with my anger and despair, and it grows to the size of a fig, an apple. "I can turn the air in a room into an inferno in a storm like this," I say. "You underestimated me."

Neev looks afraid. "I didn't underestimate you," she says. "I knew you'd find a way to—"

"It's not your turn to talk." *Treacherous little snake*. "If you're on my side, then why aren't you tied up, too?"

"You think he would leave me unchained? Not all chains are links of steel."

There's another peal of thunder, closer this time. She still won't look me in the eye, and I say, "Don't you dare. You've looked in my face this entire time as you told your lies and spun your web of treachery. Now look at me and explain why."

I can make all the threats I want, but my palms are starting to blister. Agitated, I throw the web of lightning I've created out the window where it funnels into the roiling clouds, followed by a clap of thunder so close it shakes the castle's foundation, making us both jump. I stride to Neev and grasp the front of her shirt, shaking her. Her head bobs loosely on her neck like a marionette's.

Instead of answering me, she takes out a set of keys and starts trying each one on the lock that binds the chains around my wrists. "There isn't time."

"You have to, Neev."

"You should leave me here," she says, frantically trying one key after another. "I had no doubt you'd find some way to escape, but this is faster."

"Oh, you had no doubt?" I say mockingly. "And that made your betrayal acceptable?"

She bites her lip until it turns white, like she did on the summit of Frostmead. Now I understand her strange behavior as we drew closer to Lebed. Maybe she felt some fraction of guilt.

"I tried to tell you to go back," she says.

"You did, I'll give you that. Though I thought you did it out of love for me."

She slides a small key with a starburst end into the lock, and when she turns it, it clicks into place. She yanks at the lock, tosses it to the floor, and quickly unwinds the chains around my wrists, rubbing the feeling back into my arms with her scalding hands.

My arms tingle horribly as the feeling returns to them. Neev sits down on the bed and looks at me, her eyes sorrowful. "I do love you."

"Is anything you told me about yourself true?"

"All of it. I just left out the part about Rothbart finding me begging on the streets when I was fifteen. And how he offered to save me from my growing magic if I went to the palace and fed him information."

"And you accepted his offer that easily?"

"He threatened to kill me if I said no."

"Your own father threatened to kill you?"

Neev's voice is full of disgust. "He's not my father. He just sired me. He calls me his Dendronian by-blow. Do you remember what I told you on the trade road from the city? That my grandmother was rumored to be fae?"

I nod.

"Well, there's more to it than that. She wasn't just fae. She was...well, *is* Opalista."

I stare at her in disbelief. Dendronians worship a fire goddess who goes by that name. As a land of snow and ice, they hold fire sacred the way Lazul does death. "But that would make your mother a goddess as well. And goddesses can't die."

"Half-goddesses can. Especially when they choose to. Rothbart thought if he had a child by her, he might produce a powered heir."

"You. And now he wants to use your power for himself."

She nods. "He placed a spell on me. If you kill him, I'll die too. He calls it a mortal troth. He found it in some book of forbidden magic."

"Why would he do that?"

"So that if you made it this far, you wouldn't kill him. I think he fears your power, Thedra. He knew your mother, after all. He must have feared her power, too."

My mother was fearsome, but Rothbart still destroyed her. And now he'll destroy Neev, too. Rage sparks and simmers under my skin, threatening to turn me into a whirlwind of lightning. I wish I could tear down this entire castle, stone by stone. I'd bury him beneath the rubble and incinerate the lot with fire from the sky.

"Why didn't you tell Dette all this?" I ask, my voice cracking with desperation. "She would've helped you."

"You've seen how powerful he is. He kept threatening me. Said if I didn't spy on her and send him messages, he'd kill us both. In the beginning, I just wanted to survive. I had no idea what he was planning. The attack on the trade road was the first time I saw the extent of his power."

I remember how I scorned her for saying Dette being taken was her fault. That makes sense now, too. "Did you know who he was? That he killed my mother?"

"I only knew he was a mage who wanted information about the court at Zelen. Please believe me, I didn't know what he had done until it was too late."

She reaches into the neck of her tunic and pulls out a golden chain with a locket on it. The Speaking Jewel.

I glare at her, my eyes burning with her betrayal. "I left that behind."

"I know. I took it when you weren't looking. He told me to make sure that you brought it. I didn't know then, but I think he must have had a spell on it to track us. It's how he kept finding us."

Neev pulls the long chain over her head and throws it onto the bed beside her. "Do whatever you want with it."

I throw the locket out the window. It means nothing to me now. "Is this why you slept with me? Because he told you to?"

"No." Her face crumples as she shakes her head violently from side to side. "I swear by Thorne, the night we lay together at Cliff Sedge was the sweetest night of my life."

Her lips tremble and she starts to cry, tears dripping into the cup of her gloved hands where they rest in her lap.

I sit beside her on the bed. For the first time, I feel like I can truly see her. Not just my Neev, the kind and gentle girl I fell in love with. The real Neev. Neev, the orphan, who would do anything to survive. Neev the brilliant girl of fire and light. Neev the demigoddess.

Knowing her flaws—her pain and deceit—and knowing her gifts, her kindness and strength, I only love her more. I take her face in my hands and make her look at me. "Listen, you stubborn girl. I'm going to defeat him. Even if it takes every ounce of my power. It's the only way to free Dette, and make sure he doesn't murder anyone else. It's going to storm soon. I can hit him with my lightning and tie him up with his own silver chains. Then we can take him to Zelen for trial. Will you help me?"

She nods. "But I'm not as powerful as him."

"Yes, you are. Your blood is divine and your power is magnificent. But first, we're going to find Gate and Plover. And then the library."

She blinks at me. "The library?"

"Every spell has a counter-spell."

She shakes her head. "He told me there wasn't one, but perhaps there is. Still, you don't have time to pore through every book in the library. What's left of them."

"Left of them? What do you mean?"

"Rothbart burned those he didn't find useful."

"Of course he did." I drag my fingers through my hair at the thought of what I'm about to face. Of what I may have to do. Has Rothbart cast a spell over everything and everyone I've ever loved?

Neev pulls the ring of keys out of her breeches pocket again. "I heard him tell Fen to put Plover and Gate in the dungeon. Show me where it is."

Chapter Nineteen

We slink through corridors, staying in the shadows as best we can. I wish for common magic now, even though I've scorned it all my life. The ability to glamour one's appearance, to become almost invisible in order to stay out of the way, would be invaluable now. Vanity is the only explanation for these powers not being bred into the royal bloodlines.

Through the open chamber doors, I glimpse overturned furniture, ransacked chests and wardrobes, and things haphazardly covered in white sheets. It seems Alder Tower was abandoned in a pandemonium. I wonder what Rothbart did when he took it for himself. It's said the dead walk here, but it seems so empty now, a hollowed-out shell.

We find Gate and Plover in a much different situation than I was expecting. They're in one of the cells of the dungeon, but the door is open and Gate has been freed of the web on his face. Plover no longer has the arrow through his wing. He's wearing a sling made from Gate's shirt and is lying on a straw pallet.

His face is gray and I rush to the door. "Is he alright?"

Gate looks grim. "I think so. The arrow lodged between the bones, so nothing was broken, but it was hard to remove, and he bled quite a bit. I think he's in shock."

"How did you get free?"

"Plover did it. The jailer was a pixie. He gave her a feather and asked her to take the thing off my face and set us free. When she did, we told her to flee, but there was a silver chain around her ankle, like the one on the goblin that attacked you. I broke it for her and convinced her to go back to the forest."

"With your power?"

"Agate gave her a kiss," says Plover faintly. "Pixies love mortals. She was only his guard under duress."

It seems I'm not the only one to have been underestimated. Gate looks past me to Neev, who is bending worriedly over Plover. His brow furrows. "What's *she* doing here?"

I don't let my gaze waver, doing my utmost to keep my face impassive despite my churning emotions. "She's going to help."

"Surely you don't trust her?"

"I trust her enough. Do you think I'm being foolish? Letting my heart lead me?"

He draws breath as I wait for his answer. "I don't know. But if you believe her, I'll follow you."

"Good. Let's go to the library."

A look of befuddlement passes over Gate's face. I suppress my irritation at his being the second person in three hours to show confusion over this.

We reach the library easily. A pair of double doors at the back of the room leads onto a balcony overlooking the lake. Dette and I used to study there to catch the breeze on hot afternoons. Neev and I shove the doors open now for the light. They rake aside a thick fall of dead leaves as they scrape open.

We place Plover on one of the lounges in the corner, and he lies there with his eyes closed.

The library at Lebed once held thousands of volumes. Not only books about magic but also collections on history, culture, mathematics, poetry and literature. Many of them have been taken or destroyed. Still, what looks like a few hundred are left, and I light a lamp and pore over a score of titles like *Moderate-Level Necromancy*, *Conjuring vs Elemental Magic*, and *Toxic Tracheophytes*. I find *Sylphs and Fae: A History of the Air Folk* lying face down beneath an ottoman, the book's spine broken. Rothbart either didn't see it or thought it was inconsequential enough to spare. After digging through what feels like hundreds of books, I find a volume called *Irreversible Spells and Hexes*.

I run my finger quickly down the table of contents, hoping not to see the spell Neev mentioned, but it's there, between **Maladies of the Mind** and **Mortification**.

Mortal Troth.

A binding spell. Links two mortals eternally. Ill-advised, but sometimes used between relatives or lovers to achieve a bond stronger than death. If one dies, the other must accompany their shade to the Crossing. From there, they may part or remain together, but neither may return to the mortal world. The troth requires consent from both parties, and a deal-making forged with their blood. Once made, the bond is unbreakable, even if one of the parties later changes their mind.

There's a diagram showing how to perform the spell, but there's no counter-spell. I snap the book shut with disgust. The very idea of such a permanent, irreversible spell is madness, but of course, some human thought of it and made it a reality. Humans twist everything to their own devices and to their detriment.

"Find anything?" asks Gate.

"No. And we have to get out of here. We're going to rescue Dette from that cat. And if Rothbart doesn't catch us, I want you to get her and Plover out of here. Can you do that?"

"What are you going to do, Thedra?"

I meet his gaze levelly. "I'm going to kill him. Gate, listen. You're a prick, but I like you."

The corner of his mouth lifts. "I'm touched."

"Don't make me regret this speech. I would've promoted you."

"To what?"

I was going to make him the head of my guard, but I just smirk at him. Best not to feed his ego. "If you make it back to Lazul, let my father know I said to give you a high-ranking position."

CHAPTER TWENTY

THE thunder is close to breaking when we cross the greensward to the shore where Fen is guarding Dette. I glimpse my diamond vial strung on the chain around its neck. The swirling green and purple contents sparkle even though the sky is thick with dark rain clouds.

The cat crouches when it sees us, fur bristling, and I call, “Fen, do you want to be free of that chain?”

Changing from alarm to nonchalance in an instant, it straightens, ambles, pauses with one front foot in midair, and regards me thoughtfully. As if deciding what to do with the half-raised paw, it brings it to furry lips and licks the thick pad.

“You can’t defeat him,” it says. “I’ve tried.”

“Well, perhaps you can try again.”

It looks away with a flick of its tail—the feline equivalent of a shrug.

“You don’t mind being his jailer and errand-runner?” I ask.

"The beds are soft and warm, the meat is rare, and I have free roam of the tower. Before, I could only go as far as the tree line." Fen indicates the nearest copse of trees with a tilt of its head.

"You can have free roam of all three kingdoms if you'll let me have my vial back and help me free Princess Dette. But if you don't, we'll kill you."

Fen gives Plover a cagey look and whispers, "Flee, you fool. When the mage comes, he'll put the chain on you, too."

"What is the chain made of?" I ask. "Why does it keep you captive?"

"Iron and silver. It weakens me and burns if I try to break it." Fen regards me with mild curiosity. "Who are you to promise me the run of the kingdoms?"

"King Thede of Lazul is my father."

"So, no one, then."

Tiny raindrops begin to fall. "I have the power to commune with the dead. I'm also a lightning-wielder, and there's a storm coming. I met one of your kind before. A goblin in the form of a wolf. It saw fit to help me."

"Well, Thedra of Lazul, a wolf sprite may come at your beck and call, but when unchained, I am loyal to only myself."

"I respect that," I reply. "I'm not one to stay confined inside walls myself, even when ordered."

The goblin strolls to me and rubs its large, brindled body against my calves like a common house cat. "So far," it purrs, "you've offered me no more than an empty promise."

Neev goes down on her knees beside him and removes her gloves, taking hold of the chain around his neck. Her brow furrows with concentration and the silver sizzles in her palms. The chain jingles as it drops to the greensward.

"There," she says. "The offer's no longer empty. Take them to the lookout in the High Tower. But let me go first. He mustn't know that I've betrayed him."

The lookout is reached by way of a winding stair with a wooden door at the top. Gate and I follow Fen to the top. Plover and Dette stay behind in the hidden tunnel.

The door to the lookout is unlocked, and it swings open, revealing a round room with a conical roof supported by spiraling wooden rafters, like the inside of a nautilus.

Rothbart starts as the door hits the wall and turns toward us. I see a flash of fury cross his features at the sight of me freed of my chains, but he recovers quickly and makes a bow that manages to look both lazy and graceful. "Welcome, Highness." He sweeps his arm to indicate the room. "It's nothing like the lair Mora built for me in Lazul, but it serves its purpose."

The way he uses my title is neither genuine nor obligatory. He makes it sound like mockery.

There's a chair near one of the cluttered tables. It has chains on its arms and legs, and there's a contraption attached

to it that looks very similar to a siphon, the device used to drain off an elemental's magic until they learn to control it. Ten thimble-shaped glass cups are attached to the chair's arms for placing on fingertips. Coils lead to a long glass tube that ends in a diamond vial. I wince at the sight. Having my power drawn felt like having every hair in my body slowly removed through the nerve endings in my fingertips. I learned to wield it quickly as a result.

Neev is beside the window, looking at the chair with longing. Rothbart promised her this, after all. To help her control a power that scars her every time she loses control of it. She knows he'll never keep his promise now. I wish I could squeeze her hand and comfort her, but I can't.

"Fen, what have you done with my other prisoners?" asks Rothbart, fixing the goblin with his gaze. His tone is gentle, but his eyes are dark and glittering, like a shark gone mad with bloodlust. "I only see one."

"Fen is subject to me now," I say. "Temporarily, anyway."

"Don't you know goblins are temperamental and unpredictable?"

"Yes, but I don't like putting things in chains."

"And what of Dette?" he asks. "Don't you know she can't leave Lebed?"

"She can't leave until you're dead," I say. "Rather different, isn't it?"

He gives me a cold smile. "Thedra, if you think that's all

the defense I've created, you're even less discerning than I thought."

"I know about the curse on Neev," I say. It's difficult to admit, given that it's all I've thought of since I left Lazul. "But unless you want to die, you'll return with me to face the high court's judgment."

He sighs like a teacher disappointed by a wayward student. "I'll only make this offer once more. Join me. You love both my captives. And surely a woman with your power doesn't want to be queen of a freezing, dull land like Lazul."

"No one who has seen the Glittering Caves or the cliffs on the coast of the Sapphire Sea would call Lazul dull," I say, keeping my voice even. "You call me undiscerning. Why would I join you or trust you when you killed my mother?"

I nod to Neev, who swings the window open, letting in the rain and wind. My fingertips and palms crackle, and the ends of my hair float away from my body. I don't need my vial in a storm like this, but I open it anyway, if only for the ritual of it. Gate has an arrow aimed at Rothbart, but he doesn't release it, and I know he's thinking of what happened to Plover and Ibis and the guard on the pass. *Don't shoot until his back is to you,* I told him in the library. *You're no good to me dead.*

A snap of my fingers sets my lightning free, and it rolls about the circular tower in the shape of a fiery purple ball, then leaps from floor to ceiling, spreading like a tree's branches. I move my hands in a serpentine motion and it twists and spirals at my command. I'm careful to keep it from hitting any of my companions, but I let it strike and shatter the glass phials and beakers, bottles, and books.

I sweep both hands at Rothbart, but he has a spell of his own ready, the same one he used against me in the forest. He forces the lightning back to me, and I absorb it, controlling the channel easily. But now we're at an impasse in the small room. We circle with the crackling electricity between us. My clothing hisses with static, and the arm where I was wounded in Thornewood begins to ache.

Thunder crashes as the rain breaks in earnest, and a lightning flash brightens the room. I stretch my right arm toward the window and hook two fingers in a beckoning U-shape, snaring it. I throw it at Rothbart before he can react, and it knocks him backward into one wall and breaks the connection between us. Quickly, I summon my lightning back into its vial.

Rothbart drops to his knees and collapses to the floor. His eyes are closed, but I know he's not dead because his chest is rising and falling. I walk around his inert body, giving it a wide berth. I have the chain of silver thread I took from Fen in my cloak's pocket and I take it out, moving closer. The chain is alive in my hands, moving like liquid silver. It seems to know what I want—to restrain Rothbart. Perhaps it always wants to bind and restrain, regardless of who or what is being bound.

Neev is still at the window, and I motion for her to stay

where she is. One of Rothbart's hands is on his chest, and it seems to be where he took the brunt of the strike because I can see a spidery burn. As I kneel to loop the chain around his wrist, he lunges and grabs me.

I snap my fingers as he pins me to the floor and we roll over and over in a web of electric shocks. We land with him on top, and he grapples with me for the vial, trying to pry it out of my grasp.

"Gate, shoot him!"

"I might hit you!"

"It doesn't matter!"

Gate releases the arrow, and it hits Rothbart in the back. He arches upward, screaming, and I try to scramble out from beneath him, but he's too heavy. He reaches back and grasps the arrow with both hands, pulling it out with a sickening sound of tearing flesh. This would mean death for most mortals. Everyone knows not to remove an arrow that way, but Rothbart has been draining Dette's healing power for himself, and he merely flexes his shoulder, wincing.

"I'm going to drain you to a husk," he says, stepping toward me.

In the same instant, Fen changes into his goblin form and wraps around Rothbart's legs, tripping him. I hear a light step, and Neev crosses the room in a few seconds. I'd forgotten how fast she is. In a blur of motion, she stoops and twists the vial from my hand, uncorking it.

"No," I whisper. *No. You headstrong, foolhardy girl. That's not what I meant when I said to run.*

Once again, I am back in Thornewood, with its dying trees and sickly rot. I can smell decayed leaves. And once again, there is nothing I can do.

I crawl toward her, but she throws herself at Rothbart before I can reach her, grabbing him around the neck. It resembles an embrace, a daughter thanking her father, and for a terrible moment I'm afraid she has betrayed me again, but then I hear him exclaim with rage and pain.

I hear and smell the sizzle of burning flesh, and Rothbart puts his hands around Neev's wrists, trying to pry them away from his throat. He's making a horrible sound, something between a gurgle and a scream. Neev's wrists are tiny, barely larger than a little girl's, and I'm afraid he's going to break them, but they burn his hands so badly that he lets go. The air around Neev is shimmering, building to a terrible fission.

Rothbart's skin and eyes are melting too quickly for the greenhealing he stole from Dette to repair them, and he rasps something I can't make out.

At the last second, before the room goes white hot with her rage and power, Neev forces his mouth open, her fingertips leaving livid burns on what's left of his lips and face. She tips the vial into his mouth and places both hands on his chest, infusing him with one last dose of her power. He staggers backwards as another bolt from Gate's crossbow lodges in his chest.

Rothbart doesn't implode the way the sylph in Thornewood did. My power combines with Neev's and he ignites, little bursts of blue flame kindling all over him until he bursts into flame. His body shatters like the bombs of glass and phosphorous created by our palace elementals. Neev spins away from him with the grace of a dancer and I tuck my knees and roll out of the way.

Long before I can hear or see, I begin to crawl toward where I saw Neev fall. She is reclined on her side almost peacefully, like a girl who has fallen asleep while reading in a spring glade. I turn her over and take her hands, kissing her poor, ruined palms. I stroke her face and for the first time I'm not struck by her otherworldly heat. Her body is cooling, and she is fading, out of existence, out of time.

She blinks at me, slowly. "Mortal troth. I hoped it wasn't real."

I stare at her desperately, wanting to beg her to stay with me. "Why did you do that?" I demand instead. "You did it wrong. You were supposed to run if things went sideways!"

"I always knew what I'd do. I may not be a sovereign, but I..."

She doesn't finish the sentence, but I know what she means, and I'm wrenched with the indignity of our parting after all of this.

"No," I grit out. "Not you. Stay with me."

She gives me a small, sad smile.

I know I'm running out of time, and talking quickly, I say, "I've died before. It sounds mad but the night of my death ceremony, Zori killed me. That's how I got the scar. You'll wake on the shore beyond this world. But I'll find you. I'll cross the Endless Sea. I love you, Neev. I—"

I don't finish my sentence because her head has fallen backward, her mouth gone slack. Her gray eyes stare past me at nothing, and now she fades in earnest. First her extremities, then her limbs, and finally her entire body.

In a matter of seconds, I am sitting beside her empty clothing, in a tower ravaged by fire, rain, and lightning.

Chapter Twenty-One

My face is buried in Neev's empty pile of clothes when I smell the smoke. The lookout is burning. Some of my lightning must have ignited the rafters and the dead ferns. A part of me wants to stay and let the smoke sedate me until I'm engulfed in flame. But Gate shakes me, forcing me to sit up. "Thedra, we have to get out."

We choke on dark gray smoke as he clambers down the spiral staircase, pulling me behind him. My eyes sting, streaming until I'm blinded by my own salty tears. His grip is iron, and I choke out, "Gate, help us escape!" His calm infuses my grief and terror, helping me keep my head and not panic, reminding me to crouch low on the stairwell so I can breathe.

Just when I think my lungs will burst, we spill out onto the greensward fifty feet below where we started, coughing and retching into the sodden grass. The rain has stopped, and we find Plover and Dette waiting by the boat near the lakeshore. She has shed her swan's form, and she runs to me, but this time I can't return her embrace. My arms hang at my sides like lead weights.

"Where is Neev?" she asks.

"She's gone," Gate answers for me. "The tower is burning. Hurry."

Dette takes my hand without questioning me and pulls me toward the boat. We help Plover in, and Gate pushes us away from shore and hops into the bow. The water laps gently against the sides as we row away from the isle. The tower is a flaming brand behind us, the heat rolling off it in waves.

"Were there others?" I ask.

"Others?"

"So many girls with power disappeared before you were taken. Sylphs, too."

"He said there were others before me, but they all died. Rothbart said my power at greenhealing was what saved me every time I transformed. He used it against me."

"What did he do with their bodies?"

"He threw them into the lake."

Horrified, I look at the black water surrounding our boat.

"What an accursed place," mutters Gate.

He's right, and I wait until we reach the far shore to do anything for fear of ending up in a watery grave after escaping the fire. I'm too weak to summon lightning after my struggle with Rothbart, but I promise myself I'll have one triumph over Alder Tower, even if it has torn the heart right out of me.

As Gate and Dette secure the boat, I wade into the shallows and hold my hand out over the water. I whisper the secret word and say, "By Zori's power, I summon those who lie buried here."

"What are you doing?" asks Plover, but Gate shushes him, whispering, "Watch."

A spot deep in the bottom of the lake glows. And then another. And another. The shades rise to the surface, glowing white and blue and green in the starlight. They walk across the surface of the water toward me—the daughters of earls and vassals and mages. Forcefield-makers and water-benders, spell-casters and alchemists, sylphs and mermaids.

"What do you want of us?" asks a shade with black skin and shells and bones in her hair. There are shiny, iridescent scales beside her eyes. One of the merfolk. I wonder what power he wanted from her, and if he got it.

Thinking, as always, of the nameless sylph-girl in Thornewood, I say, "Tell me your name."

"Cerith," she answers.

"And the rest of you. Tell me your names."

They reply in a jumbled symphony of sound, in different languages and voices. I turn my hand, so my palm faces up, and say the words I said to the guard on the pass. "The one who murdered you is no more. Your deaths are avenged. Leave this place and go to your resting places. Into the mountains of the sun, the depths of oceans. Across the Endless Sea."

Slowly, the shades fade and disappear, leaving the lake empty, a dark mirror reflecting the burning tower. Agate helps Plover sit with his back against the trunk of a tree and speaks softly to him, holding his hands. Dette stands watching the castle burn in silence. Then she goes to examine Plover's wound, asking if the arrow had a poison tip.

I stand apart from them, continuing to watch the castle turn into a fiery inferno. I don't want to quake and fall to pieces in front of them, but I've been holding myself together for so long, and I don't think I can any longer. Tears roll down my cheeks and I don't bother to wipe them away.

After a while, Gate joins me. "I'm sorry."

I swallow savagely, trying to hide that I'm weeping. "You don't hate her for what she did?"

"No. But it wouldn't matter if I did. You loved her."

He puts a hand on my shoulder, and my first instinct is to push him away, but I don't because I know what he's doing.

"It won't help," I say. "Let me feel it."

"It will. It helped you escape the tower. It will help now."

I nod. "All right. But don't make it a dream of her. Not yet."

"Of course not."

He keeps his hand on my shoulder, a gentle pressure. I was wrong to think it would take away my sorrow. It doesn't, but I'm calmer. He doesn't use the strong kind of magic he calls *soporific*. This is mild and tinged with heartache, like a cool cloth on a feverish forehead, or a lament sung for a lost lover.

Chapter Twenty-Two

WE are welcomed to Thistle with fanfare and celebration and after a few days of rest, Queen Akina throws a parade to celebrate Dette's safe return.

We watch the procession of horses, soldiers, acrobats, and greensmiths from the highest balcony of the palace. Thistle is a port city, and from our vantage point, I can hear the sounds of the harbor and see the tall masts of the square-sailed Zelenean ships clustered near the docks. Their colors are brilliant in the morning sunlight—snowy white, emerald, and carnelian red. I spot a little caravel with sails of pure white and bottle green sliding into port over the sparkling water to unload its cargo.

A score of acrobats begins a series of complicated death-defying acts on the paving stones below. Their tumbling is followed by the greensmiths, who make vines grow over the stones of the courtyard and up the side of the balcony to Dette's feet. The vines burst into bloom in unison, filling the air with sweet perfume.

Dette thanks them and picks one of the flowers, tucking the blossom into her curls. Dette wears a kirtle of green velvet over a gown of red silk with slits cut in the sleeves and skirt. A crown of polished acacia surmounted with emeralds is on her head, and her long hair is loose. The glossy ringlets bounce when she waves to the crowd gathered below.

I declined to be laced into a gown for the festivities but agreed to a clean tunic of pale green sateen and a new cloak, as the one I wore from Lazul was weather-stained and ragged.

Once similar feats of magic and prowess have been performed and signs of fealty made by the ambassadors of various heads of state, Queen Akina approaches the balcony, resplendent in golden robes festooned with embroidered green vines and red roses.

Akina waves to the commoners' cheering and begins a speech outlining everyone's delight and relief at Dette's return, offering special thanks to me and my three companions.

"A powerful elemental with the heart of a lion, Thedramora of Lazul is sure to have a promising career as the future leader of our ally Lazul," she says.

The crowd cheers, and Akina presents me, Plover, and Agate, adorning us with sashes decorated with Zelen's national crest. Dette lays a bouquet of blood red roses in my arms. Agate is wearing a smile brilliant enough to blind a thousand fawning admirers, but I only offer the crowd a conciliatory wave before returning to my seat. My people may be cold and stoic, but they are mine all the same. Folk of sand and frost, hard as iron and tempered diamond. There's no need for me to cater to Zelen's ripe and lusty hordes.

"Thedra the Lion-Hearted," muses Dette as I sit back down. "That suits you. Momma says the tale of the lightning-wielder who saved Princess Dette from the evil Rothbart will be told for centuries in all three kingdoms."

This is a far cry from Akina's former opinions of me, but I don't say so. "I guess it's a better nickname than Thedra the Impetuous, which is what Gate says they call me in Lazul."

Dette laughs, not unkindly. "Your impetuosity has saved my life, and I am forever grateful."

"You don't have to keep thanking me."

"Don't I?"

A servant comes by, bearing a tray of white wine and fruit and offers it to me. I take one of the glasses of wine but decline the fruit. Dette takes a plum and bites into the plump flesh.

"You should eat something," she says. "You barely touched breakfast."

I take a sip of the wine, ignoring her mothering. The drink is made from the yellow grapes in the palace vineyards, and the flavor is tart and golden on my tongue. "I didn't save you," I say. "Neev did."

"Neev betrayed me and lied to you. To both of us."

"She also sacrificed herself for both of us. She admitted

her mistakes."

"Thedra, don't make yourself sick over this."

"Over what?" I ask sharply.

"The death of someone who didn't deserve you."

"I don't think either of us can understand how few choices she had. She should be here wearing this stupid sash."

Dette's chest, pushed high by her corset, rises higher as she takes a deep breath. We've already spoken of this, and we both know where the other stands, but it keeps coming up again. The morning after we defeated Rothbart, she didn't spare a glance for Alder Tower and neither did I, despite the many happy summers we spent there. It will always be the place she was imprisoned, the Lake of Tears where she swam as a captive.

For me, it will always be the place where my dearest friend was tortured, and where I lost the girl who might have become the love of my life. Some people are so sick they have the power to stain a thing, to change it and take the goodness right out of it. Rothbart's sickness was that sort.

Agate gives the crowd one last wave and strides toward us with a swirl of his blue cape. His high black boots are polished so thoroughly they shine like jet in the sunlight. The emerald green sash Queen Akina draped over his shoulder complements his brown eyes and dark hair. He accepts a glass of wine from the servant with the tray and hands it to Plover, who still has a bandaged wing.

Plover eyes him fondly. There is a band woven of brilliant blue feathers around Gate's wrist. I don't know what they said to one another in the hours they spent in that dungeon, but it must have been fairly significant. They've been inseparable ever since.

"Will either of you be going back to Lazul with me?" I ask.

"I will, of course," says Gate, "unless Thede has an assignment for me here."

"What about Plover?"

Gate gives a blustery sigh, shooting Plover a look of affectionate exasperation. "He's not fussed about the distance, says we'll see one another next autumn."

Plover nods, but Gate sounds a bit deflated. I'm utterly bewildered by sylph romances. Apparently, some of their betrothals can last anywhere from eighty to a hundred years, and Gate and Plover are just getting to know one another.

"I heard there's food inside," says Plover. "I'm going to inspect. Join me in a bit?"

Gate nods, and Plover kisses him. The sight makes my chest ache, and I take another sip of wine, hoping to dull the pain.

"You should request an assignment to help restore Lebed as a stronghold," I say when Plover is gone. "It's only a few days from Cliff Sedge, so you could be together. And it's been years since we sent an emissary to Shoreana. Now is a perfect time. Mortal-sylph marriages are fairly rare, but I think it's only because we don't spend enough time together."

It's not just his relationship that makes me impatient for Gate to be settled in his career. Every time Akina looks at him, her eyes are bright with ambitious hunger. Someone with his gift and personality is every ruler's dream. I can't help being a bit protective of him. I found him, after all. Or he found me, depending on how one looks at it.

Gate nods, thoughtfully running his fingers over the love token on his wrist. "It's too soon to speak of marriage."

"Really? Maybe you ought to give that thing back then. Must've taken a long time for him to make."

He takes a sip of wine and watches me over the rim of the glass. "You're mean when you drink, Thedra. But I'll let it go, considering your recent heartache."

"I'm not trying to be mean. I'm happy for you."

"You're not obligated to be," he says kindly. "Considering."

Stop being so nice, damn you. "But I am. I told you he was good for you, didn't I?"

He smiles. "You can't take credit for everything. But I think you *can* take credit for this." He gestures to the flower-festooned balcony and the crowd below.

Once the crowds have dispersed, I go back to my room and collapse on the bed. Drinking the tart wine with nothing to eat has made me sick to my stomach. My ears are buzzing and there's a throbbing pain behind one of my eyes that's threatening to turn into a full-fledged headache. I get them much more frequently since I drank the cursed water of Thornewood.

I hoped to leave that place behind forever, but I still dream of it sometimes, waking with the sense of its wet cold seeping through my clothes, and the sickly sweet smell that clung to everything there lingering in my nostrils.

I ring for a page and ask him to bring me water and a loaf of bread. I'm only halfway done with the pitcher of water when he returns. "Empress Akina wishes to see you in her private council room."

I close my eyes. "I just took off my damned boots." He blanches, hesitating at my answer, and I wave him away. "Tell her I'll be there shortly."

When I enter Akina's council chamber, she's still wearing the resplendent robes she donned for the festivities. She's seated in an ornate chair at the head of a long table of polished ebony. I bow to her, no longer interested in fighting protocol, and she nods and gestures for me to sit to her left. I'm surprised to see Agate seated across from me. He tugs nervously at his uniform's high collar.

"Welcome. Would either of you like refreshment?"

I decline, and Gate refuses as well. He *must* be nervous if he's turning down food.

Akina dismisses the page and folds her ringed hands. "I've asked the two of you here because I have an offer to make."

I toy with my vial, waiting for her to offer up greensmiths and grain yields to Lazul.

"To you, Thedramora," she says with gravitas, "I offer my daughter's hand."

I gape at her. "But...a year ago, you said a marriage between us was out of the question."

"That was before you saved Dette and secured my royal line. You've proven yourself both competent and committed."

Thinking my misgivings are tidied away, Akina glances at Gate. Her eyes gleam with unveiled hunger.

I've seen that look, and my stomach churns. "What does Gate have to do with this?"

"Two wedded queens need a sire to continue their line, do they not? So, to you, Agate Mason, I offer the role of benefactor."

Gate makes a strangled sound. I wait for him to refuse, but he's staring at Akina with round eyes and an open mouth. He looks like a toad choking on a fly. His fingers stray to the bright blue band on his forearm.

"He's with someone," I say for him.

Akina dismisses this with a flick of her wrist. "Marriage isn't a requirement," she says. "All we need is your—"

"Yes," says Gate, finding his voice. "I understand."

"I know you are Lazulian. Perhaps you don't know our ways. Zelen's royal line is matriarchal. It's considered a great honor to become a benefactor."

"I am sure. But Princess Thedra, well. I mean, once we might've... But now, I see her as..."

I don't think I've ever seen Gate speechless before.

"Romantic desire is not a requirement either," says Akina slowly, as if she didn't realize she'd need to explain reproduction for this conversation and is not pleased with the task.

Gate and I look at one another, but it only draws out our discomfort.

"Well," says Akina impatiently. "I hardly thought a consultation would be needed. But I'll leave you to discuss." She rises from the chair, her layers of silk rustling.

"Wait," I say quickly.

She sits back down.

"I have three conditions."

Akina narrows her eyes. It appears she wasn't expecting this either.

"If I wed Dette, I never want to see my people suffer from famine again," I say. "We must establish trade with you. Grain, citrus, root vegetables. Even if it means you must help me take my nobles to task. It's a deal that should have been made half a century ago. Second, to your most recent proposal" —I nod toward Gate— "the laws regarding how powered children are selected in the Triumvir are long overdue for an amendment. Without them, Rothbart would never have become what he was. My mother and Neev and all his other victims would still be alive."

"What do you suggest?"

"All individuals with magical power must be trained. But they won't be separated from their families. Stop giving them preferential treatment and breeding them into the noble bloodlines. It's an ethical dilemma that has gone unchecked for four hundred years. If we don't do something, and soon, it will only lead to more problems. You have a reputation as a just and formidable empress. This would help you be remembered as a benevolent one as well."

I glance at Gate and he's regarding me with wide eyes.

Akina twists the ruby signet ring on her right index finger, no doubt to remind me of her sovereignty. "I'll bring it before the council," she says. "But you mustn't think because you're young and idealistic that you're the first to propose reform. And your third condition?"

"A ship, and a crew to man it. I want the little caravel in the harbor with the green and white lateen sails. It looks fast and seaworthy."

She waits for me to explain, but when I don't, she asks, "What for?"

"A sea voyage." I hope against hope that she won't question me further.

She eyes me with vague distrust, but one small ship can't mean much to a queen with a fleet of warships and merchant vessels in her arsenal. "Very well. One ship."

I nod. "Good. I'd like to see Dette before I give my official consent."

Akina looks daggers at me, but several minutes later I am shown into Dette's room. She's reclining on a lounge overlooking the harbor with a light throw draped over her legs and a tray of sweetmeats at her elbow. More than a month after her rescue from Rothbart's clutches, she still tires easily. Those gifted in transfiguration use it rarely because it requires so much energy. It made my mother old before her time, and Dette was made to do it every day for weeks.

She turns her head and smiles when she sees it's me. There's a twisting of string in her fingers. She loops and winds the net of strings and pulls them apart to reveal a bird that flaps its wings when she moves her fingers.

"That's clever," I say.

She pats the edge of the lounge near her feet and pulls them up to make room for me as I sit. "I could never make them as well as the other children in my father's palace, but I had nothing else to do when I was imprisoned in Alder Tower."

I knead the throbbing spot above my eye with my knuckles and she frowns.

"Headache?"

I nod. "Threatening to turn worse."

She disentangles her fingers from the string and lays her hand over the spot that hurts. In a moment, warmth grows in my temples and the pain lessens, relaxing the tense muscles in

my forehead.

"Dette, don't. You'll wear yourself out."

"I will not. It's just the muscles, not something deeper or more serious. It's here." She taps my temple lightly. "Not enough rest and too much wine, I suspect."

She keeps her hand over my eye, filling my pounding head with her restorative greenhealing. When the pain subsides, I pull her hand away from my face, but I don't let it go.

"Your mother just proposed to me for you."

She tucks a springy curl behind her ear as her dark eyes search mine. "I don't suppose you're here because you said yes?"

"I'm finished with getting engaged by proxy."

She squeezes my hand, just a little, and I can't help thinking what my father would give to be present for this moment. I wish I could make just one important decision about my life without worrying about how it might affect the crown, but it's a futile hope. One I might as well stop wasting time on.

I meet her patient, waiting gaze. "You know I'll always love you, Dette. I'll give you a political marriage if it's what you truly want. Not Thede. Not Akina. *You.*"

She looks at me levelly. "But?"

"There's something I have to do first."

She raises a questioning brow. I'm relieved to see she's not hurt. Dette knows she is first in her mother's heart, and the hearts of her people. She doesn't need to be first in mine to know her worth, but she's clearly baffled by my decision.

"I have to cross the Endless Sea."

Her expression changes from perplexity to worry. "Why?"

"You know why. You said I was infatuated with you. And you were right. But her, I... She deserves better than this. She faded before my eyes, and I promised her as she went that I'd come for her."

"Oh, Thedra." Dette cups my cheek, compassion softening her features. "Goddess knows what you saw. Rothbart—"

"Damn Rothbart! I read the spell in a book in the library, and it happened exactly as described. People have come back before. Zori did."

Dette sniffs. Zelen's goddesses are creatures of light, life, and growth. A goddess of death and resurrection makes no sense to her.

She slips her fingers free of my hand and crosses her arms. "If anyone is stubborn enough to come back, it's you. But what if you don't?"

"If I'm not back in three years' time, marry someone else."

"As the future high empress, I command you to return to me."

"Yes, Your Highness." I take her hand and lean in to kiss her cheek. The rose the greensmiths grew for her is still behind her ear and I catch its sweet scent mingled with the shea oil on her skin. My throat aches. Only three months ago, I'd have been dizzied with joy at this being the end of our story together.

Or rather, its beginning. But now my heart and loyalties are so divided, pulled a dozen directions—my duties to my people, my promises to Thede, to Neev, and now to Dette.

Seeming to sense my worry, she says, "Stop it, Thedra. You'll give yourself a headache again."

I force a smile for her. "Get some rest and don't worry about me."

Gate is waiting in the corridor when I come out of the room. He looks as tightly wound as a spring.

"How could you go off and leave me with her like that? I panicked and said no. I'm afraid she's going to have me assassinated."

I bark a laugh. "I've pissed her off lots of times and I'm still alive. Besides, did you really want to accept?"

"Of course not. The thought of being with you again...like that. Or worse, both of you."

I punch his arm, but not very hard. "Agreed. Come with me."

He follows me down the marbled corridor to an atrium flanked by twelve columns and soaring arches. The sparkling harbor is visible between two of the arches, and I point out the bright white and dark green sails of a three-masted caravel.

"See that ship? It's mine. Want to come with me?"

Gate laughs. "Where to, Thedra the Impetuous?"

"To sail the Endless Sea."

Agate's eyes widen. "Really?"

I nod.

Agate looks at me like I'm mad. "There's no goblin here threatening to snap my neck if I don't, and I can't think of a single reason why I should."

"So...is that a yes?" He gives a grating laugh, and I plead, "Come on, you know you can't pass up an opportunity for glory."

He crosses his arms. "I'll think on it."

"Bring Plover. Maybe he'll get over his fear of the water."

Before I leave Thistle, I must write a letter to my father telling him I wish to abdicate my place as Priestess of the Dead. He will be angry with me, but I saw enough death in Thornewood and on Lebed. And I was the author of some of it. I can't take my mother's place like I thought. I don't want it to destroy me from the inside like it did her. Let the people elect their own executioner.

I walk to the harbor at sunset to see my ship. Akina is nothing if not true to her word. Sailors are already unloading their goods from my vessel, and the deck has been swabbed. The pine planks gleam in the setting sun, and the green Zelenean banners are unfurled. The gang plank has been lowered, so I board, winding my way around sailors carrying heavy cargo. The deck smells of turpentine and saltwater and is sound beneath my feet. I climb into the stern, looking toward the horizon.

The sea is turning lavender beneath a peach and cornflower blue sky and my heart aches as I watch the sun sinking below the line where water meets sky. Somewhere across that wide ocean, Neev is waiting for me. I'll sail it to find her, even if it kills me.

Epilogue

We meet our first monster not five days after we set sail from Thistle. The Endless Sea is said to be full of kraken, toothed whales, and other horrors, and we've come equipped with cannons and archers. When the creature draws closer, it's revealed to be a massive leviathan. The archers nock their bows, but the boatswain raises a hand, signaling for them to hold their arrows. The leviathan is ancient, the fires in its belly long cooled. Its eyes are clouded and its ridged, scaly back is covered in barnacles.

It doesn't attack, but it swims too close to the ship, bumping into us out of curiosity. Before it descends into the deep, the creature's rock-hard hide grazes the port bow, and a flailing tentacle takes out the smaller mast.

We're forced to stop for repairs on one of the windswept outer islands. When we've dropped anchor, I don a cloak and walk the deck, impatient, but it will be at least three days before a tree can be felled and fashioned into a new mast after the ship is towed to shore for repairs. As I scan the horizon, I notice a plume of smoke hanging above one of the nearby keys. The island where we've stopped is covered in forest, but the keys are mostly rocks and scrub. I frown, studying the little isle.

Below the smoke, there's a shimmer of colors—blue and purple and brilliant umber. I keep watching it to make sure it's not a trick of the light reflecting on the water, but it continues in an endless pattern: blue on purple on orange on green. So does the billowing smoke.

I find the boatswain directing sailors in the rigging. "Will you spare one of your men to row me to that nearby key to bring some buckets?" I point toward the smoke. "It looks to be on fire and if the wind shifts, it could reach the trees."

"Yes, Your Highness. Rus!" He gestures to a wiry young sailor with a sunburned face. "Take the princess to see that mirage on the key."

I frown at the boatswain. I'm sure he's been to sea a hundred times to my one, but that doesn't mean he has to treat me like an idiot in front of the crew.

Rus looks nervous as he rows us toward the key. I try to think of something reassuring to say. "It's probably just a brush fire started by stray ash from the main island," I tell him unconvincingly.

We drop anchor in the shallows and wade onto a pebbled beach that reminds me of the shore beyond the world. The smoke plume is much higher now that we're on the key and I can see the different-colored flames flickering through the thin scrub. Heat wafts toward us in shimmering waves.

"Doesn't look much like a mirage now, does it?" I say. "Nor an ordinary fire, not with the way it moves."

Rus looks terrified. He whispers the name of a lesser sea goddess under his breath and says, "I've heard of such things at sea. We mustn't go any closer." He hooks his index fingers together, twisting them like he's pulling a knot taut. I'm not familiar with the gesture, but it resembles the universal sign against evil, like the sign for Zori in Lazul.

"You stay here, then. Or return to the boat. I have my own defenses."

"B-but Your Highness, what if...?"

"What if I don't return?"

He nods and I purse my lips, annoyed at his inability to act without orders or think for himself. "Then row back to the ship and bring help."

He scrambles obediently back to the boat, splashing through the shallows, and I go forward. The heat is so intense I have to hold my cloak over my nose and mouth to breathe, but I keep going, drawn toward the blaze. I've felt heat like this before and hope blooms in my chest. I try to tamp it down, telling myself it can't be. After all, how many times did I hope my mother would come back after she died? She only ever returned to haunt my dreams.

I pass an A-frame shelter made of scrub branches and green tree limbs. There's a spring in the center of the key, and on the other side of it is the source of the fire. It comes into focus as I skirt the spring—a being of pure flame, human-shaped, but with fire spouting from its hands and mouth. The flames engulf a pyre of driftwood and sage grass that has been built beside the spring.

I've seen fire benders and heat wielders before, but none like this. It has to be a goddess, or a godsgift gone wrong, like the first elementals. It turns in a slow circle, revealing eyes that glow like white-hot coals in a flaming face and an open mouth that spews air hot enough to boil water. I shrink away, protecting my face with my cloak.

I'm beginning to think it was stupidity that brought me here, not bravery. Gate's always saying I don't know the difference. I wish he was with me right now, but he chose to stay with Plover.

I back away on shaky legs, but it's too late. The being has seen me and comes toward me interminably fast on legs of flame.

"What are you?" I scream, my throat raw from the heat.

It stops and stands still about twenty paces away, and the flames dwindle, dying almost as quickly as they grew. Little blue flames lick all over its body, fading into threads of orange that glow, come together, and close, leaving only flesh. The fire being is gone, and a woman is left behind. Her skin isn't

burned and blackened, as one would expect, but fresh and dewy. I circle her cautiously, hand at the ready above my vial. As if lighting could do anything against a demigoddess of fire.

"Don't you know me?" she asks.

I wanted it to be her so much, I tell myself I'm imagining it. But she looks so much like Neev. The same heart-shaped face, the same large gray eyes, the same short brown hair being flicked about by the wind. But she looks different, too. She's radiant with happiness and good health. Behind her, the sea is a blinding blue beneath a cloudless sky, but she is brighter than both.

It has to be a trick. All this time I was expecting to find her a shade on a far shore, but here she is before me, vital and alive, and able to control her powers. It can't be.

My voice quakes as I say, "Let me see your hands."

She holds them out. The palms are smooth and I shake my head as tears prick my eyes. "Hers were scarred."

Before I can draw back or reach for my vial, she grabs my hand and holds it to her cheek. I flinch, expecting her face to burn me, since it was on fire only seconds ago, but it doesn't.

I don't wait another second to take her in my arms. I hold her tight, and she kisses me, and she feels like Neev. She has Neev's waist and hands and, good goddess, she has Neev's soft, sweet lips.

I draw back to look at her and take her face in my hands. "You feel real."

"I am, I promise you, I'm flesh and blood. Isn't *this* real?" She takes a step back and conjures a little ball of flame in the palm of one hand.

"But you were dead."

"I was. My grandmother, Opalista. She granted me a new body and control of my powers. As a gift for sacrificing myself to kill Rothbart. And Zori owed her a favor."

I stare at her, speechless. She gives a little half-smile that shows her dimple.

"It is you," I blurt, and it sounds like an accusation even though I don't mean for it to. She's naked, and I take off my cloak so she can cover herself.

She laughs at my dumbfounded expression as she wraps the offered garment around her chest. "I'm sorry to have ended your voyage so quickly."

I clasp her hand. "Don't be ridiculous. It's been five days and I'm already tired of the sea. It's wet and cold."

She pushes back the hair from my brow and the corner of her mouth turns up in a half-smile. "They wouldn't put a fire in your cabin?"

"Neev, I..." I'd expected months to practice this speech. I don't know how to begin. "I'm engaged to Dette," I announce. "And you know that I love her. But it's a political marriage, and she understands that. She knows how much I need the alliance to save my people."

"But will you trust me to love you, even if I'm married

to her? I want you to have a house by the sea and never know pain or hunger again. I want you to—"

"Thedra," she interjects, interrupting my blathering. "You were going to cross the Endless Sea, just to keep a promise you made to me. I trust you."

I reach out to touch her face, a part of me still unable to believe she's real. I trail my fingertips down her smooth cheek, across her lips. Her hand clasps my elbow and I let her pull me into a kiss. She tastes like the sea, like salt and sage grass and wood smoke. Her lips are soft and warm on mine, no longer burning hot.

"You told me something," she says when we part, "in Alder Tower when I was dying. And I didn't get to say it back."

I nod, my eyes burning with tears. "I remember."

"I love you too. For always."